BOOK 1 OF THE DARK ILLUSION TRILOGY

WATCH YOUR BACK

MARION HUGHES

Published in Australia by Sid Harta Books & Print Pty Ltd,
ABN: 34632585293
23 Stirling Crescent, Glen Waverley, Victoria 3150 Australia
Telephone: +61 3 9560 9920, Facsimile: +61 3 9545 1742
E-mail: author@sidharta.com.au

First published in Australia 2021
This edition published 2021
Copyright © Marion Hughes 2021
Cover design, typesetting: WorkingType (www.workingtype.com.au)

Hughes, Marion
Watch Your Back
ISBN: 978-1-925707-59-5
pp330

About the Author

Marion Hughes lives on the Mornington Peninsula, Victoria, Australia.

Also by Marion Hughes:
The Von Mueller Deception.

To Anna
With thanks.

"Over time, hidden truths morph into the dark soil of deceit into something much worse."

Between the Tides
Patti Callahan Henry

Prologue

The storm had already arrived.

'Lucinda, wake up. Quick!'

Strong hands tossed haybales aside.

'He's looking for you. Get out of here now!'

'I can't, Antonio. I've nowhere to go!' she cried, clutching his arm in the darkness.

'The barn's no longer safe. Go!'

Moments later, a screen door slammed in the distance.

'Where is she?' The voice boomed through the howling wind.

'I don't know. She went out somewhere. Ages ago.'

'You lie. Out of my way.'

Thunder drowned out the clatter of hobnailed boots across the cobblestones. A bulky figure filled the barn doorway, discernible only by sporadic flashes of lightning against an otherwise blackened sky.

'Don't make me come and get you, girl!'

But she was gone. Nimble footed, she ran headlong into the squall, until she reached the woods. *Antonio, where are you? I'm scared.* The trees shook like crazed beasts as sheets of rain swept through the clearing ahead.

For a moment, she paused. In the distance stood a high stone wall. *That's it. It has to be.* She sprinted towards the entrance where there was a heavy oak door. Tugging at the rusted handle, she pushed and heaved until it gave way with a protest. Inside was a small alcove, into which she squeezed.

'I'll be safe here,' she whispered, wrapping her arms tightly around her knees. 'I'll be safe.'

Bells jolted her awake. Confusing. Deafening. Through her blurred vision the sun's rays appeared like a kaleidoscope through the stained glass. Everything swayed before her then ... darkness.

Five days later she stood at the huge wrought iron gates clutching her small backpack, staring at the sweeping driveway ahead.

1

The children scampered goat-like up the steep track that led to the Lorenzo estate; the small boy behind doing his best to keep up.

'Hey Cara,' said the tallest of the group, 'can we go and see the spooky man's place first?'

'I don't know, Ash. We only have half an hour.'

'Oh please? I told all the kids at school about it.'

'Yes let's,' piped up his sister. 'He sounds so creepy. So does his house.'

'Oh, all right then,' Cara said, swinging around to face them. 'But don't you dare tell. Dad would kill me if he found out.'

The clifftop track leading to the Zielinski house was narrow and windy, perilously close to the crumbling cliff face. Consequently the Lorenzo children were forbidden to use it without adult supervision. However, that didn't stop them. Many times the two girls had stolen along the path instead of heading down to the beach for a swim. It was an exciting game. Everyone it seemed, wanted to know more about the mysterious resident whom no one had set eyes upon.

The Zielinski residence was set well back from the track, locked, unattended for most of the year, and badly in need of repair. The original trees were now towering giants, letting in little light. Rot had infested the wooden windows whose curtains were always closed. A perfect setting to fuel a child's imagination.

'Angelina, tell Joe to hurry up, will you?' Cara snapped impatiently as she looked over her shoulder.

'Okay.'

The thin, raven haired girl dropped a few paces behind to wait for the boy, who had fallen further behind. Leaning down she whispered in his ear and he nodded with a giggle.

'He's going as fast as he can,' she said, joining the others. 'I promised I'd play Thomas the Tank when we got home, if he kept up.'

Cara nodded. 'The house is just around there,' she said to her cousins, pointing to the next bend.

Dominic Lorenzo was standing arms crossed, on the beach below, looking out to sea where the *Jennifer* sat, glistening on moorings that were twenty-five metres from shore. A southerly wind was picking up. He gave his watch an impatient glance and turned to his brother-in-law.

'We may not be able to stay here much longer,' he remarked. 'I don't want to be caught out in this if things cut up rough.'

'I'm with you there, Mate. It takes what … four hours' sailing to get back to the marina?'

'Something like that.'

Dark clouds were already forming.

Dominic gave a quick nod towards the beach track. 'You get the kids and I'll give Jen a call to pack up on board.'

There was a nod.

As Dominic headed towards the wooden dinghy anchored close to shore, a child's scream cut the air followed by the sound of rocks and gravel. Instantaneously, both men swung around on the spot.

'Shit! The cliff face has given way!' Dominic screamed, as he tore across the sand towards the track with Peter in tow.

Dominic forged ahead like a man possessed. The overgrown path was so narrow that his brother-in-law could only follow blindly, bearing the brunt of tea tree branches flung aside that stung like whips.

As they neared the top, there came a faint sob in the distance. Both stopped in their tracks, ears straining, adrenalin pumping.

Peter pointed south to where the clifftop path narrowed and wound out of sight. 'I'd swear it came from over there somewhere, wouldn't you?'

There was a nod and Dominic was gone.

When he came to an abrupt halt moments later, Peter all but crashed into his back.

'What the – ' he edged past to see.

Four children stood riveted to the spot less than ten metres away, faces white and frozen.

'Where's Joseph?' Dominic's voice roared, as he ran towards them.

'He — he fell, Daddy,' Cara's voice was barely a whisper.

'He what?'

'Over there, Uncle Dom.'

Dominic stumbled across to the cliff's edge, forcing himself to look where his frightened nephew pointed.

'Oh God, no!'

Dominic's knees buckled beneath him and Peter instinctively ran to pull him from the brink.

'Get your hands off me,' Dominic swung out wildly. 'I've got to get down there. Call an ambulance. *Now!*' He rushed blindly back along the path that led to the beach track.

Peter McFarlane's eyes darted from child to child. 'All right. Not one of you move, you hear me?' he commanded.

There was a series of solemn nods. Hands trembling, he fumbled in his jacket for his mobile and punched in triple zero before frantically scrolling through his contacts.

'Hurry up, hurry up, will you?' he found himself kicking at the dirt.

'Madeleine speaking.'

'It's Peter,' he said urgently, 'Look there's been an accident. It's Joe. He's fallen.'

'What? Where?'

'The cliff path, just past the house. I've already called the ambulance but I don't have time to talk. Can you make it up here as soon as possible and take the children home? I've ordered them stay put but I've got to get to Dom.'

'I'll be right down.'

Peter's heart palpitated wildly as he scrambled down the cliff track. Intuitively he sensed the boy was already dead; his suspicions confirmed by the sight of Dominic Lorenzo on the rocks below, cradling the boy's broken body in his arms. *Oh Christ!* He thought. What felt like a lump of lead sat in his stomach, as he ran across the sand.

Unsure of what to do, he gently touched the weeping man's shoulder. 'I'm so sorry, Mate.'

As expected, there was no response.

'Look, perhaps you'd rather be left alone …'

Dominic slowly looked up and out to sea with unseeing eyes. 'I'll never forgive her for this. Never.'

A chill ran down Peter's spine. He knew his brother-in-law only too well. Cara Lorenzo would pay all right. She'd pay for the rest of her life.

2

Joseph Lorenzo's funeral was massive. Not content with a simple ceremony in the small church that the family attended, Dominic insisted on the best: the city's oldest and most magnificent cathedral, St Patricks. The bishop was more than happy to comply. After all, Dominic's mother, a renowned philanthropist, was one of the church's most generous benefactors.

The sight of the tiny white coffin, covered in a profusion of yellow and white flowers caused passers-by to stop and lower their heads as the solemn procession made its way up the stone steps towards the arched entrance.

The warm autumn day was too glorious for such a sombre occasion. Inside, sunlight filtered through the profusion of stain-glass windows, spilling into the alcoves that on an overcast day would have an oppressive feel. Angelic choir boy voices reverberated around the cathedral's massive interior, making spines tingle and eyes lift in wonderment.

'I commend you dear Joseph to almighty God and entrust you to your Creator. May you rest in the arms of the Lord who formed you from the dust of the earth …'

The priest's sonorous lilt became lost in the vast space; Kate McFarlane's gaze was fixed on her sister and her family, seated in the pew ahead. At one point, Jennifer reached for her husband's hand, but he pulled away. Madeleine sat ram-rod straight next to her son. Of them all, she would stand up to the test the best. Angelina's silky black hair was tied in a pony tail by a white bow as she nestled into her mother's shoulder. Cara sat motionless, six inches to her sister's right. It was she who Kate wanted to reach out and touch the most.

After the service, Kate stood solemnly beside her husband, as the coffin was carried down the steps towards the waiting hearse. Dominic, close behind, wasted no time in gathering his family and pushing them through the throng of mourners towards the black limousine parked directly behind. *Damn him, damn him to hell!* Kate thought angrily. Did he think he was the only one grieving over this whole bloody tragedy? Couldn't the bastard step away from his misery for a little while, enough to allow his wife and family the solace and support they so badly needed? *Me for instance?* Kate felt herself bristle. Since Jennifer's marriage, there had rarely been the opportunity for the two of them to spend time together.

The sisters had been close … once. They had slowly drifted apart following Jennifer's marriage eight years ago and Kate's move to London soon after that. God! Where had the time gone, she wondered.

Jennifer married into considerable wealth. The Lorenzo family owned 'Kilkenny,' a coastal property established in the 1940s by the Hardwick family, a wealthy family from Surrey, England. The property boasted a magnificent sandstone clifftop mansion, set upon a hundred acres of prime real estate. Dominic's father Vincent, married Madeleine Hardwick, the sole heiress to the property.

Born the son of a poor Italian immigrant, Vincent knew that his charisma and swarthy good looks would be insufficient to gain Madeleine's hand in marriage. First, he would have to prove his worth. He found a job in a small, local winery where he toiled from dawn to dusk, three hundred and sixty-five days of the year with the fierce grit and determination of his forebears. Time spent with Madeleine were fleeting, stolen moments.

By the time the winery's owner retired, Vincent was gifted it outright. Not content, he took out a loan for a second vineyard then a third. By the age of twenty-eight, when he finally married Madeleine, Vincent was a wealthy man.

William Hardwick bore a begrudging admiration for his son-in-law, whom he appointed his successor in time. Joint ventures were formed and Kilkenny grazing land made way for a large winery. The Lorenzo wine empire had begun. Vincent was not content with mediocrity. He wanted to have the edge. Within months, he'd headed to the Old-World wine regions of Europe to glean what he could from hundreds of years of expertise and tradition.

As a boy, Dominic worked alongside his father, showing the same determination and drive. When Vincent died of a stroke at the age of fifty-four, his son inherited a wine empire in the making.

Kate McFarlane was not envious of her sister's wealth. Jennifer was still the same kid sister who had sponsored a Sudanese child with her pocket money, brought home stray animals — and misfit classmates for that matter. A legacy of their mother. They had grown up with little and learned to appreciate what they had.

Dominic had been used to fast cars and fast women, any of whom would move heaven and earth to snare the suave heir to Kilkenny. Dominic played the game for all it was worth, discarding female companions at will once the thrill of the chase wore off. Jennifer in contrast, was a refreshing change: a natural beauty whom he had met by chance at one of his mother's charity functions.

Unlike the others, Jennifer showed little interest in him. The harder she played to get, the more determined he became. Jennifer was not easily bought and the ensuing six months' chase almost drove him crazy.

A slight smile touched Kate's lips. Her sister had forced Dominic Lorenzo to prove his worthiness, not the other way around.

Their marriage seemed fairytale perfect. Prior to Kate's departure for London, she witnessed nothing but adoration in her brother-in-law's eyes towards his beautiful young wife, and Jennifer had never seemed happier.

It took some time to learn that things were not all as they seemed.

¶

As the black car following the hearse pulled away from the curb, Kate caught a glimpse of Cara's forlorn face at the window and her heart almost broke. She had put her arms around the child at the funeral but there was no response. She shifted uneasily. Considering what the Lorenzo children had been through, she'd doubted the wisdom of them being there in the first place.

Thoughts of that fateful Saturday swirled around in Kate's mind. She had been excited at the prospect of spending time at last with her sister, nieces and nephew. The last time she'd flown back to Australia was for Joseph's christening, four years ago. She would never have dreamed that the next time would be for his funeral.

Things had started out so perfectly. She remembered sitting beside Jennifer on the deck, backs against the wheel house and chatting over coffee, while Jennifer's children played excitedly below with their cousins, whom they'd not seen since toddlers.

Kate frowned. Only now did it dawn on her that Dominic was always close by, hovering. She recalled watching the wooden dinghy as it motored towards shore, Dominic, one arm around his son, head upon head, as he steered.

'Dom just adores that boy, Jen, doesn't he?' she had remarked.

'Sure does. Spoils him rotten as well. Maybe it's the Italian father-son thing. His father was exactly the same, from what I've heard.'

The passing comment had caused Kate to feel uneasy. From what she'd seen of the boy in a short space of time, he looked to his father at every opportunity to get his own way.

If only Dominic hadn't given in to his son's whining ... just this once.

If only Cara hadn't asked that question ...

She felt a pang of despair as the scene drifted to mind.

'Can you get Daddy to row us ashore, Mummy?' she implored. 'Please? I want to show Jacqui and Ash our new ponies.'

'I don't see why not,' Jennifer said. 'It'll give us time to prepare lunch. What do you think, Dom?'

There was a moment's silence before he turned to face the children. 'All right then, but you'll be given half an hour, no more. Joseph, you're to stay here with your mother.'

'But I wanna go too.' The boy wailed. A big fat tear rolled down his chubby face.

Kate leaned over to ruffle her nephew's hair. 'Don't worry, Joe. You can have just as much fun here. Ashley has lots of games on his iPad.'

'No!' the wailing became louder. 'I wanna go with them.'

'Let him come, Dad.' Angelina stepped around from behind the group.' We'll look after him.'

'We won't be far away, Mate.' Peter added.

'Very well, then,' he said. 'But you're not to let him out of your sight, any of you. You hear?'

The group nodded earnestly.

'You're the oldest, Cara,' Dominic's dark eyes bored into those of the tallest girl. 'I'll hold you responsible.'

Once again Dominic's chilling words to her husband on the rocks came to mind. Kate prayed that they were spur-of-the-moment ones. But the frosty distance between father and daughter at the funeral told her otherwise.

9

When Kate and her family boarded the Qantas Airbus bound for London three days later, she took one last glance over her shoulder at the departure lounge.

'I'll be back soon, Jen ... I promise you that,' she uttered softly. 'And this time, we'll take up where we left off.'

Little did Kate know that the next time she set foot on Australian soil would be to attend another graveside burial at Kilkenny.

3

Kilkenny's two-storey sandstone mansion sat white and commanding, amidst well-tended lawns and flower beds.

A handful of houses sat further along the clifftop from Kilkenny to the furthest tip, where properties culminated and the terrain became a tangled, coastal jungle atop impossibly steep and crumbling cliffs.

Old, but majestic as was the era, the houses had similar features: deep front porches, high ceilings and well-worn slate floors. Most stood idle for the better part of the year, until summer, when their wealthy owners arrived with families and friends for their holidays. The month leading up to Christmas would be a hive of activity, with gardeners, maintenance workers and household staff in a frenzy, trying to bring everything up to scratch. According to the townspeople, this was the way it had always been. Those who owned the properties along this prestigious stretch of coastline were the fortunate recipients of beach houses, handed down by their families over generations. Some had enviable access to private sections of beach from their houses.

Most owners resided in the city, having amassed their fortunes in property development, stocks or shares. Although they kept to themselves when they came to stay, there was an unspoken agreement amongst them to hold on to their properties at all costs. That did not deter eager developers who constantly circled, like hyenas eyeing an ageing lion.

The clifftop residents and their extravagances were the butt of jibes, snide remarks and gossip amongst the locals, the Zielinski family in particular.

¶

The Zielinskis arrived as quietly as they left, visiting no one during their stay. It was a well-known fact they were wealthy. That had been confirmed years ago by a snippet in the society pages of a city newspaper. The locals had been incensed. How could a foreign woman have so much money, be such a snob?

The dirt had stuck.

Little did they know the tragedy behind Helena Zielinski's life. Born of Jewish-Polish descent, she'd watched in disbelief when she was a young child, as people in her town were rounded up like cattle and deported to German Death Camps during the Second World War. She'd watched her father gunned down in the street. And then came the day when her house was stormed by the Nazis and her precious violin was shattered against the wall. She was thrown out, terrified, onto the street with her mother and small brothers and taken to Auschwitz. Helena was the only one to survive.

Six years later she arrived in Australia; a wide-eyed twenty- year-old, clutching a battered suitcase. One year later, she met Stefan Zielinksi, a Polish jeweller ten years her senior, whose wife had died in the camps. Over time, they formed a bond that led to romance and ultimately marriage. With little money, they slaved in a local clothing factory until Stefan could afford his first roll of fabric to sell. This became his livelihood for two years, and then he purchased three diamonds and six emeralds They were small but of exceptional quality, as was his work. Finally, he could turn to the thing he loved doing the most.

From a humble city store, Stefan built a thriving jewellery business, the profits from which he invested in real estate. Despite living in the city his whole life, his dream had always been to own land near the sea. Opening the door of his ocean holiday house was his proudest moment. Tragically, Stefan was killed by a drunken driver as he crossed a road on the way to work one morning. The light went out of Helena's eyes after that and the place lay empty for two years before she set foot in it once more.

Like most clifftop houses, the Zielinski residence lay vacant for most of the year. But a phantom male visitor came and went intermittently. One whose face no one ever saw.

Whenever word of his return got out, rumours became rife. It was believed he was criminally insane; released some time ago from a mental institution and coming for occasional respite. A relative of Helena Zielinski, they surmised. Possibly her son.

It was late summer and the visitor was back.

4

'What's going on out there?' Dominic Lorenzo demanded as he stormed into his mother's room, pointing down to the garden where a large white marquee was being erected.

Madeleine held her head up high. 'What do you think?'

'Oh no, another bloody party.'

'And for a good cause.' Her look was steely. 'In case you haven't heard, there happens to be a famine in Sudan.' She took a sip of her tea. 'Do you expect me to just turn a blind eye, with twenty million at risk of starvation? My efforts may not account for much but –'

Dominic's fist slammed down on the bedside table next to where she lay resting.

'There's always something isn't there, Mother. I come home from the city earlier than expected and …'

'That's enough,' she silenced him. 'It's not the only reason I arranged this party, if you must know. This place needs lightening up, for heaven's sake. It's been over a year since Joseph's death. You've got to move on, Dominic. We all do. Jennifer needs you. The children need you.'

'You're right,' Dominic said wearily, rubbing his eyes with the palms of his hands. 'It's about time I made it up to Jen, I know.'

'Yes, it is.' Madeleine smiled. For all his faults and self-absorption, her son adored his wife. Obsessively so. 'The guests should be arriving about 7 pm.'

As Dominic left the room, Madeleine absent-mindedly stroked the Persian cat on her lap and looked out onto the driveway where a driver was unloading massive floral displays. Despite their differences, her son and daughter-in-law complemented each other. And Madeleine believed that Jennifer had been the key to her son's rapid rise to success as a wine exporter.

When the auburn-haired, green-eyed beauty walked into the room, eyes were riveted on her. Her good looks were not so much classical as natural. At thirty-two she looked younger than her years. It could have been her eyes that danced like a mischievous child, the almost too-upturned button nose or the wrinkle-free, creamy complexion of her Irish mother. Jennifer was petite, five-five at the most but she walked with the grace of a model inches taller. Yet it was more than Jennifer's appearance that drew people to her. She had the gift of making those around her feel special and valued. Dominic and his beautiful wife soon became part of the city 'in' set and business contacts flourished.

Jennifer's laugh was contagious. Despite the fact that Madeleine Lorenzo kept her distance from those around her, it was hard not to let her guard down with her daughter-in-law.

Initially, Jennifer was regarded with suspicion, as was every girl Dominic brought home; potential gold-diggers until proven otherwise. Most turned out to be nothing more than bimbos whom he treated as toys to be played with and cast aside once the novelty wore off.

Then Jennifer arrived: the one with the least wealth and social standing; a girl-next-door type that any mother would wish for her son.

Madeleine was aware that Dominic's new bride didn't quite know how to take her. And that was the way she wanted it. However, over time an unspoken bond developed between the two, forged from a genuine concern for those less fortunate and an innate love of Kilkenny.

Madeleine's eyes furrowed momentarily. She had heard rumours of her son's overseas "romps." Had Jennifer? She shrugged. It was none of her business. If it were true and Jennifer knew and chose to ignore it, so be it.

She had been able to.

¶

Dominic stood by the window and surveyed the scene before him. The finishing touches were being added and the guests were due to arrive in an hour. He would humour his mother once more — go along with the charity thing. He had no choice.

It infuriated him that that a large proportion of his mother's trust, shares and investments had been put aside for philanthropic purposes and entrusted to Jennifer upon her death. He hated to think how much was stashed away. It would have to be significant. But little could be done about it. Madeleine had set things up with the backing of a shrewd family lawyer. Dominic did not like the man. He had sharp, penetrating eyes that missed nothing.

Best to think of what he could control. Kilkenny would be his once Madeleine was gone, and business was booming.

Dominic eyed himself in the mirror as he headed towards the ensuite, giving a quick nod of approval. Inheriting his father's Mediterranean good looks, olive skin and masses of dark curls, he saw the way women's eyes were drawn to him, especially when he wore white, as was the case this evening. Unlike the thickset Lorenzo-males before him, Dominic was blessed with extra height and a lean physique. His dark eyes were one of his greatest assets. Deceptively innocent, they were used time and time again to charm ... and to con.

Dominic had a hold on his wife and he knew it. Money was not the attraction. Wealthy men had made moves on her before: men ten times richer than he. But her eyes remained on him alone.

'Can I come in?' he knocked on the ensuite door.

'Hang on a minute,' she said as she fiddled with her earring. 'Okay.'

Opening the door, he stepped inside and appraised his wife's elegantly cut slim-fitting black dress. Only a fine strand of pearls adorned her neck. Jennifer had never been one for jewellery, much to his frustration. He would love to have bought the most of expensive diamonds, emeralds or whatever, for her to parade her around in.

'Stun-ning!' he exclaimed.

'Really?' her eyes sparkled.

'Really. Come here gorgeous.'

'Come and get me,' she giggled.

With one step forward, he swept her up in his arms and carried her to the bed.

'I've forgotten how beautiful you are, Jen.' He tenderly stroked her face, eyes never leaving hers. 'It's all going to change from now on, I promise. You, me, the kids. I'm sorry for how I've been, it's just –'

'Sh' she said, holding a finger to his lips. 'How much time did you say till the guests arrive?'

'I didn't. But they can wait.' He rolled her to one side and planted small kisses on the back of her neck as he unzipped her dress and moved his hand slowly to her thighs.

At seven, the intercom buzzed.

'Jennifer?'

'I'm on my way, Madeleine. I was just working out what dress to wear.' She kicked at her husband's leg as he made faces, trying not to laugh. 'Yes, I'm sure he's around some-where. I'll go look. Won't be long.'

'Good one Jen,' he laughed, rolling her over on the bed once more.

'Shit, you'd better get down there, while I get ready.' She pushed him off and rushed over to the mirror. 'Bloody hell, my mascara's run and look at my hair, damn it.'

'I'm out of here,' he said with a laugh as he pulled on his underpants. 'Beats me why you wear that stuff on your face in the first place.'

'Get,' she said throwing a pillow at him.

Not long afterwards, she took one last glance over her shoulder at the bathroom mirror and muttered, 'will have to do.'

As she reached for her coat, she felt a glow of happiness. It was like having the Dominic of old back again. Things were about to change for the better. She was sure of it.

Little did she know how far from the truth that was.

5

Madeleine lay wide awake in her upstairs bedroom in the West Wing. The guests had long since gone and she stared out onto the flood-lit garden where the large marquee stood. She could just make out the three small tents at the far end of the lawn, where Cara and Angelina were having a sleep-over with a handful of children. Just as well Jennifer had ensured there were enough sleeping bags and warm blankets to go around. The nights had been exceptionally cold. *Don't forget they're children*, she thought with a smile. *When I was that age …*

Her thoughts turned to the evening just past. Things had gone according to plan. Jennifer came to life like a metamorphosing butterfly, circulating amongst the guests as if she had known them all her life. It was so good to hear the delighted squeals of children as they tore around the gardens. Oh, to be young again. She recalled the time she'd scampered around those paths as a child. Yet she couldn't stop coming back to Cara, who stood well back from the frivolity, alone and aloof. *Oh well, I suppose not everyone's the gregarious type,* she thought. *Nothing I can do about it. It's not as if I haven't tried.*

Madeleine did her best not to show favouritism towards either granddaughter but it was no easy feat. There was something about Cara. The child lacked spark and affection. None that Madeleine could detect anyway. Surely, she hadn't always been that morose. Madeleine frowned, straining to think. A hazy memory came to mind of Cara as a toddler in the arms of her mother. Hadn't there been peals of childish laughter, chubby finger tracing her mother's face, eyes glowing with mischief? Madeleine shrugged her shoulders. What did it matter now?

I'll just have to make more of an effort I suppose, she thought, as she reached for a glass of water on the bedside table. It must be hard living in the shadow of an adopted sister blessed with striking looks and natural appeal. Someone who Dominic adored.

I'll have to have a word with him, she thought as she drifted into an uneasy sleep.

§

It was nearly 3 am when she was awoken by the billowing curtain flapping against her face. 'Damn! I knew I forgot something,' she muttered as she climbed out of bed to close the window. Then something caught her eye. A flash of orange against the inky sky.

'Dear God.' She rushed to the wall and pushed the intercom. 'Dominic. Get up quick. There's a fire!'

In the distance, two dark eyes observed. Unblinking.

The marquee was ablaze. Hungry bright flames licked the canvas sides, devouring them like a ravenous wolf.

By the time Dominic ran onto the lawn, he realised there was nothing he could do. Jennifer was close behind, ashen-faced. 'The children, Dom, there's no way they'd be near the marquee, is there?'

'No, they'll be safe.' But his panic-stricken look said otherwise as he ran, a hand shielding his eyes towards the burning entrance.

'There's no one inside, thank God!' he called over his shoulder. 'Run down to the tents and get the kids up to the house. Mother's already called the fire brigade.'

By now the marquee was engulfed in flames but contained within the parameters of the meticulously manicured lawns and paved walkways.

Not long afterwards, the fire brigade arrived and proceeded to mop up and smother the remains of the marquee.

Dominic was joined by the Brigade Captain, who determined the cause to be a candle that had either tipped over or caught hold of something in the breeze; the charred piece of material found on the ground nearby was proof enough.

'Bloody prayer table,' Dominic muttered under his breath.

At Madeleine's charity events it was traditional to have

a table in one corner, adorned with a white cloth draped with gold or royal blue satin. Atop would sit a cascade of fresh flowers, the family bible and an array of candles.

The Captain needed no further explanation, having recently attended a family day at the home.

He ran one hand over his head. 'What I can't understand is why the candles weren't extinguished at the end of the evening. They were positioned pretty close to the canvas.'

'But they *were* put out. I'm certain of that,' Dominic was quick to reply. 'By my wife, not long after the guests left.'

The Captain shrugged. 'Maybe she thought she did. The main thing is that no one was harmed. You're lucky that the marquee wasn't close to the house.'

Dominic's face was dark as he walked off. Jennifer did not simply "forget" things as important as that. Something was not right.

ʛ

At 4.15 am, Dominic lay wide awake in bed and unable to sleep. Images of the night's events swirled around in his head and he thanked God that no one had been harmed. But his mind would still not rest. What *had* caused the fire?

I'll probably never know, he thought, glancing down at Jennifer, who slept peacefully in his arms. *But one thing's for sure. Next time there'll be no frigging prayer table.*

As he watched the shadows flicker on the wall, his mind

turned to Joseph. The wounds of his son's death remained painfully raw and would take years to heal, if ever. But his mother was right. It *was* time to move on.

Angelina was his saving grace. She had the knack of lifting his spirits when he was at his lowest, making him laugh at the silliest thing. But as for Cara …

Dominic's jaw tightened. Truth was, he'd been unable to warm to his eldest daughter; not since Joe's death when she appeared indifferent, and lacking in emotion. Little had changed. Tonight, for instance.

He would pretend to treat both girls equally for his wife's sake but … that was it, pretend.

6

'I hate you.' Cara shrieked, with a violent shove that sent Angelina crashing to the ground. 'I wish you'd never been born.' With a turn of her heels, she was gone.

It was three days after the party: a frigid, winter's morning, with the dew heavy on the grass. Madeleine, already up and about, happened to be looking into the garden as she waited for the kettle to boil. With a gasp, she grabbed her jacket and strode down the passage way and out onto the front lawn, where her youngest grandchild was slowly getting to her feet.

'Angelina, are you all right?' she rushed to assist.

'I'm fine Grandma.'

'What happened?'

'Nothing.' Angelina hastily brushed the grass from her jumper. 'I tripped. That's all.'

'Don't give me that, young lady. I happened to be watching out the window. Why did Cara push you like that?'

'It was nothing, Grandma. She didn't mean it.' The velvety eyes pleaded, 'It was my fault.'

'What do you mean, your fault?'

'I asked Daddy if I could change bedrooms to the one in the attic and he said I could.' There was a pause. 'I didn't know that Cara wanted it too.'

Madeleine straightened. The attic room had been her favourite too, as a child — a small, quaint doll's house, adorned with pastel floral wall paper and white furnishings, perched above like a castle turret. Here she had lived out the fantasies of an only child. Pirates sailed their ships from exotic places and stole into the cove at the foot of the cliffs in the dead of night to store their treasures, and elves and goblins inhabited the maze of gardens below.

Madeleine could hardly blame either child for desiring the room, yet upon reflection, Cara had shown little interest to this point. Madeleine frowned. The attic bedroom was not the issue here. For a moment, her heart went out to Cara who, up until now had appeared indifferent to her father's bouts of favouritism towards her sister. She turned towards Angelina and placed an arm around her shoulders. 'Well, you *are* a lucky child that your Daddy gave you the room. Perhaps you could think of a way to return your sister the favour.'

'No, it's okay, Grandma,' she said. 'I'll stay in my own bedroom and go up there to play like I do now. I wouldn't hurt Cara for the world.'

At moments Madeleine felt a sense of resentment

towards Angelina, but at times like these she could not help but warm to the child.

'Are you sure?'

'Yes Grandma.' Her eyes were solemn.

As they walked towards the house, Madeline was deep in thought. The issue was resolved for the time being but changes were called for. Soon afterwards, she paid a visit to Jennifer's room.

'I need to speak to you about Cara,' she said.

Jennifer's face was serious as she listened to her mother-in-law's account of what had transpired. Silence hung in the air before she responded. 'And just when I thought Dom and Cara were getting along. It's not that he means to favour Angelina. She's just easier all around, I suppose.' Jennifer gave a sigh. 'I guess we'll just need to make more of an effort.'

'Don't be too hard on yourself,' Madeleine said. 'Try spending more time with her. It's bound to help.'

'You're right, you know,' Jennifer said. 'Dom's involved with Angelina's dancing but we haven't encouraged Cara with anything in particular.'

'Exactly. Is there anything she's good at? Something she enjoys doing?'

'There is actually. She seems to have taken to horses the way I once did.' She paused then added, 'I wish I'd had the opportunity at her age.'

Madeleine nodded and said nothing. It had taken some time for Jennifer to open up about her past. Money had been tight in her household, with little left over for hobbies and interests. It was only by chance that she'd been introduced to the world of horses through a nursing colleague of her mother's who gave riding lessons in her spare time.

'One visit to the Equestrian centre when I was seventeen was enough to get me hooked.' Jennifer told her. 'From then on it was horses this and horses that. I must've driven Mum nuts. That year, I somehow juggled my senior studies with long stints at the stables. I suppose Mum's friend felt sorry for me because she eventually struck a deal. In return for babysitting while she was on nightshifts, I was given free dressage lessons.'

Madeline felt a pang of guilt as she recalled the conversation, reflecting upon the opportunities that she'd been given as a child. There'd been a string of ponies, a stable and ménage, yet she'd taken it all for granted. Once the last of her ponies died of old age, Kilkenny's stables had lain empty until the arrival of the girls' ponies, two years ago.

Here was the perfect opportunity for Jennifer to share her knowledge and love of horses with her eldest daughter. Hopefully it would bring the two closer. Perhaps Jennifer might consider a horse of her own one day.'

'So,' she said in her no-nonsense manner, 'would you be willing to take an interest in Cara's riding?'

'Yes, yes. Of course. I wish I'd thought of it earlier. The number of times she's stayed back with her pony, long after he's been unsaddled and fed. She's always looked for excuses to head down to the stables.'

Madeleine gave a nod. 'What do you have in mind, then. Horse shows?'

'Good Lord, no. Toby's ideal for a quiet ride out with Angelina's pony but he's certainly no show horse.'

'Well, perhaps it's worth considering a new one,' she suggested.

Jennifer's face brightened. 'That's a great idea. You don't think that Angelina would mind?'

'I doubt it,' Madeleine said. 'Right now, she's absorbed in her ballet. And then, from what she tells me, it'll be hip hop.'

Jennifer grinned. 'First I've heard of it.'

'Probably one of her phases. What was the last?'

'Tap dancing.'

'Oh, that's right.'

'And how long did that last?'

Jennifer stopped to think. 'Two lessons, I think.'

'A bit like the fad with her pony. It's been a while since I've seen her out riding.' She paused. 'No, I don't think that getting Cara another horse will worry her too much.'

'Dominic's due home around three,' Jennifer said. 'I'll mention something to him then.'

❡

The following week, a local show pony was advertised online and Jennifer took Cara to see it.

The horse was an eye-catching grey with extravagant

movement, yet it had a kind eye and responded well to all that was asked by its teenage-girl rider.

'As I mentioned when you first rang,' said the owner, eyes on the horse as it cantered a perfect circle in the arena, 'Kristy's fast outgrowing Dapper. It's time to be looking at a bigger horse.'

Jennifer nodded. Perfect sense from what she could see, yet she wasn't quite ready to make a commitment. After further discussions, the owner agreed to leasing out the pony on a six-month trial.

¶

'I don't know that we've been told the whole story,' she said to Dominic the following weekend as the newly arrived pony pranced around the ménage, neck arched and tail high. 'I think he could be a bit of a handful. I'm not sure that Cara will be able to handle him.'

Dominic shrugged. 'You're the expert, Jen. You saw the horse ridden beforehand, didn't you?'

'Yes, it did everything that was asked of it,' she replied. 'But any horse, no matter how well behaved, will try out a new rider. Cara's raring to ride him, of course but she's only used to her quiet pony. It'd be best to get a riding instructor on board from the start.'

'Whatever you think,' Dominic said and resumed reading his paper.

For a while, things could not have been better. While

Dominic took Angelina to ballet lessons of a weekend, Jennifer leaned over the ménage fence, watching with contentment as her daughter sat, eyes intent, listening to every instruction.

The new pony settled over time, as Jennifer had hoped. Cara's confidence as a rider increased day by day and before long, she was taking small rides around the property with Angelina, who had surprisingly resumed an interest in her pony.

It seemed as a breakthrough with Cara had been made at last. But it was not to be for long.

7

The girls chose to ride out. The day was cold and blustery and the horses kept a brisk pace, senses alert as they clip-clopped the path. As they turned for home, Angelina turned to Cara.

'You look so good on Dapper. Are you still taking him to the show?'

'I think so,' Cara could barely contain her excitement. 'Mum thinks we'll be ready by then. I just need a few more lessons.'

Angelina nodded. 'What's he like to ride?'

'Hard sometimes.'

'What do you mean? He does whatever you want.' Angelina gave an exasperated sigh. 'Tonto's so lazy. I can't even get him to trot.'

Cara raised an eyebrow. 'He's not lazy today.'

'That's only 'cause he doesn't want to be left behind.'

Jennifer watched from the lounge room window as the girls rode towards the mounting yard to unsaddle.

'You know Dom, bringing home that horse has been the best thing. It's so good to see those two out and about and I've never seen Cara so happy.'

'That's good, Jen.' Dominic said as he reached for another piece of toast.

He had to admit that the transformation of horse and rider was nothing short of astounding. The dressage instructor was well worth her money. Dominic thrived on success and was certain his daughter would be in line for a championship at the upcoming show.

'So, have you organised a float yet?' he asked.

'Yes. Kellie from the dressage club has kindly offered hers.'

He gave a nod. 'We'll look around for one soon, if you wish.'

'That'd be great, thanks. Once the show season starts, we'll be needing one. There's a hire place in town but the floats are pretty shoddy.'

'I can imagine.'

'Did you arrange to get the weekend off?' she asked.

He nodded. 'What time's she riding?'

'Her first event is at ten and the last around two.'

'That'll work out well actually,' he said. 'I'll bring Angie and take her on to her dance rehearsals after that.'

At the stables, Cara was about to unsaddle her pony, when there was a tap on her shoulder. 'Could I have a ride first? Please?'

Cara hesitated. 'Wait till I ask Mum. Why don't you give

him a few pats and get to know him first? Then maybe in a few days –'

'But I don't want to wait a few days. I want to have a ride now. Just a little one. She won't mind.'

'Oh, all right then,' Cara said 'but only if I lead you.'

'Thanks.' Angelina said excitedly as she was given a leg up.

'He's so awesome, Cara,' she gushed, as they walked side by side along the road. 'Do you think Mummy would get *me* a pony like Dapper? Then we could go to shows together.'

There was an icy silence.

'Cara?' Angelina persisted.

'I'm sure she would. Has she ever said no to you?'

The sarcasm was lost. 'Ooh, I can't wait,' she said excitedly. 'I'll ask her and Daddy when we get back.'

'Whatever.' Cara's eyes were dark.

The wind had picked up and leaves swirled around the pony's hooves, making it unsettled. The high-pitched chattering from its rider made things worse and Cara was quick to notice.

'That's enough for today,' she said. 'We're going back.'

'Okay. But I want to trot first. You can let go.'

'No.' Cara said angrily as she turned the horse. But it was too late. The pony, used to the slightest of rider aids, shot forward at the sudden kick in its flanks. Jerking free of Cara's hand, it tore up the driveway towards the house, where Dominic was backing the car out of the garage.

'Shit!' he yanked on the handbrake. The pony swerved to avoid the car, sending Angelina sideways onto the gravel. The unexpected movement caused the pony to wheel abruptly and gallop back to its stable mate. Dominic scrambled out and tore round to the back of the car. 'Angie!' To his relief, she was making an attempt to rise.

'I'm Okay Daddy.'

As Dominic gently picked her up in his arms, his jaw tightened as Cara ran towards him, white-faced and breathless.

'It wasn't Dapper's fault, Daddy,' she blurted out. 'He got a fright, that's all and …'

'Get inside!' Dominic spluttered. 'I'll deal with you later.'

Dominic wasn't prepared for the tilt of her head, nor the icy response. 'Not till I see that Dapper's all right.'

'Stuff the horse!' Dominic's eyes blazed into hers. 'Do as you're told!'

Without a word, Cara turned and strode towards the house.

'It wasn't Cara's fault, Daddy.' Angelina looked up at him. 'I wanted to ride Dapper. I asked her if I could.'

'Sh,' he soothed as he carried her towards the house. 'We'll talk about it later.'

'Okay. Can I go and watch some TV now?'

'No, we'll be taking you to hospital first to check things out.'

'Is Cara coming with us?'

'No.' Dominic's face was hard. 'Your sister will be staying here with Grandma.'

It came as no surprise to Jennifer that one of her daughters had fallen off her pony. She'd suffered more falls than she could remember in her riding days. It came with the territory. What alarmed her was the unexpected ranting of her husband, as he lay Angelina on the sofa.

'Angie could have been killed, for God's sake,' he said furiously.

'Dom,' Jennifer went to touch his arm but he jerked her hand away.

'You weren't driving the bloody car,' he snapped.

'No, I wasn't. Look, you've had a hell of a shock.'

'That's the bloody understatement of the year.'

The comment was ignored.

'The main thing's that Angie's Okay,' Jennifer reasoned. 'She'll probably be a bit bruised and sore tomorrow but –'

'How can you be so sure?' he demanded, 'she's going straight to the Emergency Department.'

Jennifer went to open her mouth but didn't. There was little point in arguing when Dominic was in this frame of mind.

'All right,' she told him. 'You get the car ready and I'll collect Cara from the stables.'

'Cara's been ordered to her room.' Dominic's voice was cold.

'What!' Jennifer said incredulously. 'How could you? She'll be worried sick about her pony.'

'Fuck the bloody animal!' he spluttered. 'Anyone would think that it's the horse that's injured here. It can wait till we get home.'

Jennifer met his stare head on. 'No, it *cannot* wait. Nor will you deprive your daughter of the right to see her pony. I will personally accompany Cara to the stables to check things out and then we'll go.'

Dominic went to snap but said nothing.

Jennifer fought to gain her composure. If Angelina had not been present …

She headed up the stairs. Outside Cara's bedroom door, she took a deep breath before entering.

'Come on, Darling,' she said softly. 'Let's go see Dapper.'

'But Dad said –'

'He's just a bit shocked, that's all.' She put an arm around Cara and led her towards the door. 'He'll come round.'

The words sounded hollow in her ears. *If only*, she thought.

She could feel her husband's eyes boring through her as they walked towards the front door. Things were about to become far worse.

Jennifer waited until the ponies were unsaddled and fed in their stables before taking Cara back to the house. Dominic was already in the car with Angelina, fingers drumming on the steering wheel. Ignoring him, she walked past and opened the front door.

Madeleine would know how to handle things.

Once the car pulled out of the driveway, Madeleine turned to Cara. 'Do you want to talk about things, Darling, or would you rather be left alone for a while?'

'Left alone,' came the sulky reply.

'That's fine,' she said. 'I'll be in my room if you need me.'

An hour later, she removed her reading glasses and placed them on the table before she went to check on Cara.

The familiar notes of Tchaikovsky's *Swan Lake* drifted from the music room down the passageway, where Cara sat, curled up on the window ledge, rocking to the music. Madeleine went to interrupt but thought twice and quietly closed the door.

For as long as she could remember, her oldest granddaughter had sought solace in this room, listening to music on the old CD player. Apart from Cara, the room had remained unused for years. Madeleine had considered selling her mother's grand piano and turning the room into something more practical; another office perhaps? And each time, she stalled. The old piano reflected happy memories of her childhood: of rolling around on the oriental carpet with the family dog while her mother played; carols at Christmas before dinner, sing-songs with her cousins. Perhaps one day, a family member might take to playing, she mused, with the exception of Dominic of course. Madeleine was puzzled by his aversion to music. It hadn't always been that way. She had no doubt that he would rid himself of the piano once she was gone.

For now, the music room served its purpose. Cara seemed at her happiest here, alone. Deep down Madeleine empathised with the child. She, too, was neither outgoing nor demonstrative. But it hadn't always been that way. She recalled her teenage years; the whirlwind romance with Vincent and their blissful early years of marriage. That was until … she closed her eyes as the familiar stab of pain hit again. But maybe it was all meant to be. It had certainly taught her resilience, hardened her. Never would she be taken for a fool again.

Her mind drifted once more to Cara. It wasn't as if the child wasn't given the best of everything and treated on equal terms to her sister. Well, to a degree. It was hard not to display signs of affection towards Angelina, whose effervescent presence seemed to lift everyone's spirits. Cara, on the other hand …

9

Jennifer rang from the hospital to say that Angelina's tests were clear and they were heading for home.

'Thank God.' Madelaine muttered as she put down her mobile and went to tell Cara. Hopefully things would now return to normal. She'd taken just three steps down the passageway when she stopped in disbelief. She could have sworn she heard grand piano being played in the music room. She shook her head. *That's impossible,* she thought. *There's no one in that room but Cara and she's never played a note of music in her life.* The music had stopped. *Must have been imagining it,* she thought.

When Madeleine opened the door to the music room Cara was seated, as before on the window ledge, eyes distant, arms wrapped around her knees.

'Good news, Darling,' Madeleine said, 'I've just heard from your mother at the hospital. Angelina's going to be just fine.'

Cara gave a nod, without turning.

A chill went down Madeline's spine. There was definitely something disturbing about this child. She went to open her mouth but shut it just as quickly, worrying she may say something she might regret. Quietly she left the room, her eyes troubled.

g

It was turning dark when the Range Rover turned into Kilkenny. The night chill had already set in, and condensation formed on the windscreen as Jennifer drove into the garage and cut the engine.

'We're home, baby,' Dom gently roused the sleeping head on his shoulder.

Jennifer smiled as she glanced at the touching gesture in the rear-vision mirror. But she felt a pang in her heart as she reached for her bag. Would he have done the same for Cara?

The French windows were ajar and Jennifer was quick to close them, as Dominic carried Angelina into the room and placed her on the sofa. He walked to the intercom on the far side of the room and pressed it. 'Bring Cara down would you please?'

Jennifer felt her heart sink. 'Dom, don't you think this could wait until tomorrow?'

There was no reply.

Cara was barely in the doorway before Dominic grilled her.

'So, what do you have to say for yourself?'

There was no response.

'Answer me, Cara,' he demanded. 'What in the hell do you think you were doing letting her on that horse?'

Still, there was silence. Cara's stony expression enraged him even more. He took two steps forward and shook her shoulders, his eyes boring into hers.

'Your sister could have been killed. You understand?'

'For heaven's sake, Dominic,' Madeleine stepped between them and pushed him away. 'Don't you think the child has been through enough?'

His eyes met hers angrily. 'Well, she should've known better.'

'Daddy, please,' came a small voice from the other side of the room. 'She didn't want me to ride Dapper. I made her.'

Dominic bristled. 'And your side of the story, Cara?'

Cara tilted her chin. 'What she said.'

'And have you got anything to add?'

'No.'

'Very well then,' Dominic's tone was icy. 'No one was hurt, that's the main thing. But tomorrow, the horse goes.'

Jennifer gasped. 'You can't be serious, Dom.'

'I'm serious, all right!'

'That's totally unfair and you know it.'

'Perhaps. But hopefully she'll learn a thing a two,' he continued ruthlessly. 'Who knows, maybe down the line, another horse may be in order.'

'I don't want a stupid pony anyway.' The chilling words cut the air.

All eyes were on Cara, who stood in the shadows, eyes flashing and arms crossed.

'Suit yourself.' Dominic shot back.

'That's enough! 'Madeleine snapped angrily. 'I don't want to hear another word. It's late and we're all tired. I suggest we have dinner and get an early night.'

'I'm not hungry.' Cara said. 'I'm going to my room.'

Dominic said nothing but his look was scathing as she headed towards the door.

Jennifer felt her heart plummet. At some point she was going to have to deal with Cara's anger. But now was not a good time. As for Dominic, the best thing she could do right now was to say little, at least until she had time to think.

That evening, she paid a visit to Angelina's room with a glass of warm milk and a mild sedative. Closing the bedroom door softly she paused for a moment, fingers on the handle and took a deep breath before making her way down the hallway to Cara's room. When she flicked on the light, it was obvious that her daughter was feigning sleep.

Jennifer bit her lip. *You bastard, Dominic,* she thought angrily. Her eyes swept over the recent photo of Cara and the new pony that took pride of place on her bedside table, then to the splash of navy blue in the wardrobe. She had already caught Cara parading around in her new riding jacket. Dominic was about to strip Cara of the one thing that meant more to her than anything in the world.

Not if I have anything to do with it, she thought angrily.

Jennifer gently tucked the bedclothes around Cara's shoulders and stroked her forehead. 'Things will work out, Darling, I promise,' she said softly. As she kissed her daughter's face, she could have been kissing a statue.

When the bedroom door closed, Cara lay still, tears flowing down her cheeks. *I thought you would have done more, Mum. You knew how much I loved Dapper. You could have made Dad change his mind if you really tried.*

It was some time before Jennifer made her way to her own bedroom. As hoped, Dominic was in a deep sleep. She had no desire to discuss the matter, not trusting what she might say. Slipping in to bed, she lay back-to-back with her sleeping husband. Too emotionally drained to think, she drifted into a troubled sleep.

9

In the middle of the night, a small figure crept into the bedroom down the hallway and stood beside the bed. Small fingers reached out and ran down the sleeping face. Slowly.

8

The following morning, Jennifer stood beside Dominic on the front porch watching the horse float head down the driveway.

'So,' she said, eyes blazing, 'Are you happy now?'

'No use giving the guilt treatment,' he said, 'it's a hard lesson to learn, I know, but maybe she'll think first next time.'

'I was expecting you to say something like that,' came the frosty response. 'But you know what, I hoped upon all hope that you'd have a last-minute flash of compassion and reverse your decision. How wrong I was!'

Jennifer turned on her heels and strode towards the house.

Dominic had overstepped the mark and he knew it. It would take his best efforts to get out of this one. He stood for a while, brow furrowed and arms crossed before he made his way inside.

As he entered the lounge room, he could see Jennifer's body stiffen. He halted.

'Look, I'm sorry, okay?' His words were soft. 'In retrospect, I should have handled things much better.'

There was no response.

'But I never said my decision was irreversible.'

'So, let's get things clear,' Jennifer eyed him boldly. 'After this blows over, are you willing to purchase another horse for Cara?'

'More to the point, does Cara *want* another horse?' he was quick to respond. 'You heard what she said last night.'

'If Cara's decision determines the outcome, I'm fine by that.' Jennifer said evenly.

'Me too.' He lied. 'Let's leave things at that, shall we?'

Truth was, he had felt a flicker of jealousy the moment the horse arrived and Jennifer's undivided attention turned to Cara. He didn't like the way things were heading.

Hopefully, in time Cara's interest in horses would diminish. Right now, Jennifer was a provoked tigress about to unleash, and he was in unknown territory. An uneasy feeling settled in the pit of his stomach. If he was not careful, things could turn ugly.

He made his way across the room and slipped his arms around her waist. 'Forgiven?' He planted a soft kiss on her forehead.

'Maybe.'

Strike one. He thought.

'I'll make it up to you, I promise.'

Jennifer said nothing but nodded. Dominic gently removed his arms and squeezed her hands. 'Right now,

I think Cara could do with an apology. Are you coming with me?'

Dominic could tell by the look on her face that he had dodged a bullet. The rest would be easy.

There was no answer when Jennifer knocked on Cara's bedroom door but what met their eyes when they entered the room caused Jennifer's hand to fly to her mouth. Shards of glass were strewn over the carpet, alongside the ripped photo of horse and rider. The shredded remains of a riding jacket lay atop, beside a large pair of scissors.

Dominic stood behind, a satisfied glimmer in his eyes. Strike two, he thought.

'Don't worry, Babe,' he murmured. 'She'll come around. Best to give her some space, before we deal with things. I'll speak to her in the morning. For now, let's clean up this mess.'

Angelina was still asleep when Cara came down for breakfast.

Dominic poured a glass of orange juice and placed it before her on the breakfast bench. He gave Jennifer a quick nod before he spoke.

'I owe you an apology, Cara. I had one hell of a shock yesterday but that's no excuse to come down so hard on you.'

As expected, there was no response.

'As I explained yesterday, I have no objection to another horse. That's for you to decide. Okay?'

There was no comment, just a shrug.

Strike three, he thought. This *should* mean the end of things. He had another card up his sleeve just in case.

'Meanwhile, I've organised something for all of us in two weeks' time,' he said. 'An overnight camp at the Zoo's African enclosure. The next day, there'll be an afternoon session with the handlers, including a close-up encounter with the animals.'

This time, Cara's eyes lit up.

Bingo. He thought.

Dominic had been told of Cara's obsession with African animals by her classroom teacher. The move had to be a winner. Even more satisfying was the look of approval on Jennifer's face, that had, for the past two days been nothing short of frosty.

Dominic took a moment to reflect. She was no longer the placid, easily controlled woman he first married. Not that he was particularly fazed. He would win out in the end. If she overstepped the boundaries, there were always ways and means of pulling her into line. She'd learned that long ago.

9

For the next few years, things were relatively peaceful at Kilkenny, although the simmering tension between Jennifer's daughters troubled her. Over time, she accepted that the two would never be close.

Things settled once Cara moved to secondary school. Jennifer was surprised to learn that her eldest daughter was academically bright and within the top three percentile of her class. Dominic was suitably impressed. There was a distinct shift in his attitude towards Cara, following her first semester results of six high distinctions.

'I'm proud of what you've achieved this year Cara,' he said. 'Keep up the good work.'

'Thanks,' came the guarded response.

In contrast, he was unfazed by Angelina's low-to-average marks. She only had to give him one of her smiles.

9

Summer drew to a close, followed by a stretch of glorious autumn days that rolled on like lazy waves, bringing a sense of harmony that Jennifer had not felt for some time. To her relief, Dominic began to spend more time at Kilkenny, and family outings on the *Jennifer* resumed at long last.

Madeleine watched with approval. About time, she thought. Despite the family wealth, her granddaughters were neither boastful of their possessions nor condescending towards those less fortunate. It was time to involve them in her charity work. The opportunity came soon afterwards when she was contacted by the CEO of an international aid charity, who sought permission to use Kilkenny as a venue for a gala fashion parade.

Two weeks later, he paid a visit to the property accompanied by Tony Caruzzo, a modelling agency representative. The event promised class.

As they walked over the grounds, Tony stopped in his tracks and turned to Madeleine.

'That girl over there. She's stunning. Who is she?'

Madeleine glanced over to where Angelina was frolicking around the garden beds with the housekeeper's dog. It was warm day for autumn and Angelina's cut off white shorts and pink t-shirt enhanced her olive skin and exotic beauty.

'That's my son's adopted daughter, Angelina,' she told him.

'Has she ever considered modelling?'

'Lord, no. The child's only twelve.'

The thirtyish, good-looking man's eyes were riveted. 'That's neither here nor there. We have girls starting at fourteen and –'

'I'm sure that's not the career my son envisages for her,' Madeleine was quick to interrupt.

He shrugged. 'Well, how about she does a stint at our gig, here at Kilkenny. As the school formal season is not far off, we've decided to display a range of designer dresses for teenagers. You've got no idea the amounts of money parents of seventeen-year-old girls are willing to pay these days, just for a one-night thing.'

'I've read about it in the papers, Mr. Caruzzo,' Madeleine said, 'and frankly I find the whole thing distasteful.'

The rep shook a blonde lock out of his eyes. 'I couldn't agree with you more, Mrs. Lorenzo, but at least those attending *this* function won't be out of pocket.'

'Hm,' Madeleine said with a grunt.

'So, do you think your granddaughter might be interested in modelling for us?'

'You'll have to ask her,' Madeleine replied. 'I'll get my daughter-in-law to introduce her to you when we have afternoon tea.'

Tony eyed the young beauty intently as he put forward his proposal. Undoubtedly, she was supermodel material.

'I — I don't think I could do that,' Angelina looked down at the floor. 'I wouldn't know how.'

Just look at the length of those eye lashes he thought,

before he snapped to with a response. 'Don't worry, we'd show you how. The other girls are learning as well.'

Angelina looked at Jennifer. 'What do you think, Mum?'

'I suppose it wouldn't hurt. It's all for a good cause, I suppose,' Jennifer replied. 'But you'll have to ask your father.'

Jennifer knew that Dominic would agree. He would relish the sight of his beautiful daughter under the spotlight before an admiring audience, many of them business associates of his. But it would be on his terms. The clothes would be scrutinised beforehand, and the make-up artist under strict instructions. His daughter would not be paraded like some cheap bimbo.

9

It wasn't until the night unfolded that Jennifer regretted her decision to allow Angelina to take to the catwalk.

It never dawned on her that the move would cause the slightest concern to Cara, who had merely shrugged when the idea was put forward. But when Angelina glided down the catwalk in a fuchsia pink satin dress and the audience gasped, Jennifer could feel Cara's body go rigid beside her. *Oh no*, she groaned inwardly, but by then it was too late. Dominic was already pumped up like a peacock to her other side. She could see the flash of his white teeth in the darkness as the comments began to flow.

'Is that Dominic's daughter?' came someone's voice from behind.

'Isn't that girl stunning. The one in the pink,' said another.

'She's a natural.'

Jennifer had to admit that Angelina had the edge. Her poise and graceful movement had come from years of ballet lessons.

As Angelina passed, Madeleine stiffened. The memory sprang to mind of a similar woman with a similar gait and grace and her heart squeezed with pain.

It wasn't until Jennifer turned to Cara that she noticed the empty seat beside her.

The moment the parade reached its conclusion, Jennifer headed straight to Cara's room. As expected, her daughter was long gone. There was little point in sending out a search party; Cara was more than likely in one of the caves at the beach and would return when she was ready. This had happened before, although not for some time.

'Damn,' she muttered, as she slumped on the bed to think.

In her mind she had a flash of Angelina, ten years on, dressed in corporate clothes and hosting a meeting in Dominic's board room, surrounded by admiring clients. Jennifer felt her mouth go dry. *Don't be ridiculous,* she thought. *The child's not yet begun secondary school.* But truthfully, Angelina was slowly filling the void left by Joseph's death, with Dominic doing little to dissuade her interest in his business affairs.

With a heavy heart Jennifer picked the crumpled dress

off the floor and hung it in the wardrobe, before returning to the marquee where supper was being served. The scent of freshly cut roses permeated the air and the place was abuzz with chatter. Waiters weaved their way through the crowd, trays of drinks high in hand, while a jazz quartet played in one corner.

Dominic was not hard to spot in the midst of the crowd, oozing charm with drink in hand. As Jennifer edged closer, it was clear that Angelina was the topic of conversation. Dominic beamed and nodded, one eye on his beautiful daughter as the compliments continued to flow. Jennifer could do little but play the gracious hostess at his side, grateful that Cara was out of sight. However, her thoughts were never far from her eldest daughter. *How am I going to fix this one*, she thought at the end of the evening when she found Cara's room still empty.

Dominic wasn't much help.

'I wouldn't worry too much,' he said sat on the edge of their bed to take off his shoes. 'You know what she's like. She'll be back when she's ready.'

When there was no response, he gave a sigh. 'For heaven's sake, Jen, how were we to know that she'd take off like that. Maybe the whole thing bored her. Who knows? She'll have forgotten about it in a few days. Anyway, doesn't she have exams next week?'

You just don't get it, do you, she thought, as she unzipped her dress.

Down by the beach Cara sat in the darkness holding

Madeleine's Persian cat. A blanket was draped around her shoulders. 'Just you and me, Duchess,' she said softly, 'just you and me.'

In the early hours of the morning a young couple were driving past Kilkenny on their way to the clifftop lookout.

'Joel, watch out!' the girl screamed as a white object flew through the air onto the road ahead.

The teenager swerved but it was too late as they felt the thud. He screeched to a halt and jumped out. 'Shit, it's someone's cat!' he exclaimed.

His companion was white faced. 'What'll we do?'

'Nothing we *can* do. It's dead anyway.' He ran one hand quickly over his hair. 'We'd better get out of here fast. If your parents find out we'll be in big trouble.'

He lifted the cat onto the side of the road, hastily wiped his hands on the grass and jumped back into the car.

10

The family were awoken by the noise of workers dismantling the catwalk.

'Do they have to start so early?' Dominic mumbled, as he pulled the covers over his head.

Jennifer rolled over to look at the bedside clock. 'It's ten-thirty, Dom.'

There was a groan. 'Okay. I s'pose we'd better make a move.'

Jennifer rose, dressed and headed to the kitchen where Madeleine was preparing breakfast. Angelina was perched at one end of the kitchen bench chatting animatedly, while Cara sat before her untouched cup of tea, staring out the window. Jennifer watched with a feeling of unease. She recognised that look, even if she had no idea what it signified. She sensed things were about to take a turn for the worst.

'Jennifer, have you seen Duchess by any chance?' Madeleine asked.

'No, not since last night.'

'Hm.' Madeleine looked thoughtful. 'She's usually down for her food by now, that's all.'

'She can't be far away,' Jennifer said. 'I'll go and look for her after breakfast.'

But things never reached that point. The gardener arrived not long afterwards, shifting uncomfortably in the doorway as he addressed Madeleine. 'I'm afraid, I've got some bad news, Mrs. Lorenzo. 'Your cat's been killed on the road during the night.'

'Oh no!' Jennifer gasped.

Madeleine's hand flew to her mouth and Jennifer was quick to rush to her side, to steady her.

Angelina burst into tears. 'Not Duchess!'

'What in the hell's going on?' Dominic demanded, as he pushed past the gardener and entered the room. He shook his head as Jennifer told him the news. 'I said to lock the darn thing up, didn't I?'

'But I thought we had, Dad,' Angelina said between sobs. 'Duchess was in the house before we left for the fashion parade.' She paused. 'I saw Cara holding her when I came inside later to get another pair of shoes.'

Cara looked daggers at Angelina but Dominic didn't seem to notice. 'So, you saw the cat as well, Cara?' he asked.

'You heard what she said,' came the cold response. 'I'm going outside.'

The back door slammed and there was a momentary silence.

'Everyone has their own way of grieving,' remarked the gardener, not knowing what else to say.

§

Three days later Dominic's mobile rang, as the family sat down to dinner and he flicked the on button to take the call.

'Lorenzo speaking.' There was a pause. 'She what?'

Jennifer stiffened as his eyes locked on Cara's.

He listened for a moment. 'And can you tell me what they were?'

Another pause. 'I see.' His face was grim. 'Thank you for contacting us. The matter will be addressed immediately.' Dominic punched the end button and glared at his eldest daughter. 'That was your homeroom teacher. It appears that you failed every one of your exams.'

Jennifer stared at him, open-mouthed. 'Could there have been a mistake, Dom?'

'There was no mistake.' Dominic's eyes never left his daughter's. 'So, would you mind telling me what this is about?'

Cara looked at her plate and mumbled a few words.

'I can't hear you. Look at me, damn it.'

'Dom –' Jennifer pleaded.

He gave a dismissive wave. 'Keep out of this, Jennifer. Well?' The tone was ominous. 'I'm waiting.'

Silence. A hand clenched under the table.

'Cut the crap, Cara. You've already proven what you're capable of,' he fumed. 'If you don't pick up your act then –'

'Then what?' Cara shrieked. Rising to her feet, she sent the chair reeling backwards. 'You'll send me to some snobby boarding school?'

Jennifer and Dominic exchanged a quick glance and Cara was quick to notice. 'Don't pretend you haven't discussed it. I heard you both. Is that what you want? To get me out of the way?'

'Cara' Jennifer exclaimed, but she pushed on relentlessly. 'Oh, it's all so different when I receive a distinction or two, isn't it, Dad. Suddenly, I'm something to brag about.'

'You ungrateful bitch!' Dominic exploded. 'Why can't you be more like your sister?'

'Why would I want to?' Cara screamed. 'At least I don't crawl to people. At least I –'

'Get out of here now!' he fired back.

'I'm just going.' Cara stormed out of the room, almost running into Madeleine who had arrived late for dinner.

'And you're not much different, are you.' Cara accused her, eyes blazing. 'It's Angelina this and Angelina that.'

Jennifer looked aghast. 'Cara, apologise to your grandmother at once!'

'Why should I! I meant it.'

Madeleine stood ramrod straight and with one firm movement seized her granddaughter's forearm.

'Now, I don't know what went on just now,' her voice was cold, 'but stop acting like a spoilt brat.'

Cara jerked her arm free and strode out the door.

'Hm, I'll be having a word with that young lady,' Madeleine said as she pulled out a chair. 'You can fill me in later, Dominic. Now let's get on with dinner, shall we?'

Jennifer sat deeply troubled, her barely touched meal before her. It was true that she and Dominic had considered moving Cara to a private school. Dominic argued that high fees provided the state's best teachers, who could only enhance Cara's academic potential. To Jennifer, this was simply a ruse. Dominic had always desired private school education for his children. It was an ego thing; the prestige of it all. But there was one glaring obstacle — his mother.

Jennifer recalled Madeleine's firm response when Dominic broached the subject years ago. The mention of the school, the city's most prestigious, was met with a derisive snort.

'My granddaughters will *not* be subjected to such snobbery,' she said. 'Nor will they be taken from Kilkenny to be cooped up at a boarding school, in some gloomy dormitory with Lord knows who. What was good enough for *your* education and your father's, is good enough for them.'

The subject had not been raised since, nor did Jennifer believe that Madeleine's views would have wavered.

Meanwhile, the local college attended by her daughters was reputable enough and Jennifer could not fault the dedication and enthusiasm of its young staff. Things should settle once Madeleine had words with Cara and she'd met to discuss things with Cara's teachers.

She glanced across the table to where Angelina stood behind Dominic, her arms draped around his neck.

'Got things to do now, Dad.' She planted a kiss on his cheek. 'Love you.'

Dominic grinned. 'Love you too, Angie.'

Angelina rushed around to give Jennifer and Madeleine a quick hug and then she was gone.

Jennifer's spirits plummeted. During the last hour, Dominic's blatant favouritism towards one daughter and his unconcealed disdain for the other had never been more obvious.

¶

Three days later Jennifer was going through some accounts when she heard a scream coming from the garden. With a start, she jumped to her feet, sending paper scattering to the floor like a snow storm. As she tore down the stairs and through the back door, she saw Angelina riveted to the spot and looking down, hands over her mouth. At her feet were the girls' two pet rabbits, their necks hanging to one side at an obscene angle, a trail of red seeping onto the grass.

Jennifer gasped and was quick to pull her youngest daughter's head against her chest. 'Don't look Darling,' she soothed. 'Let's get you inside.' Her heart pounded as she led Angelina into the house and settled her on the sofa.

'Who would do this, Mum?' Angelina said between sobs.

'I don't know,' Jennifer replied grimly. 'But there's some things I need to attend to. Will you be right here for a few minutes?'

There was a nod. Jennifer hurried outside to phone the gardener, who had not long arrived, and was at work in the distance near a jumble of sheds.

'Hi Ben, there's been an incident in the back garden. Can you come at once?' 'Yes, of course,' he replied.

The cold morning air chilled her, despite the first rays of sun breaking through the blanket of grey. She dug her hands deeper into her pockets as she waited.

'Holy hell!' the old gardener exclaimed when he dismounted from his quad bike and viewed the mangled mess before him. 'Christ, there's some sick people about.'

He didn't tell of the things he'd heard. What was the point in terrifying her?

'I'd be giving the police a call Mrs L. I'll deal with this mess. I'll cover 'em up in the meantime.' He took her elbow. 'Now off you go.'

'Thanks. Jennifer said gratefully. She paused for a second. 'How long ago do you think this happened, Ben?'

The gardener shrugged. 'The early hours of the morning at a guess.'

Jennifer shuddered. How many more nights until Dominic returned from the city? And why hadn't the dog barked?

12

As winter approached, a sense of unease pervaded the town, following a spate of disturbing events. Curtains were drawn, fingers pointed and tongues wagged. It was not difficult to find a scapegoat. The Zielinski residence's nocturnal visitor had returned.

Cara had been drawn to the Zielinski house for as long as she could remember. Whenever the chance arose, she would slip out quietly of an evening and head along the cliff path towards the adjoining property. When the mysterious inhabitant returned the urge to visit intensified. Not that she could see much. There was an occasional faint glow in the basement. That's where he lived.

Cara would sit metres away in the darkness, back against the old pine, legs tucked under her chin. The dank smell of pine needles, the moan of the wind, and the familiar creak of the veranda were somehow comforting.

It was as if she and the phantom resident were connected in an unfathomable way — kindred tormented souls. Who was he? What did it matter? She no longer felt the need to know. She felt in no danger. Contrary to what they said in town, Helen Zielinski's son was no crazy madman, sent here for respite. Her mother had set the record straight a long time ago. David Zielinski left for Europe years ago to pursue his career and had not been back since.

It was not unusual for Cara to disappear for one of her walks. The family learned not to ask questions. Life was harmonious that way. So, when she passed the room where they sat with their eyes glued to the larger-than-life plasma screen, no one stirred.

The night chill had already set in as she headed briskly along the familiar clifftop path, wind buffeting her hair and jacket zipped tight. It was the sound of a broken twig not far behind that caused her to jump and whirl around, her heart racing.

'Sorry.' A tall, gangly boy not much older than her materialised from the shadows, holding up his hands. 'I didn't mean to scare you.'

'You — you're in my Maths class!' she exclaimed.

He nodded and stepped towards her.

'So what in hell are you doing up here and why are you following me?'

'I wasn't following you,' he replied.

'You just *happened* to be walking along the same path after dark, in the middle of nowhere.'

'Yeah well, usually I go to the beach. But tonight, I

thought I'd come up here to check out where the guy lives, the one everybody's talking about.'

'Why?'

He shrugged. 'Something to do, I guess. There's only a few more houses along here, so it had to be one of them. And when I saw you ahead, I figured that's maybe where you were heading.'

'Well, I wasn't,' she snapped. 'Now get lost.'

'Fair enough,' and digging his hands in his pockets he walked off in the other direction.

Cara glanced over her shoulder as she continued along the path but he had gone.

§

The following morning the boy avoided her eyes during Maths and sat on the opposite side of the room. Cara noted that he kept to himself in the school yard, as did she. There was something about him, something that reminded her of herself. As the day wore on the need to approach him intensified. Did he head to the beach at night, as he said?

That night she set off to find out. The beach was deserted, apart from a lone figure perched on the sand in the distance, looking out to sea. Pulling off her runners and shoving them into her backpack, she edged along the sand dunes and down for a closer look. It was the boy. She recognised him from his lanky frame, white t-shirt and tangle of dark, wavy hair.

As Cara approached, she tensed and cleared her throat.

He turned his head at the sound.

'Mind if I sit down?' she asked.

He gave a nod.

As Cara slid onto the sand beside him, she remarked, 'You don't seem surprised to see me.'

There was a shrug. 'I've seen you here before.'

Cara wrapped her arms around her body and shoved her hands under her armpits. 'Aren't you cold?'

'Nah, don't feel the cold much.'

The two sat in silence for a while, elbows on knees, hypnotised by the crash of waves against the shore.

'Look, I'm sorry about last night. Okay?' Cara said.

He gave her a sideward glance. 'I shouldn't have crept up on you like that.'

Cara felt herself redden and she was glad of the darkness. 'You're right. I *was* going to the Zielinski house but I wanted to be alone. That's all.'

'I can relate to that.'

Cara dug her bare feet into the sand and could feel the chill seep up through the soles of her feet.

'It just takes me a while to trust people, that's all.'

'Fair enough.' The boy reached for a thread of dried seaweed and twirled it in his fingers.

'I don't even know your name,' she said.

'Will.'

'I'm Cara.'

The boy nodded, bemused. As if he *wouldn't* know. The

Lorenzo family and their millions were hardly a secret around town.

'So, Will,' she ventured, 'do you still want to see the Zielinski house?'

'Yeah. Why not.'

'You won't see much at this time of night. How about we go there tomorrow after school?'

'Okay.' The boy continued to look ahead.

'I'll meet you on the clifftop then, near my place. Make it around five.' Cara got up and brushed the sand from her jeans before heading off.

¶

The following day, Cara's class was kept in for an after-school detention but Will was waiting when she got home.

'Got held up?' he asked.

'Bloody teachers,' she mumbled, as she shoved her backpack under a nearby bush.

There was a grin. 'Usually it's my class that gets kept in.'

'Yeah, well it should be the ones who muck up. Not everyone else.' She gave a grunt. 'Well come on, the house isn't far from here.'

The two headed along the path, until Cara stopped, nodding to her right.

'Wow. The place has been let go hasn't it,' he said as they climbed through the wire fence and onto the Zielinski property.

'Yeah. But it was pretty amazing once.'

Cara recalled the well-maintained lawns and low-maintenance garden of an assortment of coastal natives, climbing roses and perennials. The wizened old gardener who tended the grounds passed away, years ago.

'It's only ever been a holiday house, though,' she continued.

'Some holiday house.' He gave a whistle as they edged around the overgrown lawn to the front garden.

Despite its age, the sprawling sandstone façade had lost little of its original charm. The blinds, permanently drawn for as long as Cara could remember, fuelled her childish imagination. What lay beyond?

As if reading her mind, he said, 'ever been inside?'

She shook her head. 'No, but I came here as a kid, to explore the gardens and stuff.'

He grinned. 'I bet you did. Do you have any brothers or sisters?'

'A sister.'

'Was she in on it?'

The silence was stony.

'I guess not, huh.' He paused. 'Can I ask you something?'

'I s'pose but I'm not saying I'll answer you.'

'Do your parents ask where you've been when you get back?'

'Screw my parents!' Cara shot back. 'First you ask about my sister, then them.'

He went to touch her arm but she flung his hand aside.

'How dare you ask about my bloody family!'

'It's just –'

'Just what?'

'I figured there was something well, not great between you and them, that's all.'

'Oh, Mr Mind reader, are you?' she blazed.

'No. It's just that I have a screwed-up family, that's all.'

'Yeah, well the world's full of fucking, screwed-up people!'

Without another word, she turned and strode towards the path.

Will watched her go. Being around Cara Lorenzo would never be easy.

12

Cara sat by the window in darkness. Life wasn't too bad. She was left alone at school which was the way she wanted it. The girls in her class gave her a wide berth. Even the most seasoned bully had given up long ago. Cara Lorenzo's tongue could lash someone to pieces in a manner of seconds.

But now there was Will. Unlike the others, he seemed unfazed by the obstacles she threw in his face. It unsettled her. With an angry yank of the curtains she climbed into bed, and lay staring at the shadows on the wall. She wondered why she'd taken him to the Zielinski house in the first place. *At least he got the message in the end,* she thought.

ꝙ

In the days to follow, Will kept his distance at school. However, by the third day, curiosity got the better of Cara.

What was so damned screwed-up about his family anyway, she wondered.

That afternoon she followed him home from school. His house, the last of three, sat along a dirt dead-end road not far from the beach, a kilometre or so out of town. It was more run down than she anticipated. Weeds choked the flower beds, the exterior was badly in need of a paint, and the windows were covered with a fine layer of salt. Cara had no idea what to expect. She crouched, hidden behind a nearby bush, peering through the branches as Will headed towards the back of the house. Minutes later he appeared, carrying two apples.

'Thought you might be hungry,' he pulled back a branch and handed her an apple.

Flustered and angry, she straightened and flicked the hair out of her eyes. 'You don't have to be so smug about it.'

'I'm not, actually. If anything, I should be ashamed that you've seen my house.'

'I couldn't care a stuff what your place looks like!' she flared.

He leaned against a nearby tree and took a bite of his apple. 'You can come in if you like. My Dad's not here.' He paused and half mumbled, 'Thank God.'

'What's with your dad?'

'Maybe one day I'll tell you and maybe you'll tell me about yours.'

Cara went to open her mouth but didn't.

He threw the apple core on the ground and headed

across the road. She followed.

'What about your mum? Is she at home?' she said from behind.

'Nope. And it's not my mum. It's Dad's partner.'

Cara nodded. 'How long's she been around?'

'Not long.'

'She okay?'

'I guess.'

'Meaning?'

He swung around, 'now who's asking questions.'

'Point taken.'

'I don't have much to do with her, if you must know. She's busy with the baby.' His eyes bore into hers. 'Now is that enough for you?'

Cara nodded. 'Sorry.'

There was an uncomfortable silence as Will opened the back door, and she followed him through the small entrance into a long, narrow passageway. As he opened the last door to the left, a heady mix of aromatic oils rushed to meet them.

'Wow,' Cara exclaimed as she entered the room and gazed at the array of leadlight lamps, patchwork quilts and handmade jewellery displayed around the room. She wandered around, touching things as if they were fragile butterflies. 'Who made all this stuff?'

'Dad's partner. She sells it at markets and stuff.'

'My God. She's talented.'

There was a shrug. 'Whatever.'

In the adjoining room, Cara spotted an old piano against the wall. 'Mind if I play?'

'I didn't know you did.'

There was a pause. 'Sometimes.'

'Go for it. I'll get us a Coke.'

Moments later, soft music wafted out into the passageway, as Will stood motionless in the doorway, cans in hand. He had grown accustomed to her frown, and was surprised by the softness on her face as she sat lost in time, fingers gliding over the keyboard. He smiled as she blew a stray lock of hair from her face, a picture of concentration. Until now, he had taken little notice of her hair. Caught by a shaft of light it shimmered like copper.

Neither heard the rattle of keys in the front door, or noticed the tall, dark haired woman who entered the room, dressed in a vibrant, African-patterned kaftan.

'That was lovely.' A deep voice resonated as Cara finished playing. 'Please, don't stop.'

Cara's hands flew off the keys as she spun around.

'I'm sorry to startle you,' the woman said. 'I'm Maggie and you are?'

'Cara,' Will was quick to intercede. 'She's from school.'

The woman crossed the room, hand outstretched. 'Pleased to meet you, Cara. So, tell me, how long have you been learning the piano?'

'I've never … been taught.' Cara's voice trailed.

'What?'

'I just hear something and play it.'

'That's wonderful, Cara. A gift. And look at your hands. They're the hands of an artist.'

Cara glanced down quickly down at them as if for the first time, grateful not to have inherited the broad, thick fingers of her father. She felt her cheeks redden as she rose from the piano stool.

'Your parents must be so proud,' the woman continued.

'They don't know I play.'

'What?' the response was incredulous.

'I don't think they'd really care much.'

'I'm sure they would.'

Cara shook her head. 'It's the way it's always been.' She quickly closed the piano lid. 'Look, I think I'd better get going.'

'Wait just a second,' Maggie lightly touched Cara's arm. 'Before you leave, do you read music at all?'

'No.'

'Would you like to learn?'

'Why?'

'Because music's within you, just as creating things is with me,' she replied. 'And because once you read music, doors can open for you. That's of course, if you want them to.'

Cara's head tilted to one side. 'I've never looked at it that way.'

'Well, perhaps you'd like to give it some thought. Let me know if you're interested. I'd be happy to help out.'

Maggie Tate thought she detected a spark of what might

have been excitement in the girl's eyes but it vanished as quickly as it appeared. *I don't know what's going on in that child's life.* She paused to reflect as she watched Cara head down the driveway, *but she's definitely troubled.*

Maggie was no gossip. She cared little about the goings-on in the town, or its residents. It was only after a discreet question here and there over the ensuing days that she learned of Cara's identity. It came as a surprise. Maggie detected none of the pretentiousness that so often went hand-in-hand with wealth. Nevertheless, the girl's aloofness and reticence to speak of her family was concerning. What on earth went on beyond the walls of Kilkenny she wondered.

Then there was the conversation that she'd overheard in the school carpark when she dropped some papers into the office. Cara had allegedly grabbed a classmate by the hair and threatened to smash her head into the lockers. 'Over some silly, passing comment,' the large woman with a mop of bleached blonde hair said. There had been no witnesses, but the victim had been threatened with far worse should she report the incident.

'Amy's mother went straight to the Principal,' the woman continued, 'but the whole thing was hushed.'

'Of course. What would you expect.' The words were laced with spite. 'That's what comes with having money.'

Was there something in what they said? Maggie chewed on her lip, as she slipped past them towards the school's entrance. Gossip, more likely than not. On the other hand, the child *had* appeared troubled. Definitely a dark horse. If provoked, could she be capable of such an act?

13

Autumn had morphed into an icy winter. Cold, south-westerly winds whipped off the ocean, bringing heavy rains. Late one afternoon, as water poured out of the broken drainpipe and onto the ground outside there was a knock on Maggie's door. There stood Cara, soaked to the skin, hair plastered to her face. 'Can we make a start?' was all she said.

Day after day Cara sat, deep in concentration, as she worked on her music theory. Soon to follow was a barrage of repetitive scales and tunes from the dog-eared music books of Maggie's childhood. It was as if the girl was starved of music and determined to make up for lost time. She spoke little; In fact, Maggie noted, Cara's behaviour was not unlike Will's.

Flames flickered in the open fireplace, casting an orange glow on the wall, as Maggie reflected on the fractured relationship with her partner's son. She doubted that he would open up to her, though Lord knows she'd tried. It was three years since she'd arrived on the scene, not long after the abrupt departure of Will's mother, Rebecca. The ensuing divorce was acrimonious, leaving Will's father, Tom, bitter and angry. She was the one to return the spark in him. With her he found love once again. Yet little was shown to Will.

It seemed to her that Tom was unnecessarily harsh towards his only son, possibly a legacy of his army days. As a captain he would have been necessarily strict, with high standards. It didn't help that Will bore a striking resemblance to his mother.

Because of Tom she felt younger than she had in years: more desirable, energised and fulfilled. Edging forty and single, with a trail of broken relationships, she'd long ago resigned herself to a childless existence.

When she found herself pregnant, it was bittersweet; the euphoria of impending motherhood contrasted against the crumbling relationship between her partner and his only son. Things had only worsened once Will reached his teenage years and started showing signs of defiance. Tom took to beating him, always behind closed doors. How could he think she did not know?

It was only a matter of time before Will retaliated. *Wait till he's bigger than you,* she thought. *Keep this up and you'll lose him altogether.*

Tom Easton had recently quit the Army to take on a position in a large security firm. Maggie knew it wouldn't last. He would move on; Army life was too deeply ingrained.

She also knew that Will wanted to stay put. He was sick of moving.

Maggie felt guilty for not being able to give Will the life he deserved, guilty for being unable to stop the beatings. And so she took to drink.

When Cara Lorenzo came onto the scene, Maggie hoped a friendship with her stepson might develop. But over time she found the relationship odd. The two spoke little and the girl often left without so much as a goodbye.

And then one day, Cara came no more.

¶

'Haven't seen you up here for a while,' Cara said without turning as Will approached from behind.

'Been a bit cold, don't you reckon?' he said as he sat down beside her under a tree.

'Didn't think the cold worried you.'

'Doesn't. But I thought it did for you.'

'Haven't stopped to think about it.' Cara tugged at a few blades of grass.

'So, you're not concerned about being here … you know, with him inside?'

'Oh for God's sake Will, lay off the guy!'

Will grabbed hold of her arm as he locked eyes on hers. 'Maybe you haven't heard, but things are happening around here again, same as last time he was here.'

Cara jerked her arm free. 'Oh really? What sort of things, then?'

'They found a decapitated cat not far from here, for one.'

'I know.' Cara paused; her eyes faraway. 'I wonder what it would be like to decapitate a cat.'

Will stiffened, unable to think of anything to say.

'Well?' Cara challenged, 'Anyone's capable of that. You, … me.'

'Maybe, but don't talk like that, okay? It gives me the creeps.'

'Suit yourself.'

The rain started to fall, lightly at first, then in heavy, persistent drops.

'You can stay here if you like,' she said, grappling with the hood of her jacket as she scrambled to her feet. 'But I'm going.'

He didn't say anything. He just watched her go.

¶

The following evening, he was there, sitting against the same windswept tree. As she approached, he turned.

'Haven't seen you up here for a while,' he mocked.

A smile escaped her lips. A brief flash and then it was gone. Will tilted his head to one side. *She should do that more often,* he thought.

Cara sat down beside him and said, 'I didn't think you'd be back, actually.'

'Why, because of all that cat stuff?'

'You think you know me, Will, but you don't.'

'Does it really matter?' he said. 'I came up here last night to tell you something.'

'Yeah?'

'I'm leaving in a few weeks.'

There was a moment's silence.

'Why?' As expected, her face gave nothing away.

'It's the way it's always been. We've never lived in a place for more than a year or so.'

Cara stared fixedly ahead. 'I thought you were happy here.'

'Since when does my happiness come into anything,' he muttered. 'Look, I don't wanna talk about it. Okay?'

'But –'

'I said, I don't want to talk about it. Don't you get that?' His eyes blazed. 'You're right, Cara Lorenzo, I don't know you at all, and you sure as hell don't know me. It's probably better that way. Huh?'

Will scrambled to his feet and stormed down the path towards the cliffs.

Cara wrapped her arms tightly around her knees and sat … still. It didn't matter. It was easier to be on your own.

Will no longer attended school, nor came to the Zielinski house. And then, two weeks later at dusk as she headed along the cliff path she noticed a lone figure on the beach below. For a few moments she paused, unsure of what to do. Then, heart pumping, she headed back towards the overgrown path that led to the shore.

He turned to face her as she flopped down beside him.

'We're all packed,' he said. 'We're leaving in the morning.'

'Where to?'

'Dunno.'

Both sat in silence, listening to the crash of the waves and watching a few gulls wheeling against the pink tinged sky.

'Well, I'd better get going.' Will lifted one hand and slowly traced his fingers over her face.

'Look after yourself, okay?'

Cara closed her eyes for a moment, and when she opened them he was already up, looking down as he spoke, 'I'll be back, someday.'

She watched motionless, fingers lingering momentarily against her cheek, as he headed around the cove and out of sight.

9

After lunch the following day, Madeleine entered the kitchen and confronted Cara.

'So, you're up at last, young lady! In case, you've forgotten, it's your turn to clean the kitchen.'

The housekeeper came four days a week and the girls alternated household chores on her days off.

'I'll do it when I'm ready,' Cara replied irritably, as she tapped another app on her iPad.

Dominic slammed his newspaper down on the table. You'll do as your grandmother says. Now!'

'I'm sick of this!' Cara screamed, eyes locked on his. 'Why don't you lay off for a change, huh?'

But Dominic was undeterred. 'You will apologise immediately.'

'And if I don't?'

Dominic was about to explode but she gave a dismissive wave. 'I know, I know. I was out of line and I'm sorry. Is that good enough for you?' Cara thumped her hand so hard on the table that the coffee she'd just made splashed across her fingers.

'Oh shit!' She exclaimed, with a jerk of her hand. With eyes blazing, she kicked at the chair then stormed out of the room.

Ten minutes later, she returned to find Angelina alone, wiping the last of the dishes.

'You're loving this, Angelina, aren't you.'

'No actually, I'm worried about you.' Angelina replied, as she folded the tea towel.

'Oh really?'

'You looked pretty rattled when you walked in last night, that's all.'

'Huh?'

'Look, I didn't know where you'd been, but you looked as though you needed someone to talk to.'

'Are you for real?' Cara said incredulously. 'So you can go straight to Mum and Dad and blab? As if I'd talk to you in the first place … about anything. And for your information I'm fine, just fine. Now butt out of my life!'

As Cara strode towards the door, she gave a shove so violent, that Angelina was sent reeling into a nearby cupboard.

'Geez, Cara,' Angelina rubbed her arm gingerly as she rose to her feet. 'There's something seriously wrong with you!'

The words caused Cara to stop dead in her tracks. 'You'll keep,' she said without turning.

14

As the year drew to a close, Cara's high marks at school drew some begrudging respect from Dominic. A month prior to her Year Twelve exams, he dropped by her room late one night, where she sat absorbed in a mathematical equation. Poking his head around the door he asked, 'Have you got a minute?'

'I s'pose.' Cara said without looking up.

Dominic entered and perched on a nearby stool, with his hands resting on his knees. 'I just wanted to ask you something.'

This time, Cara put down pen and paper and turned to face him … 'Okay.'

'Where do you plan to go from here, Cara? he asked, 'Career wise, that is.'

'Where do you want me to go?'

'That's not what I asked.'

Cara straightened. 'Okay. Am I to be in on the family business, then?'

Her directness caught him off guard.

'Is that what you want?'

'Is that what *you* want?'

'You know damned well it is. For you and your sister.'

'I see,' she said. 'Count me in then. Once I've finished my Uni degree.'

Dominic nodded with a satisfied smile.

'You'll have to work hard, bloody hard, though.' he said. 'Just as I did.'

Cara tilted her chin. 'I'm up to the challenge.'

His eyes never left hers. 'I'll hold you to it.'

Dominic rose and headed to his office, where he poured himself a neat scotch. Settling into his leather recliner, he reached for his glass well pleased with what he'd just heard. To this point, he'd not been able to gauge Cara's interest in the family firm and her direct response came as a surprise.

Angelina's future, on the other hand, was already a given. She had eyes only for the company and over time proved her business acumen. Furthermore, it took just one sultry look from Angelina for prospective clients to arrange their next meeting. And she was just sixteen. Dominic wore a wry smile as he emptied the last of his scotch and clasped his hands behind his head. The years could not come quick enough until Angelina became part of the company. Cara's quick brain and mathematical prowess would complement her sister's attributes, depending of course on how well the two could work alongside each other. Already Dominic was devising a plan to keep his daughters from killing each other — Angelina in the marketing side of things, with Cara handling the finances. Neither would have things easy. They would have to work hard as he did, and his father before him. The old adage was true. Overcoming adversity developed strength of character and, if you were lucky, wealth.

Not that Dominic wasn't born into money. His mother had ample money of her own. He just wished she wouldn't give so damned much to charity. If he had his way, he'd manage her finances more efficiently so that she could continue her philanthropy interests, while earning more from her investments. But he didn't have his way. Madeleine's mother had never trusted her son-in-law and set up a hefty trust fund for her daughter that no one else could touch.

Dominic grimaced. His mother almost smirked at him at times when finances were discussed. Well, he had all the patience in the world. She had no say over what he did once she was dead.

15

It was late afternoon when the Zielinski housekeeper glanced out the window. The wind was already up and buffeting through the time-worn trees along the cliff face, and dark clouds swirled in the distance.

How much longer can I keep doing this? Alice Hanley wondered, as she fumbled in her pockets for her gloves. Things could not have been better when she began working for the Zielinski family, thirty-two years ago. She could hardly believe her luck: a live-in position with a highly respected family in their inner-city residence. The job entailed regular visits to the family's seaside house, where little was asked apart from a weekly drive to town for supplies, cooking, and light cleaning duties. The exhilarating rush of sea air, and the ocean's distant roar were the things she missed most when she returned to the city.

Despite her wealth, Alice's employer showed none of the pretentiousness of her wealthy city neighbours. Helena Zielinski retained just one housekeeper and a full-time gardener-cum-maintenance man. There was no nanny for the Zielinski's only child … a sensitive boy with green pensive eyes.

Alice gave a smile. Despite his endearing qualities, David Zielinski was no angel. He could wrestle and scrap with the best of his mates and forever arrived home covered in scratches and grazes. These were joyous times for Alice but all too fleeting. She was well suited to her role. With her strict upbringing and no-nonsense values, she was relied upon for her reliability and discretion. Conversely, Alice considered Helena Zielinsky to be the most wonderful, generous person she'd ever met.

As time passed, Alice was able to put aside the brutality that she'd suffered at the hands of her husband and move on. She'd become part of the Zielinski family and she felt blessed. Few people led the privileged life that she did.

But now she was sixty-eight and the wintry, ocean blasts chilled her bones like ice packs. As the days passed Alice yearned to be back at her centrally heated quarters in the city to catch up on some well-deserved rest. In recent years she'd been asked to stay for longer here during winter, much to her chagrin. Nights were spent huddled over the bar heater in the living room, but Alice Handley was too proud to ask for an upgrade. Not that the Zielinskis couldn't afford it. They mainly came in the summer months when the balmy sea breeze was an intoxicating elixir, and heating was the last thing to come to mind.

Meanwhile, the cold didn't seem to affect him. Never

had. He seemed content to stay in the basement. It worried her. Why wouldn't he let her down there? Still, it was none of her business. As long as he came up for his medication. Anything was better than the Institution. The three years spent there had almost killed him. But she couldn't stop him going out at night, not like she promised Helena. She had never been able to. Plus, if his face was seen in the daylight …

16

I t was dusk when Jennifer and Cara drove back to Kilkenny, following a family weekend in the city. Angelina had chosen to spend an extra day with her father at the office.

It had been some time since Jennifer had spent time alone with Cara and the hour and a half journey seemed excruciatingly long. Attempts at light banter were met with grunts or stony silence. *What is it with Cara* she thought, *what have we done to make her like this?* Sometimes, it was like talking to someone in a dream.

As the journey wore on, Jennifer's thoughts became more troubled. Where to from here? She would have given anything to hear her daughter laugh again, watch her eyes dance. When was the last time *that* happened? Good God! It had to be the day her pony arrived at Kilkenny. Jennifer's heart was heavy as she turned into the driveway. After dinner, she found herself pacing the living room. Reaching for her keys on the table she dropped by Madeleine's room. 'I'm just heading out for some milk. Okay?'

There was a nod.

Starting the car, she reached for a CD that had not been played for some time. As the notes of her favourite Chopin *Étude* filled the air, tears filled her eyes. 'Damn it,' she muttered, wiping her face with the back of her hand.

Three kilometres ahead was a lookout, renowned for its spectacular ocean views. Despite the darkness, Jennifer swung into the empty car park. Grateful for the solitude she cut the ignition, slumped against the seat and closed her eyes. The music brought to mind the brief, rapturous affair of long ago that she'd tried so hard to erase from her memory. A brief smile formed as she recalled the sensuous touch of the fingers that traced her shoulders and gently unbuttoned her blouse as she lay in the sand dunes.

She'd tried so hard to forget her lover. But how could she? He was everything Dominic was not: sensitive, empathetic and considerate. *Fool, fool*, she muttered to herself. *Why in the hell did you let things get so out of hand in the first place.* It was never to be.

Deeply troubled over her one and only indiscretion, she vowed never again to be disloyal to her husband.

But that didn't stop Dominic's suspicions whenever they stepped out. An involuntary shiver went through her, as she recalled the handsome barrister whose repeated advances towards her led to his downfall. One swift act of revenge by Dominic brought the young man to his knees.

She was under no illusions what her husband was capable of.

What if he learned of her affair? The thought had always been there, lurking deep in her mind like some dark beast. As time went by nothing was mentioned, much to Jennifer's relief. But just when she thought that the matter had been put to rest, there'd been one or two of his cryptic comments … the looks.

Jennifer sat up with a start and her eyes wide open. No use worrying about something that might never happen. Best she got home. She'd been gone too long as it was.

Her heart was pounding as she turned on the ignition and pulled out of the car park. Once home, she headed straight to Madeleine's room and knocked on the door.

'You took a while.' The old woman's eyes were sharp as Jennifer entered the room.

'I found myself checking some emails on my phone at the store,' she lied.

'Hmm. Now sit down and tell me how things went on the trip back today with Cara. Not too well, gathering from the look on your face when you walked in the door.'

Jennifer nodded. 'I just wish she'd just open up a bit more.'

'Have you ever thought back to when *you* were a sixteen- year- old?'

Jennifer smiled and gave Madeleine's hand a squeeze. 'Point taken.'

¶

As the harsh winter winds subsided at the onset of spring Madeleine resumed her daily walks around the garden, welcoming the sun's warmth on her back at last. One morning as she rested on a wooden garden bench, she noticed Angelina heading in her direction. Immediately she was reminded of the same willowy figure, graceful walk and long dark hair of Angelina's mother. The memory brought a flood of regrets. She could well have discouraged Dominic from adopting Angelina, and have had her sent to an orphanage. But that would have been selfish. With Jennifer's failure to conceive, followed by Cara's complicated birth, Angelina came along just at the right time. Jennifer had instantly fallen in love with the child. The tiny bundle would compensate for the second child it was thought she would never have. Who would have thought that Joseph would arrive unexpectedly, four years later.

If only Angelina's resemblance to Lucinda wasn't so damned striking, she thought. *But it's hardly the child's fault.*

'Morning, Gran.'

'Good morning, Darling.'

'Mind if I join you?'

'Not at all.' Reluctantly, Madeleine patted the seat beside her. 'Now tell me what you've been up to.'

Usually, Madeleine looked forward to the times when Angelina dropped by for a chat. It took just a few minutes with her vivacious grandchild for Madeleine to feel energised and young herself. She watched as Angelina chattered about life at school and times spent with her father at the office.

'And boys?' Madeleine peered over the top of her glasses.

'Oh Gran!' Angelina said with a smirk. 'That's for you to find out.'

Angelina's eyes swept around the garden and she slipped her arm through Madeleine's. 'They're beautiful, aren't they, Gran,' she said wistfully. 'The roses, I mean. Whenever I think of Kilkenny I think of the roses.'

'Yes. Me too. Pink is my favourite. What about you?'

'Red.'

'They were your mother's favourites as well. '

'Really?' Angelina's eyes shone. 'Please Gran, tell me some more about my mother.'

'I've told you all I know.'

'Have you?'

'What do you mean?' Madeleine said quietly.

'There has to be more. More than that she was beautiful and died while giving birth to me.'

Madeleine shifted slightly. 'I'm sorry, dear but that's all there is to tell.'

Truth was, Lucinda Alcaraz had refused to go to hospital when her waters broke, and in desperation, Madeleine had called a local midwife. Lucinda's subsequent death secured Madeleine's absolute silence for a small sum of money.

'How can it be?' Angelina persisted. 'She was your

housekeeper for a year before she died. She lived at Kilkenny for God's sake.'

'Yes, she did. Our previous housekeeper, Ginny, was about to retire and move to town to be with her daughter. Your mother couldn't have arrived at a better time.'

'So who was my real father then?' Angelina challenged. 'You must know that.' She had only recently set eyes on her birth certificate, labelling her father as Unknown but Madeleine knew that wouldn't stop Angelina from searching for his identity.

'I've told you before, Angelina. Your mother did not wish to discuss it and I felt I had no right to ask.'

'That's crap!' she shouted, wrenching her arm free and leaping to her feet. Without turning she stormed down the path, ripping off the heads of every pink rose in sight.

Madelene watched in disbelief as the petals fell in Angelina's wake. For a long while she sat, motionless, eyes unseeing.

The sudden chirping of a bird brought Madeleine to her senses. *Well you can hardly blame the child,* she reasoned. It was human nature to want to know one's roots. What concerned Madeleine more was how much longer she could keep hiding the truth. Until now a comment here or there was enough to satisfy Angelina's curiosity, but not now.

Madeleine took a deep breath. No, Angelina's remorse at what she'd just done should keep her from asking again. Her hunch proved to be correct. A few words of mumbled apology from Angelina were enough. There was no mention of her mother again.

17

As the Year Twelve exams loomed Cara studied until all hours, only appearing for the occasional late-night snack, or to head out for one of her walks. Once the exams ended, Cara chose not to participate in the end-of-year mock-up day and after party. Nor was she interested in heading to the Surf Coast with her classmates during schoolies week, much to Jennifer's relief. From the stories she'd heard it would be reassuring to have her daughter home, safely out of harm's way. Little did she know that Cara had plans of her own.

Late one afternoon, Cara arrived home dressed in black with her auburn hair cut short, spiked and laced with streaks of purple, red and black.

'What the –' Dominic exploded. A vein stood out in his neck.

'A bit Goth, Dad, don't you think?' Cara gave an exaggerated pose, one hand akimbo.

Jennifer placed a restraining hand on Dominic's arm.

'Leave this one to me,' she said quietly.

'You bet I will!' He stormed out of the room.

'So what's this about, Cara?' Jennifer began.

'I gather you don't like my new hairstyle.'

'It's different.' Jennifer was careful to keep her voice neutral. 'I'm just a bit surprised, that's all. You didn't mention anything about getting it cut.'

'Oh, for Christ's sake, Mum. Do I have to tell you everything?' At that, Cara turned on her heels and strode out of the room, leaving Jennifer deep in thought. There was little about Cara that she *did* know.

¶

'Are those girls of yours out raging yet?' Jennifer's sister, Kate, asked during a Skype session from her London home.

'No, you know what Dom's like.'

'Well, don't you think he should get with the times?'

'I suppose so.'

'Jacqui's been to a few parties — screened by us first, of course. And as for Ashley, we didn't think he'd even look at a girl. It seems like he's making up for lost time.'

Jennifer laughed. 'He's what, sixteen now? I still think of Ashley as a ten-year-old. How time flies.' There was a pause. 'You're right, Kate, it's time we let go a bit.'

As Jennifer shut down the computer, she paused to reflect. The dreaded teenage party scene had to be faced sooner or later. She ran a palm across her forehead.

Perhaps things wouldn't be that bad. Dominic had already drilled the girls as to what was expected and how to handle themselves. A bead of sweat ran down her neck. It wasn't the girls she was worried about. For now there was *some* breathing space. Angelina had the year to finish and to Jennifer's knowledge Cara showed little interest in meeting up with anyone, let alone going out.

Or so she thought.

It was only by chance as she drove through town that she caught a glimpse of Cara amongst a group of others her age with similar haircuts and black garb. 'What the –' she exclaimed, turning her head as she passed.

Who were these kids? What did they get up to?

Jennifer remembered back to her Year Twelve days. With a rueful smile she recalled the school uniforms hitched up around her waist, smokes shared with other girls at the back of the oval. Her parents didn't know the half of it.

Where to from here? Jennifer had been at pains not to question Cara's comings and goings once the exams had finished and was hesitant to do so now. What right had she to intervene in the first friendship group her daughter had shown an interest in?

Dominic, however, would not see things in the same light. With a shudder she envisaged his reaction to Cara's latest fashion statement: black nails, matching lipstick and eyeliner.

Fortunately, he was away at the moment.

¶

To Jennifer's surprise Cara was invited to an eighteenth birthday party. Angelina would be attending a sleepover with classmates, so the request could hardly be refused. A discreet phone call here and there revealed that party would be supervised — whatever that meant. Jennifer knew little of the girl's parents but had no doubt that there would be alcohol. Not that this particularly concerned her — red wine was part of the Lorenzo tradition.

It was the unknown crowd that bothered her. There were so many questions she wanted to fire at her daughter. But she knew better. It would only add fuel to the fire. Still, that didn't stop her worrying.

On the night of the party, Jennifer insisted on driving Cara to the girl's house. At least she knew where to head should things go wrong. But she had to allow her daughter some trust. The deal was for Cara to return home by taxi, although heaven knows what time that would be.

Jennifer watched a movie then went to bed, where she tossed and turned, her mind flitting from one scenario to another. *Get used to it,* she thought. *There'll be more to come.*

Eventually, she drifted into an uneasy sleep.

Meanwhile, the party was in full swing. Alcohol flowed and punk rock music pumped as the group gyrated in the packed garage, arms in the air, bodies sweaty. One girl had passed out, face down in the corner beside a pool of vomit. Cara reached for another drink; her eyes dreamy and with a slight smile on her face.

9

'You have some answering to do, young lady,' Madeleine confronted Cara at the bottom of the stairs.

'Huh?' she mumbled with bleary eyes.

'You know what I'm referring to.' The voice was sharp.

'Try me.'

Madeleine was far from amused. 'I was reading until one thirty in the morning and you still weren't home. What time exactly *did* you get in?'

Cara shrugged. 'Search me.'

'Not good enough!' Madeleine exclaimed. 'You're not yet eighteen years of age, Cara. You have a duty to be home at a respectable hour.'

'And who are you to tell me what to do?' Cara fired back.

'I shouldn't have to speak to you at all.' Madeleine said evenly. 'There's no need with your sister.'

'Oh really!' Cara shrieked. 'Well it's time you knew that Angelina's not the little Miss Perfect everyone thinks.'

'What do you mean by that?'

'Oh forget it!' Cara rubbed her temples with the heels of her hands. 'Would you believe a word I said anyway?'

The raised voices caused Jennifer to appear from the kitchen.

'What's going on in here?'

'I'm just setting a few things straight, that's all.' Madeleine's eyes never left Cara's. 'And another thing, young lady you can get rid of that ridiculous hairstyle, throw those outrageous clothes in the bin, and make yourself respectable again.'

Cara put her hands over her ears. 'Oh shut up!' she shrieked. 'Just butt out of my life. You're nothing but an old woman who's stuck in the past.' She pushed past Madeleine and headed towards the door.

'I'm so sorry, Madeleine!' Jennifer exclaimed. 'I'll get Cara to apologise at once.'

'No, no need. I'd rather she goes, than listen to a forced apology.'

'But –'

Madeleine shook her head and gave a dismissive wave.

'Can we just keep this quiet, Madeleine?'

'Do you mean from Dominic?'

Jennifer nodded. 'Look, I know what she said just then was unforgivable but she's been studying hard these last few months. What she doesn't need right now is more pressure in her life.'

'Pressure?' Madeleine retorted. 'And what about the pressure she places on this family with her behaviour?'

'I know, I know,' Jennifer said with a sigh. 'I feel like tearing my hair out some times, believe me. Please, just this once?'

'Very well, but don't expect me to take sides with her once Dominic arrives home.'

As Madeleine rested in her room that afternoon, she reflected on the afternoon's events. Maybe Cara was right. *Maybe I am living in the past*, she thought. *It's time I stopped judging the girl. Time I stopped being so harsh.* It was clear that her eldest granddaughter had a mind of her own, not unlike herself at that age. But that spiked hair, drab clothes, the defiant hands on the hips … Madeleine took a deep breath. The phase would pass; fads always did. It was her relationship with Cara from here on in that was the most concerning.

18

As families prepared for their Christmas break, Cara's higher than expected Year Twelve ATAR score brought a satisfied smile to Dominic's face. And then, to Jennifer's amazement, Cara appeared one morning, her hair colour back to its original and wearing her favourite jeans and t-shirt.

'Got sick of the look,' was all she said as she walked out the door.

Christmas came and went and the summer break was all too short. Dominic took advantage of the exceptional heat by taking the family for outings on the yacht. These were the times that Jennifer treasured the most. For once, everyone seemed at peace, lost in their own thoughts as the *Jennifer* skimmed effortlessly across the waters. Could it be that the long-term rift had finally been healed between father and eldest daughter?

¶

The ensuing three years were the most harmonious that Jennifer could recall. Cara was accepted into the University of Melbourne, where she undertook a Bachelor of Commerce degree, while Angelina started work at Dominic's city office on completion of her Year Twelve studies. She stayed with her father at the family apartment, while Cara resided in the University Halls of Residence where, from what Jennifer could glean from those in the faculty, she kept to herself.

Cara was diligent in her studies, and to Dominic's delight, the faculty recommended a further two years at a graduate level on the completion of her degree. Cara's face was unreadable, while the discussions took place over the best course to choose.

'Master of Technology would be the most useful, in terms of the company,' Dominic concluded. 'The key to future proofing our business lies in the ability to adapt to change, particularly in the digital world. It's the one area we lack in expertise.'

The frigging business, always the business, Jennifer thought angrily. She turned to Cara. 'And what about you, Darling, which option would you prefer?'

There was a shrug. 'I'll give the one Dad just said a go, I s'pose.'

Jennifer felt her shoulders tighten. She had serious doubts about Cara's desire to further her studies, and technology was the subject she'd shown the least interest in.

Her hunch proved to be correct. The bombshell hit late the following year, when Cara returned home for the weekend.

'You're doing what!' Dominic exploded.

'You heard me. Taking a break next year,' came the controlled response. 'That's not asking too much is it?'

'Bullshit, Cara. You've only got one year to go, then that's it.'

'Yeah, one more year.' Cara shot back. 'But you know what, Dad, I'm over the study thing. I need a break, for God's sake! Got it?'

'I see,' the response was cold. 'So tell me, what do you propose to do in the meantime? Sit around on your arse and do nothing?'

'I'll figure something out.' Cara's eyes fixed on his.

'You'll have to because you won't be getting a cent from your mother or me in the meantime. I've been more than happy to cover your costs to this point. And it goes without saying you'll be immediately on the company payroll on the completion of your Masters, but until then …'

'I told you I'd work something out,' Cara's response was icy. 'Now, have you said all you wanted to say because I'm about to leave.'

Jennifer watched, eyebrows furrowed and arms crossed.

Had Dominic even considered the consequences of both girls working in the company, assuming that Cara *did* resume the final year of the course? Despite what her daughter had just said, Jennifer had doubts.

19

For the next few weeks, Dominic was moody and Cara was rarely to be seen. Just when things were starting to settle, the town was rocked by a series of deliberately lit fires and pet attacks. Jennifer felt uneasy. How many years had it been since the previous incidents — three, four?

¶

When the passer-by arrived on the doorstep with the body of Madeleine's Maltese Terrier in his arms, Dominic stared in disbelief. 'Oh Fuck!' Its throat had been slit and it had been repeatedly stabbed. Who would be capable of such an act of sadism? And why?

'What's wrong?' Madeline placed the tea towel on the sink and headed towards the door.

'Nothing you need to see, Mother.' Dominic made a hasty attempt to block her view, to no avail.

'No! Not Oscar!' Madeleine clutched at her chest and collapsed into his arms.

'Oh God!' the man stammered. 'I'm sorry. I found the dog near your front gate and thought you needed to know.'

'No, you did the right thing. Thanks,' Dominic said quickly over his shoulder as he eased Madeleine into a nearby chair. 'Lay him on the grass will you and scribble down your number. I'll be in touch.'

With shaking hands, Jennifer grabbed her phone and called triple zero. To her relief, two paramedics were quick to arrive and Madeleine was placed on a stretcher, lifted into the ambulance and on her way to hospital.

By the time the ambulance arrived at the hospital, Coronary Care staff were waiting, enabling Madeleine's treatment to proceed immediately.

The waiting room was crowded and Jennifer and Dominic headed to two vacant seats. The next four hours seemed interminably long, with constant announcements, an occasional child's squeal, and the incessant ping of a computer game that jangled Jennifer's nerves. The room was unbearably stuffy and Jennifer's back was clammy against the vinyl chair. Waves of antiseptic hit the air whenever a nearby door was opened. Dominic seemed oblivious to his surroundings, and sat absorbed by his iPhone, while Jennifer flicked impatiently through the outdated magazines, or occasionally rose to pour herself a cup of water.

It was late afternoon when the doctor summoned them to his office.

'We've conducted an angiogram, heart ultrasound, MRI and series of blood tests. Results show that there's been damage to your mother's heart muscle. I need to warn you both, the risk of suffering cardiac arrest is at its highest in the first few months after a heart attack.'

'I see,' Dominic's expression was grave.

'And those with damaged heart muscles, like your mother's are significantly more at risk of sudden death.'

'Oh!' Jennifer's face paled.

'So, I advise you to keep a close eye on her. No unnecessary stress.'

They nodded.

'I'd recommend a week or so in rehab for starters,' the doctor suggested.

'Out of the question.' Dominic was quick to respond. 'There's no way my mother would give her consent to that.'

Jennifer nodded in agreement. 'She'd be far more settled at home. How would daily visits from her GP do?'

'Not ideal, but it should be satisfactory. I'll organise your mother's medication in the meanwhile.'

'Wait a minute, Dom,' Jennifer touched his arm. 'How about we give Alistair McMillan a call.'

'Why involve him?' The response was sharp.

'Because he's one person in the world she trusts.'

Jennifer turned to the doctor to explain. 'Alistair is Madeleine's old GP, retired now. Those two go back a long way. Alistair's visits would be sure to lift her spirits.'

'Whatever you think. Best I get back to work now.' He

turned to face Dominic. 'Your mother will be monitored overnight and all being well, expect her to be discharged in the morning. Remember, she'll need lots of rest plus a change of pace from here on.'

'She's going to love hearing that,' Dominic muttered, as they followed the doctor down the passage.

'You're not wrong there.'

In the hospital café, Jennifer stirred her coffee absent-mindedly. What *was* Dominic's issue with Alistair McMillan? He was just as she imagined old-school doctors to be — polite, efficient and trustworthy.

It could only be jealousy. There'd been a hint of romance between Madeleine and Alistair after his wife's death to cancer, five years ago. But it was laid to rest by Dominic, who made it clear to Madeleine that his father's memory was sacrosanct. There was to be no replacement.

Madeleine was a striking looking woman, despite her age and there had been no shortage of admirers over the years. But she'd looked at none the way she did at Alistair.

As they headed home, Jennifer formed a mental tick box list of things in readiness for Madeline's return. As they drove through town, she leaned back in the leather seat and took a deep breath. *I think everything's covered now,* she thought. *The following week should run smoothly.*

§

Two days later, Jennifer walked into Madeleine's room carrying a basket in which sat a Maltese Terrier dog.

'You're not going to believe this, Madeleine, but this little guy's just been delivered by courier. It's from the Lost Dogs Home. There's a card attached, addressed to you.'

'Oh, he's so like Oscar.' Madeleine said. 'How kind. Although –' she added quietly, 'I didn't know that I would ever want another dog.'

'I understand,' Jennifer said. 'I felt exactly the same way when my Labrador dog died of old age when I was twelve.'

'And did your family get another dog?'

'Oh, yes. Mum came home with another on my next birthday.' She paused. 'It filled the gap.' She looked down at the dog in her arms. 'I'm sure that you'll find the same thing.'

'But so soon?'

'After what you've been through, it's probably just the diversion you need,' Jennifer said.

'Perhaps you're right.' Madeleine pulled herself upright against the pillows and held out her arms. 'Well, come on, hand him over. And read the card, will you?'

Jennifer smiled as she passed the dog to Madeleine and undid the envelope. 'Sorry to hear about your dog,' she read. 'Hope this helps. He was dumped and needed a good home.'

'What a thoughtful gesture. Who do you think wrote this?'

Jennifer shrugged. 'I've no idea. Perhaps the man who

found Oscar. Or it could be someone associated with your charity work.'

'Well, find out will you? I must thank them.'

'I'll try. But first, I'll call the girls to come up and meet him. They'll love him, I'm sure.'

Madeleine nodded. She looked down at the bundle of white fluff in her arms. 'I'm glad he's not a young one. Heaven forbid, I wouldn't be up to dealing with a puppy.'

Jennifer grinned as she gave the dog a pat and headed for the door. 'Will you be right with him?'

'Of course,' Madeleine replied. 'But can you do a trip into town for me? He'll need a collar and lead.'

'I'd be happy to.'

'And have you sufficient dog food in the cupboard?'

'Yes,' Jennifer said. 'I'll organise everything, don't worry. See if you can think of a name while I'm gone.'

She smiled as she pulled the door behind her. Another dog was exactly the thing for Madeleine right now.

After she'd returned from town, Jennifer called the Lost Dogs Home.

'I'm sorry, Mrs. Lorenzo,' the receptionist said. 'The donor wished to remain anonymous.'

'I see. Yes, I'll tell her. Thank you.'

Jennifer's face was thoughtful as she hung up. She walked into the lounge room where Cara was reading.

'What do you think of your grandmother's new dog?'

'Just a dog. Why?' Cara kept reading.

'Any idea who may have sent it?'

Cara looked up sharply. 'Do you think I care? She has enough money to buy a truckload of dogs if she wanted to.'

Jennifer went to speak but closed her mouth. What was the point? She wondered why she'd considered Cara the anonymous donor in the first place. After all, she and Madeleine were hardly close. In fact, they'd barely been on speaking terms prior to Madeleine's heart attack.

20

Alistair McMillan sat at Madeleine's side, holding her hand.

'I just wish I'd been here for you long before this happened,' he said softly.

The words surprised her. 'What on earth made you say that?'

'It's time I levelled with you, Madeleine.' He cleared his throat. 'You must have known of my feelings towards you all these years. '

Madeleine was instantly guarded. Since his wife's death there'd been ample opportunity to express his sentiments. And if this *was* the case, surely he must have suspected that the feeling was reciprocal. He would have seen it in her eyes. It was the reason she kept her distance when his wife was present. Women knew these things.

Madeleine gave him a direct look. 'Why didn't you speak of this before, Alistair?'

'I didn't know how, to tell you the truth,' he responded.

His eyes seemed genuine enough.

'It's not too late, is it?'

'Too late for what?'

'For us to be together.' He took a deep breath. 'Madeleine, I'm asking you to be my wife.'

'What!' The response was incredulous. 'You're not serious!'

'I've never been more serious. Who knows how many years either of us have left? Why not make them happy times? If … of course you feel the same way.'

Madeleine was silent for a moment. 'I'm not sure what to say, Alistair,' she said. 'I need time to think about this.'

Neither heard the footsteps receding down the passageway.

9

Two days later, Dominic stood before Madeleine's recliner, looking down with blazing eyes.

'How could you give Dad's Jaguar away like that?' he demanded.

'Alistair loves old cars and –'

'I bet he does!' he shot back.

The remark was ignored. 'If you recall, Alistair had one almost identical when he began the practice.'

'That's not the point,' he said sourly. 'Why wasn't I consulted?'

'Why should you be?' she was quick to respond. 'Have

you ever shown the slightest interest in the car all these years? I've no doubts that it will be restored to mint condition.'

'And what else are you planning on giving him?' he said tartly.

'How dare you!'

Dominic faltered. 'I'm sorry, Mother. I had no right to say that.'

'No, you didn't. Now leave me to rest.'

¶

Alistair was seated on the edge of the bed when she awoke.

'Did you have a good sleep?' He ran a hand gently across her forehead. 'You looked so peaceful; I didn't have the heart to wake you.'

Madeleine smiled. 'You should've. All I seem to do lately is sleep. I'm looking forward to getting some routine back into my life.'

'Slowly, slowly.'

'Always the doctor, hm?'

'Something like that,' he said with a smile.

'So what have you been up to then?' she asked, reaching for a glass of water on the bedside table.

'Nothing much, to be honest. This morning I went to check on the dog next door. They've gone away for a few days and I've taken on pet minding duties.'

The words receded into the background as Madeline

watched him talk. He was still a handsome man at seventy-seven; tall and lean with fine features and a head of thick, silvery hair. She recalled the day she first set eyes on him at the surgery. She was happily married then, with Dominic a small child. She remembered the clear, blue eyes that locked on hers as he crossed the room, hand extended. One touch was enough to send her pulse racing and she found herself fighting for composure. Apart from Vincent there'd never been another man in her life, but in a split second everything changed. She left the surgery in a daze, palms clammy on the steering wheel as Dominic chattered alongside, rolling a small toy in his fingers.

'Have you given further consideration to my offer, Madeleine?'

The words jolted her back to reality.

'Of course I have, Alistair,' The reply was hasty. 'You took me by surprise, that's all. I still need more time.'

'Take all the time you want.' He covered her hand with his. 'I want you to be sure, my Darling.'

The unexpected term of endearment produced a rush of warmth and for a moment, Madeleine considered giving her consent. It had been years since she'd felt so desired. The love she'd once shared with Vincent wilted like a flower once she learned of his infidelities, despite his pro-testations of love and promises of reform. The blackmail incident with an attractive, young prostitute came close to destroying her. But she paid up. Other women may be able to forgive such indiscretions but not Madeleine. Vincent's meaningless caresses and fake love making left her cold. By her late forties, sex was no longer part of her life.

Alistair McMillan filled the void — an imaginary lover she dreamed of at night and fantasised about during the day. Family visits to the surgery were made with excited anticipation. Like an infatuated schoolgirl she searched in hope for the slightest glimmer of interest on his part, but as the years passed, she resigned herself to being a trusted friend and nothing more. And now the opportunity was at her fingertips to be with the man she'd loved for so long. What was holding her back? She gave his hand a squeeze. 'I knew you'd understand and I promise I'll have an answer soon.'

He nodded and went to rise. 'Right now, you look as though you could do with some more rest. I'll be back first thing in the morning.'

Madeleine put up a hand. 'No, don't leave yet. There are a few things I wish to discuss first. It's to do with the children's camp.'

'Are you sure?'

'I'm sure,' she said with a smile, gesturing towards her desk near the window. 'In the top drawer there's a rolled-up map of Kilkenny. Can you bring it to me please?'

'Of course.'

For some time, Madeleine had considered donating a portion of Kilkenny for a holiday camp for young cancer victims and their families. The idea first came about when Alistair was still in practice. He'd spoken many times of the need for positives in the lives of his young cancer patients and their families. She saw the despair in his face when they didn't make it. It was something she'd thought about a lot over the last few weeks.

Cancer research was high on Madeleine's list of philanthropy projects. If she could provide cancer support as well, she'd be well satisfied. She'd briefly discussed her thoughts with Alistair a few days ago. He was still in contact with the Oncologist at the Children's Hospital, and had other connections that may be useful as well. It was time to discuss her plans.

Madeleine reached for her glasses and unrolled the map. 'This would be the most suitable spot, I think,' she said, tracing her finger around a section in the bottom left-hand corner. Ten acres and well-sheltered, with direct beach access.' She frowned. 'Subject of course to what the family have to say.'

'You don't think they'd agree?'

Madeleine hesitated before she replied. 'I have my doubts, to tell you the truth. Dominic would be the first to protest.' She gave a grim smile. 'The thought of giving something away for nothing … especially prime beach-front real estate.'

'And Jennifer and the girls?' he inquired.

'Jennifer has philanthropy at heart so I doubt that she'd object,' she paused. 'But as for the girls, it's hard to say, really. I'd have to ask. They love this property. I don't think either would wish to see any of it go, even if it's only ten acres.'

'I see.'

'I'll speak to them about it tomorrow.'

'And Dominic?' he said carefully.

Dominic's words the previous evening echoed in her mind: *And what else are you planning on giving him?*

'He'll be approached when the time is right.'

adeleine watched from her window until Dominic's car disappeared down the driveway, then called Jennifer through the intercom. 'Are the girls home yet?'

'No. They shouldn't be far away.'

'Could you send them up when they arrive?'

She leaned back against the pillows and reflected on what she'd hidden from Angelina all these years — from all of them. If Dominic knew it would kill him. Images came to mind of the bedraggled young girl with large, frightened eyes who stood on her doorstep all those years ago, clutching her small backpack as if her life depended on it.

Just as well the convent was miles away, Madeleine thought. It was a miracle that Lucinda had not been traced. The Benedictine nuns had seen to that, as was their way. Not like these days.

If only I'd not been home to answer their call, she thought.

With a shudder, she recalled the tell-tale welts and blue,

black, blotches on the young woman's face and neck. An illegal immigrant who'd fled with her family from Brazil, the nuns had said.

How much more had they been privy to and not disclosed?

Madeleine shrugged. It was probably the case for many others passed on by the nuns from time to time. It was not her place to ask. Everyone deserved a second chance. Yet she often found herself speculating on the girl's background.

'Tell me about your family,' she said one morning as Lucinda tended to her room. 'Do you have any brothers and sisters?'

'My family are dead.'

The bitterness in the girl's voice was out of character and took Madeleine by surprise. She never asked again.

As Madeleine gazed out over the garden, she felt her heart squeeze. *You were more than just a housekeeper, Lucinda,* she thought, *you became the daughter that I'd always wanted. Not that I told you that.*

Lucinda had seemed so content in her new job. She was young and beautiful, with the world at her feet. She could have moved on at any time, but didn't.

Madeleine recalled the growing sense of unease that prompted her to ask, 'Have you ever thought about settling down one day; starting a family, perhaps?'

'No!' The response was sharp. 'Men give pain. Only pain.'

'I see.' Was all she could think of to say.

It was little wonder then that Lucinda showed scant interest in flirting. Not that this deterred every hot-blooded male on the property. It only made some of them more determined. Madeleine saw the yearning in their eyes whenever the Brazilian beauty with the long dark hair and graceful walk passed by. Vincent was no exception, yet Madeleine doubted that he would make a move on the girl. He wouldn't dare. Not after his previous indiscretion that had led perilously close to a divorce.

When Madeleine learned of Lucinda's pregnancy twelve months later, her heart bled for the young woman who stood trembling before her, unable to meet her eyes.

'You must tell me who the father is, Lucinda,' she prompted gently. 'I won't tell, I promise and to be honest, I don't care. Vincent and I will support you through this. You have my word.'

At that point, Lucinda burst into tears and fled to the servants' quarters.

Madeleine thought at first that Lucinda had been accosted by one of Vincent's business associates who sometimes came to visit. She recalled in disgust their leering eyes, when Lucinda filled their wine glasses at dinner… the pudgy fingers that lingered too long on her arm, and lewd remarks that were met with collective grins of approval. They were in their fifties for God's sake — balding men with thickened waist lines … as was Vincent.

It took seven months after Lucinda's death before she finally confronted him.

'Answer me, you bastard. Be a man for once.'

'Of course, I never slept with her,' he snapped. 'That's what you want to hear isn't it?'

'Look at me, Vincent, look at me. See! You can't.'

'Does it matter anyway? I'm the devil if I do, the devil if I don't.'

'Don't try that one on me. I saw you coming out of her cottage. More than once.'

'I can't deny that. I was often there fixing things. Helping out.'

'Helping out's right,' she retorted scornfully. 'Get out of my sight, Vincent. I can't bear to look at you!'

Vincent Lorenzo died without revealing the truth, six months later.

It took a familiar gold earring embedded in his slipper for Madeleine to receive the closure she so badly needed.

The secret that Lucinda Álvarez carried to her grave stabbed like a dagger through Madeleine's heart every time she set eyes on Angelina. But the child was the innocent one in all of this.

Angelina would never be without.

¶

The sun was casting its last rays across Madeleine's room as she sat, deep in conversation with her two granddaughters.

'But you can't carve up Kilkenny, Gran!' Angelina exclaimed in alarm.

'I didn't say I was doing anything at this stage,' she said irritably. 'I'm just seeking your opinions, that's all.'

'But you know how much this place means to both of us.'

'Speak for yourself, Angelina,' Cara's response was icy. 'Kilkenny is *my* birthright, not yours.'

Not quite, Madeleine thought quickly.

'And you've just been fortunate enough to tap into it.' Cara continued relentlessly.

'Stop that right now!' Madeleine snapped. 'That's a nasty, vindictive comment and you know it. Apologise to your sister at once.'

'Fat chance of that.'

The expression on Cara's face only incited Madeleine's rage and her response was swift. 'Just remember this my girl. A will can always be changed … It takes just one phone call.'

A hush fell over the room.

Madeleine rolled her eyes. 'Look, I'm not in a mood for all of this. As I said before, I was just seeking some opinions, for heaven's sake. Now leave me to rest, would you.'

Cara was the first to depart, knocking over a bedside table in her wake as she stormed out of the room, but not before she shot Madeleine a look that caused her blood to run cold. *I swear that girl would kill me right here and now, if she had the chance,* she thought with a shiver.

Angelina remained motionless in the shadows, eyes fixed on Madeleine. She thought of Alistair McMillan, who had departed not long ago. *What else were you two planning that we didn't know of?* she wondered. Without a word she quietly made her way out of the room.

As Madeleine listened to the footsteps fading down the corridor, she took a sip of water and leaned wearily back into the pillows. The ten-acre section of land in question was on a separate title from the rest of the property: the site of the original winery set up by her father almost thirty years ago. It had been long left idle once Dominic invested in other projects and moved to his city office. She hadn't expected such a strong response from her granddaughters. After all, the area was rarely visited these days, and the remaining few buildings were badly in need of repair.

Madeleine chewed at her lower lip. If only they knew what she suspected of her son over recent years: things he'd let slip. She could only hope that she was wrong. Very wrong.

Once she was gone, Kilkenny was Dominic's to do with as he wished. Reaching for her phone on the bedside table, she scrolled through her contact numbers and called the family lawyer.

'Hello, Xavier, it's Madeleine. I'm sorry for the late call but I need to speak to you.'

'Of course. You're not too late. I always stay back on Fridays. So, what's on your mind?'

'I've been thinking about my Will over the past few days and I'd like some amendments made, in regards to Cara and Angelina.'

'I see. Go on.'

There was silence at the other end once she'd finished.

'Are you certain about this, Madeleine?'

'Oh yes. Quite certain.'

'Very well then. When do you want this done by?'

The response was quick. 'As soon as possible. 'That's if it's not too much of an inconvenience.'

'No, it's only a matter of inserting a clause into the existing document.' There was a pause. 'But as your lawyer I feel obliged to ask, is there anything you'd like to come in and discuss, Madeleine?'

'No.' The response was firm. 'I just want the matter to be dealt with as soon as possible. Send me the document by express mail, would you, and I'll have it signed and returned.'

When Alistair McMillan called later that night, he sat quietly as Madeleine spoke of her granddaughters' responses to their proposal.

'Don't worry about it,' he said. 'You expected as much.'

There was a grim nod. 'Yes, but I'm not done with yet. When you drop by tomorrow, bring in your bank account details would you? I've another plan in mind.'

§

After Alistair left the following evening, Madeleine became uneasy. Perhaps she'd acted too hastily. As she reached for the light switch and sank into the pillows, the familiar smell of his French aftershave lingered, comforting her. *Things will be just fine*, she convinced herself.

But sleep was fitful.

She awoke to a chorus of noisy twittering in the garden below, and as the sun's first rays spilled out from under the curtains the thought of another day's rest was too much to take. By nine she was up and dressed, sorting through some papers and starting on her emails.

'Can't that wait?'Jennifer asked as she entered Madeleine's room with a breakfast tray.

'It's high time I got back to things,' came the gruff response, 'have a look at all those emails would you!'

Jennifer gave a smile as she glanced over Madeleine's shoulder. 'I know what *that's* like,' she remarked.

'Anyone would think the damned things haven't been checked for weeks, not days.'

'How about I give you a hand to sift through them this afternoon.' Jennifer suggested. 'I've nothing else on.'

'Would you?'

'Of course,' she replied. I'll be back after lunch. Would you like the door left open or closed?'

'Open, thanks.'

As she buttered her toast, Madeleine reflected on how lucky she was to have a daughter-in-law like Jennifer, whom she knew with certainty would expand her philanthropy projects long after she was gone. Dominic would not get his hands on one cent of her trust fund. She had made sure of that years ago. She knew that it riled him to see his wife privy to plans and schemes that he wasn't. The thought brought a satisfied smile to her lips.

❡

The afternoon's activities left Madeleine drained and tired.

'You've been a wonderful help, Jennifer,' she said as she placed her hands on the desk's edge and rose stiffly from her chair. 'I think I'll lie down and rest for a while.'

'What about dinner?'

'I'm not all that hungry to tell you the truth. Perhaps I'll have something light for supper.'

Alistair's face registered concern when he stepped into Madeleine's room a few hours later. 'You look so pale, my Darling.' He strode quickly to her side. 'Is everything all right?'

'Oh yes,' Madeleine managed a smile. 'I just didn't get a great deal of sleep last night, that's all.' She paused. 'To tell you the truth, I've been having second thoughts. About the money I mean. Perhaps we should put things on hold for a while.'

'Shh,' he soothed, 'it was a splendid gesture and will make a great difference. We've plenty of time to put things in place but right now, getting you better is the number one priority.'

He could see that she was struggling to stay awake. 'Best I leave you to rest now,' he said. 'I'll be back first thing in the morning. We can talk about it then if you wish.' He paused. 'Unless of course you'd like me to stay.'

'No, you're probably right. I'm sure I'll feel better after a good night's sleep.'

'All right then.' He fetched a bottle of medication from his brief case. 'I dropped off your script as you asked. Here's your next lot of pills.'

'Thank you, Alistair,' she reached out and touched his arm. 'You're special, you know that?'

'Have you only just worked that out?' He said with a twinkle in his eye as he placed the bottle on the bedside table.

After he had planted a soft kiss on her brow and left the room, Madeleine stopped to reflect. Why was she yet to accept his marriage proposal? Damn Dominic to hell. *He* had planted the seeds of uncertainty by insinuating that Alistair was nothing more than a gold digger. She frowned. Alistair *was wealthy* in his own right. Wasn't he? She shrugged. She'd always assumed so following the sale of his surgery and house in the well-to-do side of town. Regardless, his wealth would pale into insignificance compared to hers. So what if she agreed to his proposal; how best then to safeguard her assets? A prenuptial agreement was out of the question; she considered the idea abhorrent and distasteful. There would have to be another avenue. She straightened the covers with one hand. No use thinking about it now. She'd cross that bridge when she came to it. Nevertheless, her eyes remained troubled. Already she'd electronically transferred a hundred thousand dollars to his account, a transaction of which Dominic knew nothing.

What If she died tomorrow? Disturbing thoughts began

tumbling around in Madeleine's mind, and as she felt her heart begin to race, she reached for her pills with a trembling hand.

No, no, she reassured herself. That was not the Alistair that she knew and loved.

¶

It was an unusually hot night for January and Madeleine rose at midnight to open the window. As she lay back on the bed, and felt the balmy sea breeze upon her face, she smiled and slowly drifted off to sleep.

At 3 am. the door to her bedroom slowly opened. The wind billowed the curtains around like sails as the figure stood for a moment in the doorway then stepped inside the room. The door clicked softly behind. The dog looked up from its basket, gave a quick wag of its tail and went back to sleep.

Madeleine stirred and looked up. 'Oh, it's you,' she murmered sleepily, 'what on earth are you doing here at this time of night?'

22

I t was the housekeeper's scream early the following morning that sent everyone scrambling from their beds and rushing to Madeleine's bedroom.

'Oh my God, no.' Jennifer said with a choked gasp as she pushed past the others to the bed to check Madeleine's pulse. 'She's quite cold,' she said through her tears. 'It must have happened some time ago. Dom, call Madeleine's doctor, would you?'

He nodded, leaving the room to fetch his mobile.

'She just looks like she's asleep, Mum,' Angelina stifled a sob, 'I just want her to wake up.'

'I know you do, Darling.' Jennifer reached for her hand and gave it a gentle squeeze. 'Now go and get dressed, girls. There's nothing more to be done here. You can say your goodbyes after the doctor has visited.'

Dominic arrived soon afterwards. 'Basinger's on his way.'

He stood for a few moments, eyes on Madeleine's

peaceful face. *Where did you and I go so wrong, Mother?* He wondered. Thoughts tumbled through his mind. Would things have been different if his only sibling, Francesca, hadn't died of cot death when he was five? Would having a daughter have made Madeleine more tender? More loving as a parent?

Perhaps he should have been more understanding, more forgiving. But it was hard, bloody hard. She'd been tough as a parent — uncompromising and cold. He'd come to resent her domination in the same way his father had. Both had been just as powerless to change things.

'Dom?' Jennifer looked at him with concern. 'Are you all right?'

He nodded. 'It's just so unexpected. When I called by her room last night, she looked so damned well.'

'I know,' the response was soft.

'Even when they said that another attack was on the cards, I don't suppose I really believed it.'

'That makes two of us.' Jennifer glanced towards the bed. 'Madeleine was so strong.'

She turned and gently touched his face. 'Come on, let's go and get dressed before the doctor arrives. I'll join you in a minute after I've straightened the covers. Madeleine would have liked things left neat and tidy.'

Dominic's eyes rolled.

'Oh, and I'll contact Alistair.'

'What for?' Dominic responded sharply. 'That can wait.'

'No.' The comeback was firm. 'Alistair's hardly left

her side since this all happened. I'm sure he'd want to be here.'

Dominic's face was dark as he walked out the door.

Propping herself on the edge of the desk, Jennifer reached for Madeleine's mobile.

Outside everything seemed so normal when she rose to draw back the curtains. The gardener, oblivious to the situation, was starting up the ride-on mower in the garden below while Madeleine's dog ran in circles, yapping at his side.

The dog! I'd clean forgot about it, she thought. *Must have run out of Madeleine's room when the housekeeper went in. One of the girls must have let him out.*

The familiar scent of roses wafted from a vase nearby and she absentmindedly reached to touch a petal. Wistfully, she thought about the years spent working alongside her mother-in-law and she felt a great sadness that those days were at an end. *I won't let you down Madeleine. Your Trust will live on,* she thought as she wiped a tear from her cheek with the back of her hand.

Not long afterwards, Dominic and Jennifer escorted the doctor to Madeleine's room to conduct his examination. Twenty minutes later he stepped outside. 'You can come in now.'

At that moment, Alistair appeared at the top of the staircase and Jennifer motioned him to join them, much to Dominic's ire.

'This is a case of sudden cardiac death,' the doctor told

them, closing the door behind him. 'Not surprising really, given the events of last week. The likelihood of a reoccurring episode was always on the cards.'

'Yes, but so soon?' Jennifer asked.

'I agree. It *was* unexpected. Madeleine seemed to be responding well to treatment and I was hopeful of a few more years yet. Still, one never knows.'

'So, are you planning an autopsy?' Dominic was quick to ask.

The doctor adjusted his glasses and looked surprised. 'Do you think that's necessary? I'm recording this as Death by Natural Causes. There's nothing of note that would warrant further investigation, unless of course you make a formal request.'

'No of course we won't.' Jennifer was quick to respond. 'None of us wish for such an invasive procedure unless it was strictly called for, do we, Dom.'

'No, but –'

'And you, Alistair?' she asked.

Alistair immediately shook his head. 'I wouldn't wish for that. No.'

The doctor cleared his throat. 'Right. I'll just fill out the death certificate then.' He reached for his bag. 'And my deepest condolences to all of you. I've not been long in this town but from what I've heard, Madeleine was an exceptional lady.'

Dominic said nothing. His eyes were locked on Alistair McMillan.

23

Madeleine's funeral was conducted according to her wishes: a family only affair at the local Catholic church followed by a graveside ceremony at Kilkenny's cemetery. Set in a sheltered gully well back from the house, the setting was a remnant of a bygone era where family dynasties were laid to rest alongside their favourite workers. But only four gravesites stood at Kilkenny: those of Dominic's father Vincent, still-born sister Francesca, Joseph and now his mother. The word 'Kilkenny' was chiselled into a large stone at the entrance gate, and a weathered wrought iron fence marked its perimeter. One large shade tree stood in the corner.

The parched, summer grass crunched underfoot as the family filed solemnly through the gate and lined up beside the open grave, beside which sat Madeleine's coffin topped with a mass of roses.

Barely able to accept the finality of it all, Jennifer felt a numbness she had not experienced since her mother's death, fifteen years ago. The priest's words of solace faded as images of Madeleine flashed through her mind.

How *was* Dominic feeling, she asked herself. When it came to his mother, he was a closed book. She'd noted a slight change of expression when he first entered the cemetery but that was only when he set eyes upon Joseph's grave. Otherwise there was no sign of emotion, not even when Madeleine's coffin was lowered into the grave or as he watched Angelina's trembling face when she stepped forward, tossing a rose to pay her last respects.

Jennifer wondered what had transpired between Dominic and his mother all those years ago to make him so unfeeling.

The gardener waited until the family had returned to the house before he shuffled down the path to the graveyard to pay his own respects. He noticed someone in the distance seated on the ground between Joseph and Madeleine's graves. He blinked. Even from that distance, his ageing eyes told him that something was not quite right. He crept closer, then stopped in disbelief. By the gravesite Angelina was seated cross-legged in the dust. She was half-turned and oblivious of his presence. Her eyes were glazed and fixed downwards, her movements mirroring something he had seen before. What was it? He strained to think. *Ah that's it.* He recalled the day many years ago when he had visited his six-year-old grandson at his primary school. In the school yard was a small boy sitting in the dirt with a stick, making circles in the ground before him, over and over. 'Oh, that's Jacob, Dad,' his daughter explained later. 'He's severely autistic. His behaviour is his way of doing things.'

But Angelina wasn't autistic. So, what was wrong with her? He was disturbed by the circling motions she made as she rocked, one hand on Madeleine's grave, the other on Joseph's.

I suppose everyone has their own way of grieving, he thought. But the sight of the beautiful young woman clothed in black, sandals filled with dirt, was deeply troubling.

Careful not to be noticed, the gardener edged towards the path and headed for home. The visit to Madeleine's gravesite could wait until the morning.

¶

Madeleine's memorial service was held two days later in the same cathedral as Joseph's funeral, seventeen years prior. It was a warm day and the sun spilled down through the vast stained-glass windows, casting bright rays of light on to the carpet. As the slow tolling of the bells subsided, a throng of mourners began making their way down the aisles, to the spine-tingling chorus of the choir. The boys, clad in robes of white with blue sashes, assembled to one side of the pulpit. Masses of pink roses stood on marble stands near the sanctuary, and on a table nearby stood an enlarged photograph of Madeleine taken in her twenties in the garden at Kilkenny.

The affair was much bigger than any of the family had envisaged. A sea of people, many of whom Dominic had never set eyes upon were in attendance. Madeleine's philanthropic efforts reached far and wide and the eulogies revealed achievements that not even Jennifer was aware of. It staggered her to think how much money Madeleine must have poured into the community over the years; as it would Dominic who sat, seething, by her side.

¶

Three days later, the family sat in the lounge-room at Kilkenny as Madeleine's lawyer, Xavier Reardon, read her will. Dominic's stony face belied the rage swelling inside him as the contents were revealed. Kilkenny would be his, as expected, but little else. His mother's trusts and personal assets were well and truly out of reach. He cringed as the lawyer revealed the vast sums of money bequeathed to charities: sixty thousand dollars to one, forty thousand to another; the list went on. Even Madeleine's forty-five percent shares in his company were to be passed on to Jennifer.

It was his mother's ultimate revenge.

You bitch. He thought in rage. *You fucking bitch!*

The final blow came when Cara and Angelina were to receive one million dollars on their respective twenty-fifth birthdays, to do with as they wished.

There was a simultaneous gasp from the girls.

'What!' Dominic exploded, 'that's preposterous. There's got to be a mistake.'

The lawyer leaned back in his chair, hands clasped, and peered over the top of his glasses. 'There's no mistake, Dominic.'

Dominic's face contorted with fury. Something did not add up. For all her idiosyncrasies, his mother was no fool. She of all people would acknowledge that a twenty-five-year-old was in no way mature enough to handle that amount of money. If anything, he would have envisaged a trust fund, enabling the girls to live off the interest until they were older.

It took every bit of Dominic's self-control not to jump up and smash the lawyer into the wall. *You've known about this all along, haven't you,* he thought, infuriated that the little man opposite knew things he would never learn. He fought for calm.

'I see.' His words were icy. 'Well that's that then.'

Jennifer quickly glanced at the lawyer, choosing her words carefully. 'It's a very generous offer of Madeleine's and it will be greatly appreciated by the girls in the years to come. It just came as a surprise, that's all.'

The lawyer nodded. 'I'm sure it did.'

When he read Madeleine's final words and went to close the folder, Dominic said, 'so there's no more?'

'No. Were you expecting more?'

Dominic's expression was steely. 'Possibly.'

Later, as Jennifer turned down the doona and slipped

under the covers, Dominic stood quietly by the door. 'You know Mother wanted to marry him, didn't you?'

'Who, Alistair?'

There was a nod.

'Really? How can you be sure?'

Dominic's eyes were cold. 'Because she told me, four days ago. Asked me how I felt about it.'

Jennifer was almost too stunned to speak. 'And what did you say?'

'I said no, in no uncertain terms, of course.'

'What?' Jennifer said with a gasp. 'But why? If that's what would make her happy in her final years –'

'I'm sure it'd make McMillan happy as well,' his words were laced with sarcasm. 'I did some investigating when he started visiting Mother. Did you know that he is almost penniless?'

'Oh!' The words caught Jennifer by surprise.

'After he sold his practice, he tipped most of the profits into a building society that eventually collapsed.'

'But surely that's not his fault.'

'Perhaps not. But he owns his house and that's about it. Oh, and you didn't know about his son, did you?'

'Which one? Alistair had three sons from what I remember.'

'The youngest. The drug addict. He'd been bleeding his father dry for years. People always said that the break-ins at the surgery were inside jobs.'

'What are you getting at, Dom?'

'When I related all this to Mother, she had no idea. Would you believe that?' He paused. 'That was on the night she died.'

Jennifer felt the blood run from her face. 'You don't think what you revealed to her had anything to do with her heart attack?'

'Not bloody likely. You should have seen the look in her eyes. McMillan would have been confronted about it, don't you worry. The moment he walked through her door.'

'I still don't see where you're coming from, Dom. What went on between the pair of them is hardly our business.'

'Oh, I think it is,' Dominic snapped as he flung back the covers and climbed into bed.

'What are you getting at?'

'Did you notice how quick McMillan was to dismiss my suggestion of an autopsy.'

'You're not saying he *killed* her?'

'Think about it,' Dominic's voice was cold. 'Maybe he wanted to wipe his hands of her once he'd been confronted, and his little secrets were blown sky high. Have you considered that?'

She stared, open-mouthed as he continued relentlessly.

'All he had to do was get her blood pressure soaring. Say something, do something like hide her pills. I don't know.'

Jennifer was aghast. 'I can't believe you just said that!'

The comment was ignored. 'I'll tell you one thing though. If I find out that McMillan got one cent out of her more than that car …' he flicked off the lamp switch.

Jennifer lay still, watching the shadows on the wall that moved eerily like phantom waves. She didn't dare tell him about the piece of paper that Madeleine took from Alistair and promptly shoved under the covers when she entered the room unexpectedly, a few days ago. *What was on that note,* she wondered. Numbers of some description.

24

For several days after the reading of the will, Dominic was silent and moody and the others avoided him. And then he left for the city. For six months he worked long hours in his office without a break, and visits to Kilkenny were rare.

Not to be deterred, Jennifer insisted that his birthday be held at home.

'There's a new Italian restaurant in town and I've booked four places,' she said over the phone.

'Sounds like I've not got much choice in the matter.' Dominic's tone was teasing.

'Nope.'

There was a sigh at the other end.

'I'm sorry, Jen. I've been neglectful. Haven't I. It's about time I returned home for a while to be with you and the girls.'

To Jennifer's surprise, Dominic remained true to his word for the next three weeks.

9

One evening after dinner, Jennifer approached him in his study.

'Almost finished?'

'Just about,' he said. 'We're all set to sign a substantial deal and I'm going over the final details.'

Jennifer placed his coffee beside him on the desk and glanced at the computer screen. 'Is that the one you spoke of a month or so ago.'

He nodded. 'It's thanks to Angie that we nailed the contract. She's a natural when it comes to dealing with clients.'

'I can imagine that,' Jennifer responded with a smile.

'To be honest, she's become a real asset to the company. She's got such ambition, such vision for the future.'

'That doesn't surprise me,' Jennifer said, 'you only have to think back to when she was a little girl; we could hardly keep her away from your office.'

'Yeah but ...'

'You're thinking about Joe again, aren't you,' she said.

Dominic's eyes were pained. 'I had such plans.'

Jennifer slid onto his knee, draping her arms around his neck and burying her head into his chest.

'I know you did, Darling. And I miss him too. So very much.'

With a choked sob, Dominic wrapped his arms around her and held her tightly, his chin resting on her head, eyes far away.

Neither spoke for some time but Jennifer savoured the moment. It had been so long since he had reached out to her.

Now was not the time to tell him about Cara. Her decision to work at a local show jumping stable had come like a bolt out of the blue. The hours would be absurd: four-thirtyish starts with late finishes, and the pay lousy from what she'd said. The job involved stints away as a strapper once the show jumping circuit began. How long would that last? She didn't say; three, perhaps four months of the year? Jennifer had her doubts when she first learned of it. But Cara was twenty-four, old enough to make her own decisions. Jennifer could only hope that the move wouldn't unsettle her daughter to the point of dropping out of her studies altogether. If that were to happen, her prospects within Dominic's company were next to none. It didn't bear thinking about.

Dominic would have to be told sooner or later. She shuddered to think of his response.

Little did Jennifer know that another incident involving Cara would occur before she had a chance to broach the subject: one that would unleash Dominic's fury like no other before it.

ꝯ

Dominic had booked a weekend at a city hotel to celebrate their wedding anniversary. No expense was spared.

Jennifer gasped as they walked through the door. The apartment boasted uninterrupted views of the city from its floor to ceiling windows. The décor was contemporary, and white leather furniture sat on the Moroccan rugs scattered around the polished timber floor. She glimpsed a spa through a far doorway.

'Do you like it?' Dominic caressed the nape of her neck. Jennifer savoured the moment. It had been so long since they'd been away together.

'I love it. Thank you, Darling.'

'Good.' His hand slid around her shoulder. 'Now come on, let's take a look around.'

A bottle of French champagne, a bouquet of red roses, and a small box with black ribbon sat on the bedside table in the master bedroom.

Dominic lifted the box and handed it to her. 'It's for you. Go on. Open it.'

Jennifer carefully untied the bow and lifted the lid. Inside was a silver, diamond-encrusted bracelet and matching drop earrings.

'It's beautiful,' she lifted the bracelet from the box. 'But you shouldn't have.'

'It's nothing.' Dominic made a dismissive wave. But Jennifer was aware of the gift's value. She recognised the diamond company logo in the box. She felt a pang of guilt as she watched Dominic fasten the bracelet around her wrist, and thought of her mother and the years she'd worked as a nurse on night shift, struggling to make ends meet.

Extravagances such as these were only dreamed of. They had little, but appreciated every bit they had. Most importantly, they were loved. Holidays were rare, yet Jennifer never felt deprived. Her mother always made sure there were small outings and treats.

It was through their mother that Jennifer and her younger sister learned the value of money. She recalled as an eight-year-old being told, 'Learning how to save is very important, Jenny. Come, and I'll show you.' She headed across the kitchen and pulled three jars down from the shelf.

'From now on, I'd like you to divide your pocket money into three. One lot for each jar — one for savings, one for spending and one for helping others. Never forget the last, Darling. There're always people in the world worse off than us. I think it's up to all who can, to help out.'

Jennifer hadn't forgotten all those years. She thought of Madeleine's Foundation. *I'll do my best to make you proud.*

Her father was something else: a broken man, wallowing in self-pity, sitting by while his wife worked herself to exhaustion. He'd been in a serious car accident, leaving him with loss of movement in his left arm and a few plates in both legs. *You could have worked but you didn't,* she thought with bitterness.

If it hadn't been for the alcohol, maybe he would have. And now her mother was dead, without doing any of the things she'd planned.

Jennifer glanced down at her bracelet. She couldn't

recall her father giving her mother jewellery of any description, or any gifts for that matter.

He was now living the good life, courtesy of her mother's life insurance, flitting around Europe with his second wife, twenty years his junior. Jennifer was sure he'd be piling gifts on *her*.

Just wait until the money runs out, she thought.

At least he'd been deprived of the thing he wanted most — to accompany her down the aisle at one of the most talked about, extravagant weddings of the year. Nor would he play a further role in her life. He and his grasping wife would never get the opportunity to mingle with high society.

'A penny for your thoughts,' Dominic touched her nose with his finger tip.

Before Jennifer had time to think of a response there was a knock on the door.

'That'll be the porter with our luggage,' Dominic said as he headed towards the passageway.

At eight o'clock they took the lift to the restaurant located on the third floor. The place had class. To the right of the main foyer was an elegant bar where diners clustered in groups, cocktails in hand before making their way to the main restaurant. Dress was formal and Jennifer was glad they'd packed evening wear. The room was abuzz with chatter and the smell of expensive perfume hung in the air.

As they followed the waiter to their table, Jennifer slipped her arm through Dominic's. She felt fortunate to have a husband whose eyes were for her alone when they were out together.

Dominic was well pleased. He noted the admiring glances from men as Jennifer passed. He was glad she'd chosen her deep red, off-the-shoulder dress: his favourite. Her hair was swept high on her head and the diamond drop earrings and glittering bracelet complemented her outfit perfectly. She was the epitome of elegance. He scowled at a man seated nearby whose eyes lingered on Jennifer's décolletage as they went past. His hand covered hers possessively and he felt a nervous tingle down his spine. If Jennifer was ever to leave him, there'd he another male by her side in an instant. Deep down he feared that one day she might get sick of their lifestyle and just walk out. He thought of the weeks, sometimes months he spent away from home. How many other wives would put up with that?

It was time to think about an overseas holiday. Just the two of them. No business involved.

The waiter stopped at a table by the window and pulled out Jennifer's chair. Silver gleamed amongst the pink orchids in the candlelight and before her lay a fan-shaped linen napkin.

Jennifer watched as Dominic studied the wine list. He wore a charcoal grey, handmade Italian suit, a white shirt and a steel grey silk tie. His chin was dark with stubble against his olive skin, and his raven hair, now tinged with grey, had barely receded. Jennifer felt her heart skip a beat. The years had only made him more handsome.

'Cocktails for starters?' he looked up at her.

Jennifer nodded. 'A Margherita for me.'

'And I'll have a martini. We'll have pinot noir with dinner.' Dominic pointed to his favourite selection.

'Yes, Sir.'

As the drinks waiter took the wine list and headed towards the bar, Dominic glanced at a couple seated nearby. The man had just finished his soup and was dabbing at his mouth with his napkin. Dominic thought of his father all those years ago, seated at the table in his work clothes at lunch, soaking up the remains of his soup with a piece of bread in his thick fingers and slurping it into his mouth. He winced.

'So, what's planned for tomorrow?' Jennifer's words brought him back with a start.

'How about a sleep-in for starters.'

'I like the sound of things already.'

'Then a buffet brunch, followed by a late afternoon massage for two.'

'Now you're talking.'

At that moment, a waiter arrived with two leather-bound menus and placed their napkins on their laps.

Over dinner they clinked glasses and Dominic held her gaze in the candlelight. He had never seen her look so beautiful. 'It's been far too long since we've done this hasn't it.' He said, reaching for her hand. 'I'll make it up to you. I promise.'

Jennifer wondered why his words gave her a feeling of unease.

Later as they finished the last of their wine, Dominic glanced at his watch. 'Eleven already. Shall I order coffee or would you rather head back to sample the champagne and chocolates?'

Jennifer ran her foot slowly down his leg under the table. 'The champagne sounds good.'

Dominic grinned and signalled to the waiter for the bill.

A handful of diners remained, chatting over dessert as they headed towards their room. As they passed the foyer Dominic's thoughts drifted back all those years to his parents. He strained to think of the last time they'd spent time away together. It certainly would not have been in a place like this. Did his mother resent not living the lifestyle she'd been accustomed to? If so, she never said.

On their final night, Dominic and Jennifer made a last-minute decision to head home to avoid the next day's peak hour traffic. Dominic called Angelina to see if she wanted a lift, but as expected she was out on a date. Commitment was something Angelina did not adhere to. Not that she could be accused of leading men astray. She made it clear from the start that freedom was her number one priority.

Meanwhile, she mingled in social circles from time to time with Jennifer and Dominic. Heads turned whenever the stunning beauty entered the room, but hopeful young suitors were under no illusion about the scrutiny they'd face from Dominic Lorenzo should they be lucky enough to land a date. Older men weren't about to test their luck. One look from Dominic was enough to halt them in their tracks. It didn't stop them from fantasising, however. Jennifer could see it in their eyes. She noted their wives' frosty looks and grips firmly on their husbands' arms when Angelina headed in their direction.

It was after dark when Jennifer and Dominic left for home.

9

At Kilkenny, a thick fog had settled and the cold wintry air was a sign of things to come. Cara pulled another jumper over her head and headed down the stairs to the lounge room, where Madeleine's grand piano had been relocated following her death.

Madeleine's second floor apartment was now occupied by Dominic and Jennifer, with the West Wing refurbished into two large private living areas, one for each daughter. This seemed to decrease the tension between the siblings … just.

No one knew that Cara spent hours seated at Madeleine's piano late at night. But only when no one was about.

Usually, she liked the curtains open so that she could glance across the illuminated garden but this evening she drew them tight and turned the gas heater on to full. Kilkenny's high ceilings had always posed a heating problem, but now a flick of a switch could fix things in seconds. As she passed the original open fireplace, she wondered how people coped in those days.

Selecting an armful of sheet music from the music cabinet, she lifted the piano lid and settled in for the evening. There she sat, lost in time. Eyes intense, fingers like gentle ripples across the keys, she was too absorbed to hear the car pull up in the driveway outside two hours later.

As was customary, Dominic stopped near the front door to let Jennifer out while he parked the car. She took just two steps and stopped, stock-still as the haunting notes of Beethoven's *Moonlight Sonata* flowed out to meet her.

'Who in the hell's playing in there? Dominic's angry voice from behind cut through her wonderment like a bird shot in mid-flight.

'I've no idea.' She swung around, 'I wasn't expecting anyone. Were you?'

There was no response as Dominic pushed past and strode towards the house.

What the hell? Jennifer thought as she took off after him.

As Dominic flung open the loungeroom door the music stopped midstream, and a chair scraped abruptly on polished timber. Dominic stood frozen in the doorway, blocking Jennifer's view; the muscles in his neck as taut as a coiled rope.

'Dom, what's wrong?' She pushed past to see.

'Oh!' her hand flew to her face.

Cara snapped the music book shut and it slipped through her fingers, crashing onto the floor with a thump. With a reddened face she scrambled to pick it up.

'Cara, who taught you to play that?' Jennifer asked incredulously, 'It was beautiful.'

'I had some lessons at school, that's all.'

'I see,' Dominic said coldly, as he stepped into the room.

'What's wrong?' Cara said, her eyes darting from one parent to another. 'Have I done something wrong?'

The words were ignored by Dominic as he turned to Jennifer. 'So, am I supposed to believe you know nothing about this?'

'Are you accusing me of covering this up?' she felt her nails digging into her palms.

'Well, are you?'

'No, I'm not,' she fired back.

'Does it matter anyway? I think that the situation speaks for itself.'

'Huh?' Cara said, bewildered. 'What are you on about?'

'Why don't you ask your mother.' With a scathing look at Jennifer, Dominic swept out of the room, slamming the door behind him.

Cara turned to Jennifer. 'Mum?'

Jennifer's mouth went dry and she could feel her heart thumping wildly against her chest. She was unprepared for this. *Come on, think damn it,* her inner voice commanded. *Say something. Anything. She won't check any of it out.*

'I think that your father was shocked to hear you play, that's all, Darling,' she told her. 'I mentioned piano lessons years ago and he wasn't that keen.'

Jennifer could feel her cheeks redden. Only a smidgeon

of what she'd said was true. She *had* considered asking him, but knew it wasn't worth her while. Not if he heard the things that she had; Cara as a toddler, singing note-perfect or perched on the piano stool as a five-year-old, making up tunes with her chubby fingers. It'd been so long ago and she'd witnessed no further signs. Until now.

Cara's voice jolted her back to reality. 'Why wouldn't Dad let me have lessons, then?'

'Oh, I think that goes back a long way to when he was a child,' Jennifer lied. 'Piano lessons were forced upon him by Madeleine and he hated them. I guess it just turned him off.'

'Was he any good?'

Jennifer's response was hasty. 'I don't know. Madeleine never said.'

'It's really affected him, though, hasn't it,' Cara said. 'I mean, he can't stand listening to music; any kind of music.'

Jennifer held her head high as she met her daughter's eyes.

'Regardless, you're to keep playing. Promise me that?'

Cara nodded. *Yeah, I'll play,* she thought *but next time I'll be more frigging careful, that's all.*

Jennifer was still awake when Dominic arrived home at around 3 am. He was silent when he climbed into bed and his breath smelled of whiskey. Jennifer reached out but he recoiled at her touch.

In the morning he was gone.

When would he be back and what was she in for when he returned?

For some reason the thought did not trouble her the way it once had. She was up for the challenge. In any case, his mind would soon be preoccupied with work matters. She sensed that big changes were underway in the company. It was something he'd let slip at the weekend when he'd had a glass or two too many. Lorenzo wineries was expanding to become Lorenzo Enterprises, whatever that meant. He'd mumbled something about property development and big money coming in but would say no more.

What in the hell was going on?

9

It was two weeks before Dominic returned home, walking in the door as if nothing had happened. Mind games as she'd expected. But she too could play.

'Well, aren't you going to ask what I've been up to at the office?' he remarked with a hint of arrogance, after he'd taken his things upstairs and come down for coffee.

'I knew you'd tell me in your own time,' Jennifer replied evenly.

Dominic met her eyes with a cold glare. 'I see.' He walked over to the coffee machine and made himself an expresso. 'I've been doing some thinking while I've been away. Quite a lot, actually.' He pulled up a stool at the kitchen bench.

Jennifer felt a sense of unease.

'I know all about Cara taking on that shit job at the stables,' he said coolly. 'She said it'd be only for a year or two but you know something?' His voice raised a notch. 'I don't care a stuff if she finishes her degree or even gets to work at the company. She can do whatever she friggin' well likes from now on.'

Bastard, she thought. Dominic at his best.

'What's got into you?' she played at being ignorant.

'You're the best person to know that.' He paused and his tone was menacing. 'I always get my facts together first, Jen. You of all people should know that.'

You're enjoying this, aren't you, she thought.

She shot Dominic an icy glare and strode out of the room before he had the chance to continue. Heading outside, she stopped on the porch to grab a coat and found herself rummaging in a nearby drawer for a packet of cigarettes. *Shit has it come to this*, she thought in disbelief. How long had it been? One year? Two? It was a wonder the packet was still there. It was getting dark and the wind was arctic. She fastened the zip up to her chin as she headed down the track towards the beach. Making her way around the shore line she chose a sheltered spot and sat in the sand, arms locked around her knees, watching the trails of smoke blend into the night fog.

For a moment her senses were blissfully dulled by the constant crashing of the waves against the shore. Then she thought about Dominic's reaction to hearing Cara play and a great weariness overcame her. What was he going to do? Order a DNA test? For now, there was a more pressing issue: Cara's decision to postpone her course.

She thought of Dominic's smug expression when he broached the subject almost as soon as he entered the house. For a few moments she sat, seething. Had he been truly serious about employing Cara in the first place?

She rubbed her neck and reached for another cigarette. The answer was probably yes. She recalled the proud look on his face when he learned of Cara's VCE results; the way he'd sat head-to-head with her in his office, animatedly discussing university courses. It all seemed so long ago. Back then, Cara had shown an enthusiasm for her studies that Jennifer hadn't expected and her intellect wasn't lost on Dominic either. A few bragging comments here and there to his work colleagues and Cara's forthcoming position within the company became a highly anticipated one.

Jennifer thought a truce had finally been reached between father and eldest daughter in the ensuing years; the all too brief summer days spent aboard on the *Jennifer*; brown eyes challenging green as they debated controversial issues over the dinner table. But it all stopped abruptly.

In retrospect Jennifer knew she'd been naïve to assume that the rift between the two would *ever* be healed, even before he'd heard her play. It began all those years ago when Dominic sat on the rocks, cradling Joe's broken body in his arms. She, more than anyone knew that Dominic did not forgive or forget. But to bestow a life sentence of pain and guilt on an eight-year-old? All she'd noted was Dom had shifted his preferences from one daughter to the other.

Maybe if Cara had played into his hands, flattered him

in the way that Angelina did, things would have been different. But Cara was not one to kowtow to anyone. His orders were met with silent resistance, and later a feisty defiance. His sarcasm no longer had an effect either. It was almost as if she rose a notch to his challenges.

She glanced at the dark sky. *Can't stay here forever,* she mumbled, rising stiffly to her feet. Her fingers were already numb and she blew hard on them before shoving them into her pockets. With a heavy heart and not knowing what to expect when she got home, she trudged through the sand towards the path.

She didn't notice a figure standing high on the cliffs above, watching.

It was already nine when she opened the back door and walked quietly into the hallway. Damn! The bedroom light was on. She had hoped Dominic would be in the study as was usual for this time of night. She frowned and headed up the stairs, steeling herself for what was to come.

But she needn't have worried. There were no barbed remarks, no silent treatment. Dominic was sitting on the edge of the bed holding his head in his hands. Upon hearing her enter, he rose to meet her and gently pulled her into his arms. 'I'm sorry, Babe,' he murmured, 'Forget what I said before. It was a heat of the moment thing, that's all. You mean the world to me and I'd never do anything to jeopardise that.'

'I know.' She closed her eyes and pressed against his chest, lost momentarily in time as her arms reached up to lock behind his neck. But a flicker of uncertainty followed. It was not like him to back down this quickly. She sensed that there was something else.

Well, she'd worry about that later. For now, there was a reprieve.

Jennifer awoke during the night and sank back on the pillows, feeling needed and satisfied. Dominic's love making was never better than when he was apologetic. But soon there'd be another outburst and then another apology. Ultimately it was Dominic who controlled things; controlled her.

And she was no longer willing to take it.

Jennifer clasped her hands behind her head on the pillow and found her thoughts straying to another time when there'd been a choice. She'd opted for the money; the lifestyle. But what if she'd chosen otherwise? A face flashed through her mind: a handsome, young man with thoughtful eyes and a sensitive expression. She forced the memory from her mind.

Sleep was disturbed and sporadic.

25

Dominic sat in his expansive apartment watching the city come to life below. Things at Kilkenny had gone according to plan and Jennifer was once more under his control.

But the real challenge was yet to come. There was no way she'd agree to his latest plans. He'd need to tread carefully; tell her just enough to keep her off his back. If he wasn't so obsessed with her, he'd simply file for divorce and forge ahead. But he was consumed by jealousy. Jennifer was his and his alone. Nothing would alter that. He remembered the brash young barrister who'd been foolish enough to make a move on her, when their paths had crossed at social gatherings. He recalled Jennifer's subtle body language, the flick of her hair. She should've known there'd be consequences. By the time Dominic was through, the city papers were riddled with details of the barrister's shady past, including string of sexual allegations from former employees, two underaged. A messy and costly divorce soon followed.

Dominic frowned. That was years ago. If the same thing happened now, how would she react. Would she be the one to file for a divorce?

The possibility had never crossed his mind before and it was quickly brushed aside. It wouldn't come to that. There was too much at stake. Meanwhile, he had the best of both worlds …

Raquel was the perfect mistress; had been for the last two years. Discreet and smart, she knew exactly what was expected and kept her end of the bargain. In return were gifts, travel and a generous remuneration.

For Dominic, the set-up couldn't be more perfect. It was all too easy to add a last-minute booking to his flights and accommodation abroad.

Raquel had been an asset when it came to clinching business deals. He noted the looks of envy from prospective clients when the tall beauty, twenty years his junior, graced his side. But there was more to Raquel than good looks. Articulate and witty she held her own at dinner whether conversations turned to business, politics or world affairs. She'd done her homework.

The best part was when they headed back to their hotel at the end of the evening. He thought of Raquel, lying naked beside him on the bed, one leg draped over his, tequila in hand, murmuring risqué utterances in his ear. The sex to follow was whatever he wished it to be — sensuous, passionate or erotic.

Dominic had often wondered why he'd not yet tired of

her. Most likely it was because she asked no questions and didn't overstep the mark. Not like the others. He frowned. Well they'd learned of his suppressed temper all too late. Learned that he wasn't one to be messed with.

As had Jennifer.

But what if Jennifer learned of Raquel and the ones before that. Would she discreetly ignore it as *his* mother had? He'd find a way of dealing with it. Jennifer knew she was the only one he truly loved.

Dominic's father had had an eye for beautiful women and so did he. With wealth came the opportunity for easy pick-ups, though with discretion. But his father had no finesse. Dominic made certain no one could say that about him.

He wondered how his mother, one of the most striking women of her time, had become attracted in the first place to a penniless, Italian migrant. It wasn't his father's looks, that's for sure. Dominic recalled photos of him as a young man — short and swarthy, with a mop of thick dark curls. He did however possess expressive, large brown eyes; eyes that Dominic had been lucky to inherit.

He surmised that his father's initial grit, determination and hard work must have earned his mother's admiration and respect enough to agree to give her hand in marriage. It was through him that Lorenzo Wineries were born and came to flourish.

Dominic glanced at the photo of himself and Jennifer aboard their yacht. What was it that kept him straying? It wasn't that he cared for the women. Perhaps it had something to do with the adrenalin rush that came with covering his tracks. He'd come close at times, seen the questioning eyes of his colleagues. Raquel was, so far, nonexistent. Times spent with her had been meticulously planned and had so far proved watertight. Not that this sat comfortably with him. It was only a matter of time before their affair was exposed. For the time being things would go on as normal but she would play no part in his future plans.

Once again, he felt blessed. Blessed for his wealth, good looks and sharp intellect.

A smugness overtook his face as he leaned back in the chair, hands clasped behind his head and thought once more of Jennifer. She'd come around. Simple as that. But he'd have to be good. Better than good. No matter, he could always raise himself another notch.

¶

From the moment the new business manager entered the office, Angelina disliked him. She bristled at the beaming smile on Dominic's face as he strode across the room to shake the man's hand. She was still fuming over her father's abrupt dismissal of the previous one who'd held the position since she was a child. No reason had been given for his termination and it irked her that she'd not been consulted. She had a feeling that all was not what it seemed.

It wasn't as if Paul Anderson wasn't impressive. Quite

the contrary. He was tall and younger than expected, maybe early fortyish with dark hair showing its first signs of grey. His charcoal suit could belong to a newsreader.

It was the man's air of assertiveness that she disliked the most, not to mention the way that his eyes lingered on her low-cut blouse. She was surprised that her father hadn't noticed but his business associate of ten years, Lee Farrell, did. Angelina saw Lee's jaw harden as he stood in the corner, arms crossed while the introductions were being made.

It was only at the last minute that he stepped across to offer his hand.

'I've heard so much about you both,' Paul Anderson said when Dominic left the room to take a phone call.

'Oh really?' Angelina said coolly. 'Well, perhaps you could fill us in a bit about yourself. Dad certainly didn't.'

For a moment the man lost his composure. 'Where do I start? Well, I've been in the game for the last fifteen years if that helps.'

'Finance game?' Angelina shot back.

'I seem to get the impression that you're not overly happy with my appointment, Miss Lorenzo.'

'You can call me Angelina,' she said, not taking her eyes off his. 'Let's just say I was surprised by the suddenness of it all.'

'Perhaps you can let my past performance speak for itself. If you care to look through my records …'

He went to reach for his briefcase but Angelina gave

a dismissive wave. 'I have little interest in resumes, Mr. Anderson. Time can be the judge.' Paul Anderson glanced uneasily at Lee Farrell, whose face registered nothing.

At that moment Dominic re-entered the room.

'Well, if that's everything, Dad, we need to get back to work,' Angelina said, not attempting to hide the frostiness in her voice.

As the door clicked behind them, Dominic frowned. 'Not the warmest of receptions, I'm afraid.'

There was a shrug. 'I expected as much from what you said. So, what exactly did you tell them?'

'Very little.'

There was a nod. 'Good.'

'We'll have to be careful, though. Angie's no fool, Paul.'

'I gathered that.'

'She's used to being part of the decision making.'

'Leave it to me. I'll figure things out.'

Dominic nodded. It was a relief to finally have Paul on board. The pressure of the last few weeks had taken its toll. He had no doubts that Angelina would investigate Paul's credentials but she'd find nothing. It had taken him three years to learn the truth.

Paul Anderson was in fact Paul Guthrie, the son of a successful financial advisor who loved fast money, fast cars and beautiful women. But his father had become too greedy and paid the cost — a six-year stint behind bars for money laundering and fraud.

Paul's mother walked out years ago after learning

of her husband's infidelities, leaving Paul to live the high life with his father, a lifestyle neither was willing to relinquish.

'Should have been more bloody careful in the first place,' his father said on the day of his prison release. 'But it wasn't all a waste of time, my boy. Amazing the contacts, you can make on the inside.'

By the time Leonard Guthrie died of a heart attack, aged fifty- six, Paul knew the ropes, had access to his father's hidden bank accounts, and was well entrenched in the underworld, particularly throughout Asia. However, he'd managed to maintain a squeaky-clean record by managing the finances of a large, reputable company that imported goods from Bali and other parts of Asia. The job entailed frequent trips abroad, providing Paul with the perfect opportunity to develop his clandestine operations.

'Take a seat, mate and I'll get us a whisky.' Dominic walked to the crystal decanter on the sideboard and reached for two glasses.

It hardly seemed like three years since he'd first met Paul in Bangkok whilst investigating the expansion of his wine exports. He remembered the meetings that followed and the heady excitement of listening to Paul as he outlined the millions that could be made there in the short-term. Within six months, Dominic had siphoned money out of an account that Jennifer knew nothing about, to buy his first block of offices.

It did not take him long to fall under Paul's influence

and plans were soon underway for property development throughout Asia and Third World countries.

Little did Dominic know that he was slowly becoming entrenched in a deadly game where corruption, drugs, Asian Triads and the Russian Mafia ruled behind legitimate operations. But by this time, it was too late. The wine export industry no longer held appeal; there was too much hard work for little return. He wanted excitement and the same adrenaline kick that he got from his women.

Raquel took no part in his trips to Asia. Instead, he bedded exotic women recommended by Paul. They were clean but the price tag for peace of mind was exorbitant.

Dominic was about to buy into ventures bigger than he'd envisaged but it was becoming increasingly difficult to cover his tracks. The time had come to rid the company of James Stanford, his long-serving business manager, and slot Paul into the role.

Dominic knew that he was walking on the wild side. Such ventures would come at a huge cost. Money he didn't have. He could only borrow so much. Kilkenny would have to go. He recalled the look of surprise on Paul's face when the subject came up and he could understand why. The stretch of land upon which Kilkenny stood was gold on the property market. He only had to advertise and he'd be swamped by celebrities, movie stars and the like who'd been circling like vultures for years. He'd get to name his price.

'You're not regretful about selling the place, are you?' Paul had said.

'Nope. It's Jen and the girls who'll be the issue.'

'I can see why. You're sitting on one of the most beautiful properties in that stretch of the woods.'

'I'm well aware of that but to be truthful, I've a gutful of bad memories when it comes to the place.'

'Oh?'

'A domineering mother for one, a son I adored who fell to his death on the cliffs. I could go on.'

'I think you've made your point. But how are you going to get around your wife and kids?'

'There's still quite a bit of thinking to do on that one.'

Dominic placed the lid on the decanter and walked across the room, drinks in hand. 'So, it's finally official,' he said. 'Welcome aboard, mate.'

There was a clink of glasses.

26

Winter arrived bringing extremely cold temperatures. In the Zielinski house, Alice Hanley sat huddled near the heater in her bed-sitter, rubbing her arthritic hands. It was getting dark and she just wanted to sleep. But first he needed his medication. She frowned. Was he swallowing the pills or hiding them in his mouth then spitting them out later, as he'd done at the Institution? Of late she'd noticed a shift in his behaviour. He'd been moodier and had all but stopped talking. Of more concern was his tendencies to venture out late at night. Early that morning, she'd awoken to the creaking of floor boards on the veranda as he made his way towards the front door. What time was it. Two o'clock? Three?

What was he up to and where did he go?

There'd been another spate of disturbing crimes in the town. Young women had been stalked, residents had awoken to find intruders in their houses and there'd been three stabbings. Fingers soon pointed in his direction.

This was nothing new. It was an unfortunate coincidence that similar disturbances had flared up in the past when they'd come to stay. Last time there'd been the attacks on pets. Now there was a missing girl to contend with.

Would they ever leave him in peace? Years ago, he'd been cleared of a murder that had made headlines around the country. A local woman had been strangled and her body discovered in the bushes aligning their property. Their house had been searched and a sample of his DNA was taken and put on the police database. There'd been no match, as she'd expected. He wasn't capable of murder. Was he? Alice felt a tight knot in the pit of her stomach. She'd never trusted the doctors and the way they'd experimented with his medication as if he were some kind of lab rat. One brand in particular had caused a string of abusive outbursts and he'd hurled a chair at a psychiatrist for no reason.

She'd told him about the recent rumours — begged him not to go outside until things settled, to no avail. If Helena knew, she'd put a stop to the visits. *God knows it would make things easier.* Alice thought of her warm room back in town. But she couldn't tell. She knew how much this place meant to him.

Alice shifted uncomfortably in her chair as she thought of the small girl who'd recently wandered off from the local caravan park while her parents shared drinks in a nearby van. A fisherman on the beach allegedly heard a child's scream coming from the clifftop near their house and had alerted the police.

Despite an extensive search of their property and surrounding area, the child was never found. But that didn't stop the gossip. Alice would never forget his haunted face when he was dragged out of the house that night and taken to the police station for questioning. His version of the night's events had been unwavering. But had he lied? There were times he was simply unable to recall recent events. Not that she told *them* that.

She thought with unease of the underground bunker hidden deep in the sand dunes on the perimeter of their property. She'd all but forgotten about it until last summer when Helena Zielinski brought an old friend to stay. Her friend's grandchildren soon learned of the bunker's existence and set off with great excitement to find it. The "cubby cave," as it had always been known was built by Stefan Zielinski as a treat for his children, soon after the house was constructed. Growing up in Poland during the Second World War, Stefan had played with his friends in similar bunkers in the woods on the outskirts of town. The location of Poland and its constant partition by its enemies, Russia, Germany or Prussia, led some people to have escape routes or places to hide.

Sadly, Stefan died before he could spend time in the bunker with his children. Visiting the secret "cubby cave" was one of the things the Zielinski children and their friends looked to most when they came to visit. But amazingly, it had remained hidden from locals for all these years.

From what Alice remembered it was an elaborate construction — as would be expected from Stefan Zielinski, who had a fascination for architecture and design.

Well camouflaged by native grass, with a trapdoor and descending iron ladder, the bunker was supported by reinforced concrete beams and fitted with complex air holes. It comprised two interconnecting rooms that were high enough to stand in. Over the years it had been fitted with a table, chairs and two bunk beds, plus bits and pieces brought down by the children over the years. Alice had always shivered at the thought of the children's sleepovers down there. It was pitch black and oh so cold, but the children seemed not to notice.

Is that where he headed at night? And should she tell?

♪

Cara waited until the headlights of her mother's car disappeared down the driveway before making her way to the living room. She had three hours to play. Jennifer never returned from her Thursday night meeting until, at least, eleven. Lifting the piano lid, she reached for a folder of music and settled in for the evening.

As a child, she'd sat for hours in the piano room, listening to her mother's classical music CDs and the desire to play like that herself one day had never waned.

It was Maggie Tate who'd instilled in her the need to master the basics. *There are no short cuts,* she'd said. *Sheer slog is what's called for. And years of it at that.* The words had done little to deter Cara. With determination and hard work, she worked her way through Madeleine's books of scales and elementary pieces and onto more challenging works. She had little patience for sight reading but the gift of perfect pitch enabled her to self-correct by listening to the recordings.

She glanced at the collection of classical CDs on the shelf. When was the last time her mother had listened to them? It was so far back she couldn't remember.

9

In the basement there was darkness, apart from a warm, strong glow from a single lamp on the desk. But he could not work. There was a restlessness within, compelling him to venture out once again into the darkness. As if drawn by an unseen force, he removed the matted rug from his knees, rose and went to the cupboard to get his coat. He liked that coat. Long and black, it blended with the night.

He knew he shouldn't leave the house. Perhaps he *had* done the things he was accused of. He *was* capable of it. Especially when he'd taken his medication and he found himself wavering between fantasy and reality. He hated the effect the drugs had on him but taking them was a condition of his release. Not that he swallowed them every time. He suspected that Alice knew but she never said.

It was never long before the cravings returned. And when things became too much and he found himself reaching for a handful of the pills that were stashed in his drawer, he couldn't be sure of what he might do or say.

He recalled the night he'd found himself standing over the mutilated dog, staring at his blood-soaked hands in disbelief. Looking around wildly to see that no one was about, he'd fled into the darkness towards the safety of his house. Down in the basement, he'd fumbled for the light switch and flung his coat on a nearby chair. Slumping onto the bed, he'd reached into the drawer and with shaking hands, pulled out a bottle of pills.

The events of that evening were to haunt him for days to come and random, confusing thoughts plagued his mind.

I couldn't have done it. I love dogs. There was no knife in my hand. No, but I could've disposed of it beforehand.

Not trusting what he might do he tried not to venture out after that, but the need for freedom and the rush of salt air against his skin became too much. By the sixth night, he was reaching for his coat.

He had no idea how many pills he'd swallowed, but next thing he was running away from an hysterical woman on the beach. *I don't think I followed her,* he thought. He vaguely recalled someone ahead in the distance and he had no idea how he'd caught up so fast. But he recalled the terror in the woman's eyes as he went to pass; the way she swung around, her hair swirling in the wind. And the scream. He'd awoken many times since, in the dead of night, haunted by that scream. *I think I touched her arm,* he thought in angst, *to console her but that's all I did … wasn't it?*

But what of the two gashes on his face the next morning. He felt his jaw clench. It could've been a tree branch, he consoled himself. God knows it was dark enough.

§

Two nights later, all was quiet as he edged his way up the stairs and along the passage to the doorway.

Hypnotically he walked through the back yard, feeling the crunch of pine needles under his feet. A large tree near the back gate creaked like a rocking chair in the wind. On the main road, he pushed on until he reached the imposing wrought iron gates of Kilkenny. There he stood for a few moments, staring up the driveway, paralysed with fear. He'd moved through the grounds many times in the darkness, but he'd made a vow year ago not to venture near the house, not trusting what he might do. He'd broken the vow once and he was about to do it again.

He wanted to turn and head back but was powerless to do so. As if in a trance he headed along the boundary fence to the side gate and reached for the rusted handle.

He'd gone only as far as the driveway when he heard the haunting sounds of a Chopin *Nocturne* wafting across the lawn. Like a sleepwalker he drifted towards the house and stood motionless … watching.

The curtains to the large bay window were open and Cara sat, absorbed, her fingers floating over the keys like a bird skimming.

Slowly he moved closer, chills coursing through his body, emotions spiralling out of control. He wanted to reach for her, wanted to stroke her hair but he knew he had to get away … fast. With a sob he turned and ran blindly into the night.

27

ee Farrell watched Angelina walk past his office and he felt a familiar longing.

He was forty-two and she twenty-five. Surely that wasn't too much of an age difference these days. But he'd been an uncle figure to the girls over the years, therein lay the difference.

As he watched Angelina grow Lee had no doubts that she'd turn into a stunner. He envied the stream of young men vying for her affections and wished that he was one of them. But his fantasies would remain well hidden; he wasn't about to jeopardise his relationship with Jennifer and Dominic.

Lee reflected on the years he'd spent with Dominic's family and his efforts in persuading Cara to step aboard the family yacht. From what he'd heard she'd rarely done so since the day of her brother's death.

His heart had reached out to the withdrawn, moody child who'd been through God knows what, and he went out of his way to encourage her at the helm. Eventually his efforts paid off. Cara took to the sport in the way that he'd hoped and he became a regular guest aboard the *Jennifer* when the family set sail.

Cara had always been a closed book and Lee was not one to pry. It took time to earn her trust and he liked to think that she'd reach out to him should the need arise. It wouldn't be her father she'd turn to. He wondered what in hell had transpired between those two over the years. Dominic rarely spoke of her and he knew better than to ask.

He'd seen little of Cara since she enrolled at university, and he'd looked to taking up their relationship where they'd left off once she joined the company.

His thoughts drifted to Angelina and he felt a trickle of sweat run down his back. If only her office wasn't on the same floor as his. The familiar light footsteps and lingering scent of her perfume as she passed drove him crazy.

Lee ran a hand through his hair. He'd better be careful. There was Eleanor, his wife of nine years, who missed nothing.

His love of sailing began as a twelve-year-old when he was introduced to the sport under a scheme for disadvantaged children. Raised in a high-rise Sydney slum to an alcoholic mother and unemployed father, he vowed to rise above his circumstances. Children in the block were easy targets for local gangs and drug runners so Lee kept to himself. Born with a sharp intellect and inquisitive nature, he was content being indoors, reading and studying.

The school that he attended comprised a high proportion of students who had similar backgrounds to his, or were migrants. Subsequently student drop-out levels were high, much to the disappointment of the dedicated team of young teachers determined to see their students achieve. It was Lee's homeroom teacher who noted his potential and stepped in as a mentor. Within six months he was offered a sailing course that would ultimately change his life.

A two-week stint aboard the *Wild Winds 3,* and the chance to step aboard yachts moored at the marina opened Lee's eyes to a world of prosperity and wealth. *One day I'll be part of all this,* he thought.

With fierce determination and grit he worked his way through high school and on to university. In his final year it was his good fortune to meet Eleanor Farrell, a wealthy socialite, ten years his senior.

He'd heard that the rich chartered luxury yachts during the summer months and he figured that becoming a crew member during his summer break would be his best hope of making contact. His irresistible charm and rugged tradesman good looks were enough to ensnare Eleanor, whom he met at a luncheon at the yacht club prior to his boat's departure. 'Here's my number if you're interested when you get back' she'd said softly, as she pressed a card into his hand.

From there was no turning back. Against her father's will, Eleanor married him the following year. But not before a prenuptial agreement was drawn up.

Lee lived the high life but he knew he'd lose everything if he left Eleanor. And so, he stayed years with a woman he'd never loved, socialising with the wealthy and enjoying the luxuries he'd become accustomed to.

Sooner or later, he knew that he'd need to find work. He couldn't live off her forever. Not that he wanted to. It wasn't a good prospect.

Bored and in need of mental stimulation, by chance he spotted the opening for a business advisor at the Lorenzo Wineries' Head Office. He applied for the job with little hope of success. Although he possessed the relevant qualifications, he lacked experience. However, his charisma and ambition won him the position. Wasting no time, he applied himself diligently, all the while charming his way into Dominic's personal life. Promotion and pay rise followed. At the back of his mind he thought it prudent to invest in stocks and shares, just in case.

Lee was by now an expert yachtsman thanks to Eleanor's list of yachting connections. Passing on the finer points of sailing to his boss worked to his advantage. As Dominic's time became more taken up by business matters, Lee was given unrestricted access to his yacht the *Jennifer,* a sixty-five meter doublemasted Herreshoff schooner. Things couldn't be better.

He'd dreamed of owning such a yacht but the price tag was way out of reach. It was a pity that Eleanor didn't share his love of sailing or she might have been cajoled into buying one. But she became seasick just setting foot on a boat. He'd surmised long ago that his wife's obsession with yachts was a prestige thing: the chance to cultivate connections with the well to do.

Her favourite pastime was socialising at the yacht club, much to Lee's annoyance. He'd rather be out sailing or competing than sitting, listening to idle chatter. But living the high life had its sacrifices — charming Eleanor's chardonnay drinking friends was one of them.

He saw the way Eleanor gloated when he joined their table. She was the envy of them all. Most had middle-aged husbands who'd let themselves go — too much red wine and fancy dinners. He on the other hand, was toned and tanned, complimenting his good looks. From a distance he could pass for a crew member fifteen years his junior. And he used it to his advantage. There was no way he was about to jeopardise his standing with Eleanor. It had taken too long. The yachting scene was a haven for young beautiful women, opportunists like himself. There'd been occasions when he'd been tempted to have a one-night stand. But he'd not succumbed and avoided temptation.

Lee returned to his emails and clicked on one from Dominic. He frowned as he scrolled through the message. Why was Dominic about to make another trip to Bangkok and what would he be doing there?

❡

He came in the darkness. It was Thursday evening and

he knew that Cara would be alone in the house. He'd wait until Jennifer's car disappeared down the driveway, then make his way to the large bush on the lawn where he'd settle on the grass to watch her play. After a while, he'd find himself closing his eyes and with arms wrapped around his knees, he'd sway to the music. Time would disappear like a drifting feather.

On this night his mind was reeling. He'd taken a double dose of medication after a sleepless night; one of many when the visions returned to haunt him. There he'd be, pinned against the wall of the dark alleyway in Prague as the two thugs growled threats in broken English. He could hear the raucous banter of drinkers nearby as he cowered, screaming to be spared. There'd be the agony of his head smashing against cobblestones and the glint of silver under murky yellow light. As his mind filled with red, and he recalled an unmistakable metallic taste, he'd be met with the most chilling image of all: the two severed fingertips that that lay inches from his eyes. Then nothing.

'I would've kept my word, you bastard,' he cried out writhing in a tangle of saturated sheets. 'But you had to strip me of everything that mattered.'

With eyes darting wildly in the darkness, he willed his breathing to slow and sat up, relieved of the opportunity to escape the nightmare.

The music had stopped. It was the dampness seeping through the ground below that broke his reverie. Opening his eyes he lifted his wrist, straining to make out the time.

Jennifer would be back soon. He recalled the first time he'd watched her arrive home. The moment her headlights appeared in the driveway, he scrambled to his feet and ran to the cover of the pergola that lay in darkness. He caught only a glimpse as she entered the house but it was enough to send his mind racing.

He knew it was wrong to watch her like that and resisted the urge to do so again. Until now.

Jennifer's mind was troubled as she pulled into the driveway. Two nights ago, Dominic's mobile rang as he was eating dinner. He was quick to recognise the number and headed out of the room to answer the call, mumbling something as he went about an urgent business matter. But Jennifer was not so easily fooled. She'd seen that look on the faces of men who liked to stray.

Once she'd activated the remote to the garage and parked the car, she sat in darkness for a few moments before grabbing her bag and car keys. But as she went to step out of the car, something caught her eye in the rear vision mirror. She thought that she could see a shadow moving across the lawn. Tentatively she slid out, edged her way along the garage wall and peered into the darkness. Nothing. She frowned.

Probably a dog, she thought. It wouldn't be the first time that people had taken a short cut through Kilkenny to get to the beach. She wished Dominic was home. Once again she recalled the call he took at the restaurant and thoughts began to tumble around in her mind. Where *was* he tonight? And why was he spending more weekends in the city?

As she entered the house, Jennifer heard the door to the piano room close, followed by Cara's light tread up the stairway. She walked wearily to her room and undressed before heading to the ensuite for a shower. *Damn it, I forgot to feed the dog,* she thought. Grabbing her robe from the nearby chair, she pulled it on and hastily tied the belt as she set out for the kitchen.

He watched from the darkness, not five metres from where she stood at the window, bare-footed on the cold floor and hair loose around her shoulders as she opened the can of dog food. He felt his heart begin to pound. The back door was unfastened. More often than not they neglected to lock it once the dog was let out for its nightly walk. After the recent events in town, he thought they'd be more careful.

In effect he could enter the house at any time.

Fighting to control his feelings he waited until the kitchen light went out and turned for home.

28

The room was abuzz with chatter as Dominic and Jennifer crossed the floor to greet their host.

'Welcome and thanks for coming.' The tall, silver-haired man stepped forward to shake their hands. 'It's good to see you both.'

'And you as well, Oliver.' Jennifer replied with a smile.

'Claire will be sorry she missed you. She's attending a fashion parade for her favourite charity this evening.'

Jennifer nodded. Oliver's wife was often out on these occasions but his get-togethers continued regardless.

'Well, pass on my best wishes to her, would you?' she responded. 'I'll drop by to see her when I'm next in town.'

'She'd like that. Now let me show you over the place.'

'Thank you. I'm looking forward to seeing it. Dominic has told me so much about it.'

The penthouse apartment was one of eight, encompassing the entire sixty-third storey of a newly constructed residential and commercial tower. Jennifer had no doubt that what she was about to see would be amazing. From what she'd heard, Oliver placed a two-million-dollar deposit on the place when he was first shown the plans by the Singaporean developers four years ago. God knows how much it was worth now.

Oliver was a heavy investor in stocks and shares, spending six months respectively in the city and in New York. He was also a philanthropist who'd been a close friend to Madeleine and remained a patron of her two main charities. He held parties from time to time and Jennifer and Dominic were amongst his regular guests. The affairs were lavish, befitting his social standing. Jennifer had quickly warmed to Oliver's circle of friends. Most were rich, some immensely so, but one would never know. Unlike others she'd met, they never bragged or put others down.

Dominic gave scant thought to the matter. A party was a party. As long as the alcohol flowed freely and there was a chance to expand his business connections, he was content to settle in and mingle with his customary charm and wit.

It had been some time since they had stepped out socially. Dominic seemed to have lost touch with many of his acquaintances and showed far less interest in attending events he once enjoyed. It therefore came as a surprise when Oliver's invitation to dinner was accepted so readily.

'It's about time we went to the apartment for the weekend,' he'd said. 'Oliver's just flown in from the States and he's keen to show us his new place.'

Jennifer stood on the plush carpet, barely able to take in

her surroundings. She'd only seen such luxury in American movies or *Vogue* magazines. The scent of fresh blooms wafted through the air. She smiled. Oliver's wife Claire loved flowers and an arrangement was always present in their house, even in her absence. For a moment, Jennifer stood lost in thought, reminded of the roses in Madeleine's room.

'This place is something else, hey?' Dominic squeezed her hand as they followed Oliver out into the passageway towards the lift.

She could see the hunger in his eyes when they stepped out on to the top floor, comprising a large heated swimming pool, gymnasium and private cinema.

'Wow!' she exclaimed, 'it's like a resort. Can *anyone* come up here?'

'No. just the eight of us. Only those with penthouses have access,' Oliver explained, smiling and reaching for her hand. 'Here, come and take a look at the view.'

He led her to the floor to ceiling plate glass window to observe the outline of the city from the spectacular backdrop.

'It's beautiful Oliver, it truly is.'

'Yes, it's not bad, is it' he said as he sat on the window ledge, looking into the distance as the sun cast its last rays. 'You know, I feel at peace in this place. Perhaps it's the views over the bay. I don't know.'

¶

The words echoed in Jennifer's mind as she dressed for dinner the following evening. She couldn't begin to imagine what it would be like to live in a place like that. *If I were Oliver, there'd be less time spent in New York from now on,* she thought with a faint smile as she fastened an earring.

Dominic had booked a table in a newly refurbished hotel across the other side of town. 'I hope you'll like it,' he said. 'I've never been there but from what they say at work –'

Jennifer held a finger to his lips. 'I'll love it.' She said. 'Everywhere you take me is special.'

At eight, Dominic popped his head around the corner. 'Are you ready? The taxi's arrived.'

She nodded and grabbed her bag from the chair.

It had rained heavily for the past hour and the taxi's windscreen wipers worked furiously as the driver pulled out from the kerb. Although the downpour had ceased by the time they arrived at the hotel, the cold night air went straight through Jennifer's woollen dress as she alighted from the taxi and she wished she'd packed her coat. A car horn blared in the distance as they hurried towards the warmth of the hotel.

Over dinner Jennifer found her troubles drifting away as they sipped their wine and spoke freely, the way they used to do. And over coffee when he leaned forward, hands clasped, and looked softly into her eyes she felt her heart melt. It had been so long since she'd felt so desired.

Later, Dominic looked only at her as he led her to the

dance floor, oblivious of the women who flirted with their eyes. And when the music began and he pulled her close, lips pressed against her hair, she wondered how she could ever have doubted his fidelity.

But her sense of complacency was to be short-lived. Once the band had played their last number and Dominic escorted her to their table, they were approached by a patron whom she recognised from Dominic's work. He'd clearly had too much to drink.

'Hey Dominic, where've you been of a night when you're in town. I've tried your apartment a number of times but you're never home. Thought you might've liked a drink after work.'

Jennifer thought she detected a flicker of alarm on Dominic's face but it quickly vanished.

'Have you thought of trying my work number?' he snapped. 'Some of us *do* stay back late, you know.'

'Hey, don' be like that.' The man swayed, wiping a sleeve against his mouth. 'It's not like I was suggesting an affair or something.'

'Well, *I'd* suggest you handle your drink a bit better, Gareth.' Dominic's words were cold. 'Now if you'll excuse us.'

His hand was firm on Jennifer's arm as he steered her away.

As they sat in the back of the taxi for the trip home across town, Jennifer pondered over what the man had said. Exactly what *did* Dominic do of a night when he was in town. Angelina said that he sometimes stayed back at the office but she was only there some of the time. Right now she was in no state of mind to think clearly. As she lay her head on his shoulder, she found herself mumbling between hazy thoughts, 'you wouldn't, would you?'

'Wouldn't what?'

'Have an affair behind my back.'

'And risk losing you?'

'You haven't answered my question.'

'And you should know me well enough not to ask. You mean everything to me.'

She felt his lips press against her forehead as she drifted off.

Dominic sat beside her, eyes dark, watching the blur of lights flash by. This was too close for comfort. He'd been far too careless over his affair with Raquel, had taken her to way too many places. One day he would come unstuck. If Gareth had dropped by the apartment last Friday night, for instance …

Raquel would have to go. There was too much at stake.

That night as he turned off the bathroom light and climbed into bed where Jennifer lay sleeping, the scent of her favourite Chanel against the sheets unsettled him. I'd better make it up to her tomorrow, he thought, as he laid an arm around her and pulled himself close.

Jennifer awoke to a tray set with a white linen napkin, red rose, freshly brewed coffee, juice and hot rolls from the bakery down the street.

'Hey,' she said, rubbing her eyes as she sat up, 'is this for real?'

Dominic sat on the edge of the bed and reached out to stroke her face. 'You deserve it, Babe. I've been spending far too much time away from you.'

'I must admit, it's been pretty lonely at Kilkenny.'

Dominic started to say something but stopped himself.

'Yum,' she said as she took a bite out of the roll that he'd buttered, 'that takes some beating.'

'Good. But save some of your appetite for later. I've booked us into *The Windsor* for lunch before we head back.'

'My favourite,' she said with a smile. 'Thanks Dom.'

'You're worth it, Babe.'

The morning was spent wandering around the city arcades, hand in hand, stopping for coffee and shopping. So far, so good. And the meal couldn't be better. He would have liked a few more days together in the city but she was keen to get back to Kilkenny, as always. He would have to make his move soon. Would have to wait until the right moment.

29

Two days later, Jennifer rose from the table after dinner while Dominic was reading the paper. 'I'm just going for a walk along the beach. Shouldn't be too long.'

'Mind if I come?'

The words surprised her. He never accompanied her on her daily walks.

'Of course not,' she replied. 'I'll just get our coats.'

A fine misty rain had just started as they headed down the path and she dug her hands deep in her pockets.

As they walked along the shore, Dominic took a deep breath and mentally rehearsed what he was about to say. But it no longer sounded right. He had no doubt that he was in for a fight whichever way he played things. The first words she spoke didn't help.

'You know, I had the best time in town at the weekend but couldn't wait to get back home.' She took one hand from her pocket and hooked it on his elbow.

He stiffened. What he wanted to say was, 'Yeah? Well

it's a pity the same doesn't go for me,' but he held his tongue.

'There's something about the place, I don't know,' she continued, oblivious to the rigidity of his body. 'I can understand why the girls never stay away too long.'

The silence that followed was the calm before the storm. By the time his words came out, it was too late. 'Well perhaps it was time you all stopped living in the past and got with the real world.'

She stopped abruptly and turned to face him. 'What's that supposed to mean?'

'Look, I've been thinking about this place for a number of years now and –'

Her hand dropped from his arm. 'And?'

'Weighing things up, I suppose you could say. I'm hardly ever here now and to tell you the truth, *I* don't really miss it.'

He watched as her face blanched, and wondered how far to push. But he had already opened up a can of worms.

'So, what exactly are you saying?'

'Have you ever wondered how much this place is worth?'

'No, I have *not*!'

'Well, perhaps it's time you knew. It's worth millions. Millions that could be better spent elsewhere.'

'Such as?' she fired back.

'Such as the penthouse directly below Oliver's for a start. The sale didn't go through and it's on the market again. We'd sell the apartment as well of course. There's been no shortage of offers: Chinese and Indian businessmen seeking accommodation for their kids near the Uni. We could pretty much get what we wanted for it.'

'Oh I see!' she yelled, 'so that's what this weekend was all about was it? The so-called "house warming" at Oliver's, the new emerald earrings. I should have known.' She turned to go but he grabbed her arm so tightly she felt like he'd cut off the circulation in her arm. His eyes blazed into hers.

'Cut the crap, Jennifer. I saw your face light up when you saw that rooftop setup, and your eyes feasted on that view. I thought you'd enjoy being neighbours of Oliver and Claire.'

'I don't believe this!' She jerked her arm free.

'Take a look around our place,' he snapped. 'The house is badly in need of repair and the buildings around the property are so old they're falling down. It'll cost a fortune to fix everything.'

'Money I'm prepared to spend.'

'And have you thought about me? Where do I come into the equation? All the years I've worked without a break to build up the business. And you? You never had to work a day since you married me. Just walked around, enjoying the views with my mother.'

She slapped his face and he stood, stunned for a moment.

'Just how much money do you need for me to buy you out then?' Jennifer said through gritted teeth. 'Can you tell me that much?'

'So, do I take that to be a no?' Dominic's voice was cold now.

'You can bet on it.'

Dominic needed every bit of restraint not to hurl her into the cliff face. Instead, he grabbed her chin and twisted until her eyes smarted.

'Very well,' his eyes were inches from hers, 'You've made things perfectly clear. But you haven't heard the last of it. Not by a long shot.'

His hand dropped to his side and he strode away without looking back. Jennifer stood, her lip trembling as he stormed out of sight.

High on the cliff face the man blended into the inky darkness like a panther. He had watched the couple arguing below, until the sun's last rays disappeared across the horizon and listened as words of heated conversation hit the still night.

When he heard footsteps crunching up the narrow path, the crash of branches in their wake, he pulled himself hard against the trunk of a nearby tree. As he watched Dominic pass just metres away, a rage burned up within that he'd never felt before. It took every ounce of self-control not to jump up from behind and strike him down. But now was not the time. He clenched his fists and closed his eyes, envisaging his hands tighten around Dominic's neck until the last bit of life drained from his body and it slumped like a rag doll into the dirt.

When the time came, he'd be prepared. *I've got nothing*

to lose, he thought.

Jennifer walked blindly into the night, her mind a turmoil of emotions. She should have read the warning signs years ago. Dominic had never talked with pride about Kilkenny in the way that his mother did, and since her death little had been spent on maintenance. At the back of the property bracken ferns proliferated like the rabbits that inhabited its gullies. Fences were down and the roof of the old winery had collapsed in a recent storm.

And as for the house, Dominic was correct. It would take a considerable amount of money to restore the place to its original glory. The recent renovations to Madeleine's quarters proved that.

A simmering anger welled inside her as she walked. Stuff him. If he really wanted to sell the place, he would have one hell of a fight on his hands. But where the hell would she get the money to buy him out?

She took a deep breath, and, forcing all thoughts aside, turned her attention to the rhythm of her feet in the wet sand.

The man followed some way back in the darkness, thoughts hazy. He should never have followed her in the first place. But his medication gave him a loss of inhibition and sense of daring. She'd been walking for some time now and was heading around the cliffs towards town. If he was to approach her it needed to be soon. His steps quickened. But what if he did catch up? What then?

Jennifer sensed something. She spun around. There was

a shape of someone in the distance. At first she thought it was Dominic, but instinct told her otherwise. Her throat went dry. Apart from the two of them the beach was deserted. Her heart began to pound. There'd been reports of a stalker in the town, obscene phone calls to young women and a case of rape.

She quickened her pace but a fleeting glance over her shoulder told her that the person behind was gaining ground. She started to run, pulse throbbing, legs struggling against the heaviness of the sand and knowing full well she could not last. Twenty metres ahead she stopped for a few seconds, bending over and gasping for breath before she pushed on once again. Then an unexposed rock caught her toe, causing her to trip head first into the sand. Gritty particles stung her eyes and lodged in her mouth as she struggled to rise. But something caused her to freeze. A shadow loomed over her, like an ominous cloud. His short, ragged breaths cut the air, filling her with fear but it was the slow stroke of a hand over her hair that sent her scrambling to her feet, screaming and thrashing, braced for a struggle.

Then he was gone.

¶

Dominic swilled the last drop of whisky, slammed the glass on the table then headed up the stairs to the bedroom to pack. Clothes were flung on the bed which, with one hand he swept into a bag.

Normally, he would have stayed and ridden things out. But not tonight. He had never seen Jennifer so enraged, never witnessed such resistance. He pressed a hand against his still burning cheek. She'd changed and he needed to as well. Pretty damned quickly. Ashamed as Dominic was to admit it, emotions had always ruled his head as far as Jennifer was concerned. Well that was about to cease. A few days in the city before his flight to Bangkok would harden his resolve. The new deal would whet his appetite and provide ample time to consider his future moves when he arrived home. He had no intention of contacting Jennifer before he left. Let the bitch sweat. As he grabbed his bag and made his way down the passageway, Cara stepped out of her room.

'Dad, where are you going? Where's Mum?'

'Down on the beach, somewhere. Who knows?'

'What? You left her down there in the dark? After what's been going on around here? How could you! She could be attacked down there, even killed.'

There was a pause before Dominic spoke. 'Let's get things clear,' he said menacingly, 'It was your mother's idea to stay there and not mine. Have you got that?'

'That's still no excuse not to go back to check.'

Dominic's face contorted with rage. He lurched forward and grabbed a handful of Cara's hair, causing her head to fling back and eyes water.

'Dad! Let go.'

'What your mother and I do is none of your business. Have you got that?'

'I *said,* let go of my frigging hair!' Cara's words were low and ominous.

Dominic dropped his hand and met her eyes in a deadly gaze.

'If you're that worried about your mother, go look for her yourself. I've got things to do in town.'

He slung the sports bag over his shoulder and strode down the passageway.

Cara watched, eyes blazing and heart pumping. 'You don't care about her at all, do you.' She muttered. 'You don't fucking-well care!'

She waited until the sound of the engine faded before putting on her jacket and heading outside. For a moment she stood, looking around in the darkness. She sensed that something was wrong. It was over two hours since her mother had left for her walk. There had obviously been a massive argument but Cara was yet to understand how her father could leave Jennifer like that.

Walking briskly to the garage, she took a torch from the shelf and made her way down to the beach. There was no sign of her mother. It was eerie shining the torch on the rocks, seeing the light bounce off the water like a ping pong ball. Cara was used to being down there alone in the dark. But this time it was as if she was invading someone's privacy. *Maybe she's already home,* Cara comforted herself, as she headed back to check. *You're probably worrying about nothing.* But the house was empty.

With a frown, Cara grabbed her car keys and headed

towards town. As she turned on to the esplanade, her lights picked up someone walking across the foreshore. She knew that walk. But what on earth was her mother doing so far from home. It was only when she drove closer and she saw the dishevelled hair and look of fear on Jennifer's face, that her heart lurched.

She screeched into the kerb and jumped out. 'Mum, are you all right?'

'Cara! What are you doing here?'

'Just a feeling I had,' she said. 'Something's happened hasn't it. I can tell by the look on your face.'

'I thought I saw someone in the bushes back there, that's all.'

'And?' Cara looked at the sand on Jennifer's clothes.'

'I fell over as I was walking on the beach, 'Jennifer said quickly. 'Must've tripped on a rock or something.'

'You're not hurt, are you?'

'No, I'm fine.'

'So what are you doing this far from home?'

'I walked further than I thought, that's all,' she said. 'It was dark and I could see the lights of town ahead. It made no sense to turn back.'

'How come you didn't have your torch with you, Cara persisted, 'or at least your phone. The light wouldn't be that strong, but enough to see you home.'

'I know, I know. It's something I always drum into the pair of you, isn't it.'

Cara shot her a wry look.

'To be honest, I had planned to go out for just a short walk.'

Cara went to say something but stopped short.

'Look, we'll talk about it later. Right now, I could do with a hot shower. Let's go, shall we?'

There was a nod and they headed towards the car.

Neither spoke until they turned in the driveway.

'You and Dad had a row, didn't you,' Cara said, eyes ahead.

'Why, did he say something?'

Cara said nothing, just waited until they drew closer to the house.

'Is your father still here?' Jennifer felt a flash of panic when she saw the lights in front room.

Cara hesitated. 'Look Mum, it's none of my business, I know, but I get the feeling it was more than just a tiff between you two down there. I've rarely seen him so fired up.'

Jennifer ran a palm across her forehead. 'It's been a long day, Darling and I really don't feel like talking about it right now. Okay?'

'That's fine.' Cara's tone was cool. 'Perhaps you can tell Angelina. She'll be home in the morning. Don't worry, I'll be gone before then.'

'Cara –' Jennifer went to touch her arm but was shrugged aside.

'I hope you sleep well.' Cara locked the car door and walked inside.

Damn it. Jennifer thought. *The one time she reaches out to me, shows some concern, I do this.*

She so badly wanted run to after Cara, grab hold of her hand and say, 'I didn't mean what I just said. I *need* to talk to you; tell you what happened. I'm scared and I don't know what to do next.' But she didn't.

With a sigh, she walked towards the veranda, undoing her coat.

30

Jennifer's sleep was fitful and disturbed. When she arose and drew back the curtains, Cara's car was already gone. She sat on the window ledge, face pressed against the glass and looked out into the foggy morning. She had no doubt that she was in for the fight of her life. And she had no idea where to start.

A glimpse of her reflection in the window elicited a groan and she lifted one hand to her tangled hair. As she rose, a glimpse in the mirror confirmed the worst. She looked like she'd been sleeping rough. Particles of sand were wedged into her pasty skin that contrasted sharply against the black circles under her eyes. Six hours ago she had fallen exhausted into bed, without bothering to shower — something she never did.

She quickly showered and dressed, then made her way to the kitchen, hoping her drawn appearance would go unnoticed. She was wrong.

'Mum, are you all right?' Angelina walked in soon

afterwards.

'I'm fine. Just a late night that's all.'

'Looks like it. Where's Dad?'

'He's gone back to the city.'

'When? Last night?'

'He didn't arrive at the apartment when you were there?'

'No.'

'I see.' Jennifer's hands tightened.

'I thought he was staying here for the weekend.'

'It's a long story,' Jennifer said wearily, as she poured herself a glass of water. 'I'd rather not talk about it just now.'

Her words were ignored. 'The pair of you had an argument, didn't you.'

'You could say that.'

'Come on Mum. Out with it. If it's any consolation, he's been snappy at work as well.'

'Oh?'

'There's more to this, isn't there. I can tell by the look on your face.'

Jennifer ran a hand through her hair. 'Yes, there is.' She motioned to the chair opposite. 'You'd better sit down. I suppose you need to know sooner or later.'

Angelina's reaction to Dominic's plans was disbelief, as expected. 'That can't be right! There's no way he'd sell this place. You know what Dad's like. He gets all these ideas and goes at them like a bat out of hell then moves on to something else.'

'I'd like to believe it this once … but I don't.'

Angelina sat seething beside her, arms crossed and eyes dark. Paul Anderson was behind all of this; she was convinced of it. The man seemed to have some kind of hold on her father. Until he arrived, her mother was the centre of Dominic's universe. He knew how much Kilkenny meant to her; to all of them. But now was not the time to let emotion cloud her judgement. Paul's time would come.

'Don't worry Mum, we'll figure something out.' Angelina turned to look at Jennifer. 'You won't hear much about it anyway, until Dad gets back.'

'Gets back from where?' Jennifer said in surprise.

'He didn't tell you about his trip?'

'No, he didn't.'

'He's flying to Bangkok in a few days.'

Jennifer raised an eyebrow. 'Oh? For how long?'

'Five days, I think.'

'Why?'

'Some business deal he's ready to sign.'

'Do you know what it's about?'

Angelina shrugged. 'Must be big though. As I said before, he's been as edgy as hell at the office.'

Jennifer frowned. *What else was going on?*

Angelina interrupted her thoughts.

'Try not to dwell on it for now, okay? I'm heading back to the office in the morning and I'll figure something out then.'

'But I thought you were staying for a few more days.'

'Not now I'm not.' Her face was grim. 'Does Cara know about this?'

'No, I didn't get a chance to tell her last night.'

'Well, let her know. Between the three of us we'll come up with something,' Angelina assured her, 'just wait until Dad's gone away. Okay?'

Jennifer nodded, grateful not to have to think.

'Right now, you look as if you could do with some sleep. You look like shit,' Angelina said bluntly.

Jennifer gave a weak smile. 'That bad huh?'

Angelina nodded. 'That bad. Look, go back to bed for a while. You've nothing else on for the day, have you?'

'No.'

Angelina rose and pulled Jennifer to her feet. 'Off you go. I'll be up to check on you later.'

Sleep came easier than Jennifer thought. She woke to the sound of rain beating against her window. Her bedside clock that told her she'd been asleep for five hours. *Shit, that long,* she thought, pulling off the doona and swinging her legs to the floor. Still dressed in her jeans and sweater she splashed cold water over her face, ran a brush over her hair and went downstairs. Angelina was nowhere to be seen. The rest had left Jennifer energised and ravenous. It had been close to twenty-four hours since she'd last eaten and she headed for the kitchen to heat up some soup and make herself a sandwich.

As she cleared away the last of the dishes, her eyes caught sight of her mobile and she thought of Cara. She knew she wouldn't rest until her daughter knew of Dominic's plans to sell but a phone call was not the way to do it.

At least I can make a time to meet, she thought.

Her call was met by Cara's message bank. She waited. 'Hi Cara, it's Mum. Give me a ring, will you?'

An hour passed then two, and the call had not been returned.

Jennifer's brow furrowed. That was not like Cara. Admittedly they didn't contact each other much, but her calls were always answered promptly. Reaching for the phone once more she put a call through to the show jumping stables.

'Good afternoon, this is Jennifer Lorenzo,' she said, 'I've been trying to contact Cara but haven't been able to get through. Is everything all right?'

The man at the other end sounded surprised. 'I thought she was with you for the weekend.'

Jennifer felt her heart beat quicken. 'Well she was but –'

'She's probably headed off to town then. She does that sometimes on her days off.'

'To our apartment?'

'Nah, some other place she hangs out at.'

Jennifer was bewildered. 'Do you know where it is?'

'Not really. Cara likes to keep things private. But I do have the number if that helps. She gave it to me in case of an emergency.'

'I'd appreciate that. Thanks.' Jennifer reached across the table for a pen.

For a few moments, she sat still, struggling to take in what she'd heard. Where *was* this place and why had Cara kept her visits a secret? With a sinking heart, she realised that she didn't know her daughter at all. Cara had never confided in her, never looked to her for support. What if she was in danger?

At the end of the call she clicked on the Google icon and began a search. *God, where do I start? There's so many of them,* she thought, as she scrolled down. One website in particular caught her eye. It looked professional enough. She hit the call symbol and waited.

31

Cara wandered through the city streets. It was close to midnight, but as usual for a Saturday there were plenty of people around. It was the third time she'd gone to the city on her rare days off and she had no intention of divulging her whereabouts. The family apartment often stood empty but chances of an unexpected blow-in were always on the cards.

Instead, she opted for a one-bedroom apartment at a shady boarding house not far from the CBD: all that her limited finances allowed. Apart from the occasional shouting match two doors down from hers, or a drunken resident in the passageway trying to find their room, there was little noise apart from the hum of traffic outside that she'd grown accustomed to.

As she headed towards the seedier side of town a wave of garlic met her nostrils, causing her mouth to water. She glanced at the pizza shop, already filling with customers. She decided to pick one up on the way back. By that time she'd probably be ravenous. As she dug her hands further into her pockets, thoughts came to mind of the evening just passed. What was the row between her parents about this time? It was always her father who ended up with the upper hand and her mother the one to back down. *Why do you keep putting up with it* she thought? *Why don't you stand up to him for a change? Like I did last night …*

Cara was used to Dominic's threats but he'd never laid a hand on her before.

Her face burned with anger as she walked. One thing was for sure: that time would be the last. With a shiver, she reached for her hoodie. She'd forgotten how cold the city could be at night. As she headed towards the river she noted a lonely figure huddled beneath the bridge under a thin blanket. An empty wine cask lay alongside.

With a pang of guilt, she thought how it was only fate determining those born wanting for nothing and those confined to a life of hardship. With the roll of a dice she could have been either.

The irony was that she was as good as on the streets herself the longer she deferred her course. *Suck it up, Dad,* she thought with a wry smile. The decision had been worth it; never had she felt such a sense of empowerment over her father.

Cara's pride didn't allow her to access her inheritance. She preferred to live frugally than to be in a position for Dominic to make snide comments. She could have sought part-time accountancy work. This would have appeased

Dominic to some extent. In contrast, a job in a show jumping stables was the ultimate kick in the guts. Perhaps that's why the offer was accepted so readily.

The summer show jumping circuit was about to begin and that meant six to eight weeks on the road, strapping for the stable's riders and their mounts. The pay was lousy and the food average, but it was enough to survive on. It was horses that made the job worthwhile.

When her pony was so cruelly taken from her as a child, it was as if part of her was ripped away as well. When she'd stolen out to the stables in the early hours of the morning to say her goodbyes, she thought her heart would break. It took a long time for her wounds to heal but she had moved on. She had to. She'd all but forgotten the joy that horses brought to her life until she was around them once more.

Cara glanced at the hazy lights on the river. Jack Gallagher would have long departed the country by now. She felt her anger rise as she reflected on how easily she'd succumbed to the charms of the accomplished thirty-five-year-old Irish rider who'd flown out to present a series of show jumping clinics.

As she walked along the darkened city streets, Cara recalled with bitterness the night she was led by Jack's hand to his room. It wasn't supposed to be like that ... was it? Her first experience of sex in a sordid cramped bottom bunk surrounded by a pile of dirty clothes, carelessly tossed on the floor beside a half-read *Horse Deals* magazine.

For days after they first met, she dreamed of making love with the handsome Irishman; the grass under the stars perhaps, or in the sand dunes against the pounding of the ocean.

But this … It started out as a stubby or two and moved onto stronger stuff, the swift loss of inhibition, the memory of being thrown against the wall, hands ripping at her blouse, pulling down her jeans, words that seemed far away, almost surreal. 'God you're beautiful,' fingers groping under her pants, probing until they found an opening, and thrusting harshly inside her.

She'd screamed at him to stop, furious at her slurred words and blurred sensations, but he'd continued regardless.

One swift slam upwards with her knee, sent him hunched over, writhing with pain.

'Don't you *ever* touch me again. Got that?'

'You friggin' frigid bitch,' he looked up, gasping. 'Who'd want you anyway.'

Maybe no-one, Cara thought, as she waited at the traffic lights alongside a couple deep in conversation, *but at least I'll be the one calling the shots.*

A bar nearby was in full swing and she pushed open the door and headed for the counter.

'I'd like a drink thanks. Something strong.'

'What type?'

She shrugged. 'Whatever. Surprise me.'

'Hard day, huh?'

'Could say that.'

The bartender looked with some concern at the young woman perched on the stool in front of him. This was not the part of town for a single woman. It was frequented by prostitutes, pimps and drug dealers. Yet there was something about her ... she looked as if she could hold her own.

He reached for a brown bottle on the top shelf and unscrewed the lid.

Cara sat, letting the effect of the second drink take over. A hazy recollection of a moment long ago washed over her. The fleeting touch of fingers tracing her face. An opportunity lost. It brought to mind the text she received out of the blue, not long after he'd gone. He'd wanted to see her again. Wanted to extend the relationship. *Why didn't I reply?* She asked herself. *Why did I reject him like that?* He was the only person she'd felt close to, wanted to be close to.

She thought of the dark unruly curls, the grin that could be so infuriating and her heart skipped a beat. She found herself wondering how much he'd have changed; what they would say to each other if they met now.

For a moment she had the urge to reach into her pocket for her mobile but stopped herself. She'd had her chance and blown it. Will would have moved on long ago. It was all too late.

A thirty-somethingish man edged his way through the crowd to order his drink and turned to face her.

'Here by yourself?'

She was quick to note his eyes on her low-cut shirt.

'What does it look like?'

He grinned. 'Wanna dance? No strings attached.'

He looked pleasant enough: his strong, tanned features and lean build indicative of a tradesman.

'Why not.'

She noticed the white line against the tan on the ring finger of his left hand as she rose.

The strobe lights, upbeat music and loud voices overwhelmed her and she was soon laughing and dancing, lost in time, the raw, sweet odour of sweat engulfing her senses.

'Want another drink?' he leaned towards her ear to be heard as the band paused for a break.

'Yeah.'

She felt strong fingers wrap around hers as he led her through the crowd to the bar.

When they returned to the dance floor the effect of the double shot of tequila was already kicking in. *So, I'm frigid am I, Mr. Jack Gallagher,* she thought with anger. *That unattractive, huh?* Well we'll see about that. She returned the man's smile, not resisting when his arms wrapped around her and pulled her close. She closed her eyes, allowing herself to be carried away. She didn't care that hands were reaching under her blouse and moving in slow sensuous movements around her back, didn't pull back when she felt the touch of his lips against hers.

As the night wore on Cara lost track of the drinks consumed. She vaguely remembered stumbling out of the bar on closing time, strong arms around her shoulders to prevent her from sliding to the ground. There was a blur of voices, the clatter of a rubbish bin in a distant alleyway … then nothing.

And in the early morning when she awoke in a cheap motel with his leg sprawled over her naked body, fractured images of the night returned: of him throwing her onto the bed, wrenching her legs apart and boring into her. She was grateful that she'd been too drunk to feel anything but the self-loathing that most consumed her.

Cara bit her lip with shame. She couldn't recall how she'd got there. Didn't even know his name. Well too bad. Life went on. *If you could just see me now, Dad,* she thought. Careful not to wake the man, she slid from underneath and tiptoed across the room to get her clothes.

32

In the early hours of the morning Lucas Grady switched off his camera and headed towards his car parked around the corner and out of view. He felt sorry for Jennifer Lorenzo. Who wouldn't? As a private investigator he got calls like hers almost every week. What was wrong with the kids of today? Not that Cara Lorenzo was a kid. She was twenty -six. Old enough to know better.

He recalled the anguish in Jennifer's voice the previous night when he'd rang her to tell of the sleazy bar and how easily Cara allowed herself to be picked up. He didn't relish the thought of showing her the footage.

More out of curiosity than anything else he'd agreed to take on the Lorenzo woman's case. Jennifer and her husband often graced the society pages, yet she was not linked in any way to the bitchy set of wealthy women known around town, many of whom he'd had dealings with in the past. From what he'd read she had done a significant amount of philanthropic work.

From the photo that Jennifer had sent him of her daughter, there were distinct similarities between the two. Cara Lorenzo was every bit as good looking as her mother but in an unusual way. Perhaps it was her eyes, green and vivid. Her auburn hair was richer in colour and a tad more luxurious. You didn't see hair much like that these days.

As he observed her the previous evening, she had just worn blue jeans and a white shirt that displayed more than a hint of cleavage. There was no sign of make-up or jewellery, apart from a pair of plain, silver hoop earrings. She possessed natural poise; carrying her slender frame with the grace of a martial arts expert. He noted that her fingers were long and tapered. An artist perhaps?

Lucas had almost willed her not to accompany the stranger out of the bar at the end of the night. However, it soon became apparent that this was no naïve young woman. Cara Lorenzo's body language told him she knew exactly what she was doing. And when he followed the pair down a nearby laneway, he knew where they were headed. There were no boutique hotels in this part of town, only a motel well known for paedophiles and prostitutes. He'd heard of schoolgirls making out with God knows who in their lunchtimes to earn a quick buck. The thought sickened him and he quickly forced it from mind. Leaning against a fence in the darkness, collar turned up and camera poised he prepared himself for the long night ahead.

As the evening wore on, he found himself wondering what a girl of her standing was doing in this part of town. Probably a falling out of some description; rebellion against a strict upbringing perhaps? He'd seen it all with wealthy families — lies, drug addiction, prostitution — it happened to the best of them.

The Lorenzo woman had been beside herself with worry when she rang that afternoon and he could understand why. Her daughter was supposedly working in some stable out of town while taking a gap year. Nothing unusual about that, but it appeared that she'd had been living some sort of double life. Oh well, that was for them to work out. For him it was another successful outcome. The young woman was unharmed and alive. Others weren't so lucky.

It was late Sunday afternoon and it was unlike him to agree to a weekend consultation. He'd already given her the answers she wanted; there was no urgency to meet so soon. God knows, he was tired enough. But there was a vulnerability in her voice, a desperate need to talk to someone. He envisaged his wife in the same scenario. What was the go with her husband, he wondered.

Lucas wasn't sure what to expect, but when his doorbell rang he was pleasantly surprised. The woman was refreshingly disarming, with a natural beauty.

'I can't thank you enough for agreeing to my job at such short notice,' she said as he ushered her inside.

'No problem. Glad I was able to help.'

He showed her inside. 'I think you'd better take a seat. There's some footage from last night I think you should see.'

He saw the way she trembled when he pulled out a chair and his heart went out to her. He too had a daughter, not much younger than hers.

Placing his laptop in front of her he clicked on a file.

'It's taken from when your daughter entered the bar until she left with someone she'd met around 1.30 am.'

'Oh my God!' Jennifer's hands flew to her face as she watched Cara swaying drunkenly against a tall, lean man, whose hand slowly moved over her rear end as they walked. They stopped at a flashing neon light that said 'Barker St Motel' and entered.

Not long afterwards, a light went on in the room furthest away and a curtain yanked shut.

The next image was of Cara, dishevelled and wide-eyed, edging her way out of the motel and running up the street.

'That was at 5 am,' Lucas said. 'She headed straight back to the boarding house to collect her things and then drove off. I tailed her to the stables.'

Lucas's voice was gentle as he handed Jennifer a glass of water. 'Perhaps it's time you two had a chat.'

'Yes, yes, you're right.' She paused. 'I can't thank you enough for everything you've done, Lucas. After we first spoke, I came so close to pulling out. I'm so glad I didn't.' But her mind was in turmoil. How would she face Cara?

Jennifer gave a sigh as she pulled out of the underground car park and onto the street. The last thing she felt like facing was the long trip ahead and her timing couldn't have been worse. It was just on five and the weekend traffic heading out of town was just starting to build. If it was a week later Dominic would be in Bangkok and she'd head straight for the apartment for the night. But he was there. Just minutes away. With a shiver, she dismissed the thought.

By the time she'd driven through the CBD, cars on the ramp leading to the freeway were at a standstill. A car horn blared from behind, making her jump. 'Give me a break,' she said, glaring into the rear vision mirror. 'I'll move when I can.'

Even the weather was against her as she eventually found her way into the traffic and headed for home. It rained on and off for most of the journey and her nerves were jangled by the drivers who tailgated or cut in front of her at the last minute, leaving little room to stop.

As she neared home, Jennifer felt drained and empty. Instead of relief, she was wracked by an overriding sense of guilt.

What would Cara think if she if found out what her mother had done? The act had been an extreme invasion of privacy, a betrayal of trust. Would she understand or turn away once and for all? It would be easier not to say anything.

However, deep down Jennifer never doubted that the talk with Cara would have to take place; but when and under what circumstances?

By the time she pulled in to the driveway, she could hardly think straight.

Angelina was asleep on the couch but awoke to the jingle of Jennifer's car keys as she entered the room.

'Oh hi, Mum.' She sat up, rubbing her eyes. 'Must've dozed off. What time is it?'

'Eight-thirty.'

'Shit. That late. How did your day go with Laura?'

'Good.' Jennifer felt a knot in her stomach as she spoke. It was not like her to lie like that. She could only hope that Angelina didn't run into Laura Gibbons any time soon. 'She asked me to stay for dinner.'

'I'm glad, Mum,' Angelina said. 'It would've given you a chance to get your mind off things.'

'It did actually,' the response was quick. 'So what time are you leaving in the morning?'

'Early, I imagine. Around seven.'

She nodded. 'Well, get me up before you go, would you.'

'No worries. Would you like me to make you a coffee?'

Jennifer shook her head. 'I had one not so long ago. I think I'll just head straight to bed. I can hardly keep my eyes open.'

She ran a hot bath and lowered herself down into the welcoming warmth of the lavender scented water. The troubles of the day seemed to melt away like snow in springtime as she lay, eyes closed and lost in time.

Things'll be okay she thought, as she climbed into bed and pulled the covers up tightly around her shoulders.

Sleep was instantaneous.

33

Dominic was edgy as he called Angelina into the office. He had hardly slept over the weekend, knowing that he'd blown things well and truly with Jennifer. He regretted his loss of control and his cutting words to her; regretted taking off in her car without going back to check that she was all right. Well, there was no turning back now. He had to face the music. His last hope was to convince Angelina to stand with him against Jennifer for the sale of Kilkenny. And how in the hell was he to do that? For once, he had no clear-cut plan. His head began to ache. Things could swing either way. He was floundering and he didn't like it.

'You wanted to see me Dad?'

Angelina looked particularly attractive as she appeared in the doorway. Her hair was swept back in a chignon at the base of her neck and she wore a black pin-striped skirt and jacket, with higher heels than normal. She was an asset to the company all right.

'Yes Angie, come in and close the door, will you?'

Angelina walked over and sat on the corner of his desk. In the past, he'd found this ritual slightly amusing, audacious almost, but this time he was unnerved by it.'

'It's about you and Mum, isn't it. She rang me.'

He could feel beads of sweat forming on his brow.

'And what did she tell you?'

'About you wanting to sell Kilkenny.'

'I see. And how did you feel about it?' Dominic could feel his pulse race.

'There's got to be a reason why you'd make such a decision. Something big.' Her almond eyes lowered for a moment than met his coolly. 'Would I be right in saying it's more than just the penthouse at Benson Towers?'

Dominic paused for a moment before answering. 'Look, I'll level with you, Angie. I have a chance to make it big time. I know how much Kilkenny means to you but –'

'You don't have to explain, Dad. If that's what you think is best.'

'You mean you'd be willing to –'

'Give up Kilkenny?' she interrupted 'Why not? I'm hardly there these days.' She paused. 'I wouldn't have thought it Dad, but the city's grown on me. The lifestyle, the nightlife.'

Dominic could barely contain his excitement as she went on. This was far from what he'd expected.

'But what about your mother?'

'Leave her to me. That will take quite some thinking

about.' Angelina smiled to herself as she left the room. It was easier than she'd thought.

'By the way,' Dominic said as she reached for the door, 'I like that outfit.'

'Thanks,' she turned and gave a half smile.

¶

Angelina drummed her fingers on the table beside a cold cup of tea and plate of half-eaten sandwiches. There had to be some way of finding out her father's plans. Two options came to mind and she decided to go for the first. Dominic was at a meeting with clients in the CBD so it should be safe enough. Uncurling her feet from under her, she rose from the sofa and fetched her car keys.

All was quiet in the office block as she made her way up the elevator to the eighth floor … the location of Dominic's offices. She doubted that his computer password was the old one. Paul would have made sure of that. Since his arrival everything had been shrouded in a cloud of secrecy.

There could be something in his filing cabinet; she had duplicates of her father's keys. If not, she would push until she got answers. Tricky but not impossible.

The doors opened and she stepped into the passageway, then stopped with a frown. There was a light spilling under the door to Dominic's expansive office. As she walked noiselessly along the carpet, she heard his voice. Damn it. He must have cancelled his dinner and decided to work back instead. She would have to come back another night. But another voice caused her to freeze. A woman's voice? 'What the hell …' she muttered under her breath and crept to the door to listen. And what she heard caused her stomach to turn.

'My God you're beautiful, Gabby. Have I ever told you that?'

'About a million and one times,' came the sultry reply. 'You know, I never feel comfortable in your office. I thought you said that it's no longer safe here.'

'I know, I know. It's just that my luck changed today. I think everything's about to become seriously good. I felt like being reckless.'

There was a pause and sound of a zip being undone, followed by a moan.

Feeling revulsion and anger Angelina turned from the door. So this was what he had been up to all those times 'clients' came to town. What else was he up to that she didn't know about?

34

Angelina waited until two days after Dominic's flight to Bangkok before she made her move. It was a foggy, autumn day when she made her way along the passage to Paul Anderson's office, adjoining her father's.

She tapped the door lightly.

'Who is it?'

'Angelina.'

'Oh. Come in.'

As she opened the door and entered the room, she sensed an immediate sexual tension. So far so good. Her pinstripe suit once again proved useful. This time though, her long hair hung loosely around her shoulders, its freshly washed shampoo scent permeating the air.

'If you're looking for Melissa, I let her go to lunch early,' he said, a little too quickly.

Even better.

'No, it's you I've come to see actually.'

'Oh? Well close the door and take a seat.'

'Thanks.' Angelina took her time walking across the room and sat in the chair opposite. She could see him swallow as she crossed one leg over the other, watched his eyes fix on the fine gold chain around her neck and his efforts to restrain himself from looking lower.

Angelina was enjoying herself.

Paul Anderson had fantasised over being alone with a stunning woman like this for years. And now the opportunity had come, he felt himself blushing like a schoolboy. It was no different to the time when he was fifteen and the new history teacher came into the room. Even now he remembered the long, silky brown hair, short skirt and coral pink painted nails.

'Are you sure I haven't come at a bad time?' She snapped him from his reverie. 'I could come back later if you are busy.'

'No … now's fine.' His shirt was clammy against the leather chair.

'I've come to see you about Dad, Paul. I'm worried about him, to be honest. I wonder whether he should've gone away this time.'

'Oh? What makes you say that?'

'He seems to be under a lot of stress lately, that's all. Usually he confides in me but this time he's been like a closed book. I thought you might be able to fill me in, that's all.'

Angelina could see a reluctance creep over his face and was quick to speak. 'I know all about Kilkenny and I'm okay about the sale.'

He was surprised. 'Are you sure about that?'

'Quite sure. The city's my home now.'

Paul frowned for a moment. There shouldn't be too much harm in divulging a few things. From what Dominic said the day before he left, once the deals had been signed, Angelina would be in on everything from then on.

'What would you like to know?'

Angelina twirled a lock of hair in her fingers. 'About the Bangkok deal for starters. What it's about, how much we're up for, who's involved.'

Paul shifted uncomfortably.

'Oh, come on, Paul. Cut the crap.' Her eyes bore into his, unnerving him. 'It's about time you levelled with me. It's not hard to put the pieces together. What you and Dad are up to is hardly legit and I'm fine with that. In fact, the thought of being part of it blows my mind.'

Paul sat in stunned disbelief, not knowing what to say.

'Come on, Paul. Out with it.'

Angelina received only a sketchy outline of what she wanted to know but enough to plan her next move. There were two deals, one on Tuesday, the other, two days later. One thing that staggered her was the amount of money involved. No wonder her father had been so testy.

'You know, Paul,' her voice was sultry as she stood to leave. 'I've changed my mind about you. I think you and I could work well together.' She flicked back her hair. 'Really well, if you know what I mean.'

'Me too.' The words barely came out.

❡

Paul phoned Dominic in Bangkok.

'I thought you might like to know that Angelina paid me a visit just now.'

'Oh?'

'We discussed the sale of Kilkenny. I was surprised that she was okay with it.'

'Me too, to be honest, when she mentioned it just before I left,' Dominic replied. 'Like I said Paul, she'll work in just fine with us.'

'I can see what you mean now,' Paul said.

When Dominic finished the call, his thoughts turned to Cara. He could not see her consenting to Paul's covert operations or being part of anything illegal for that matter. Unlike Angelina.

Lately he had considered dismissing Cara from the company altogether given her surly, insolent attitude and lack of interest. But it would be necessary to go through the murky, legal procedures. He smirked with grim satisfaction. He held one trump card. One that could bring Cara to her knees and cast her out onto the street. And Jennifer knew it.

❡

At the end of the day Angelina waited until Paul stepped into the elevator and headed for home, then walked into Lee Farrell's office.

He looked up in surprise. 'I thought you'd already gone, Angie.'

She closed the door quietly behind her, walked over to where he sat and perched herself on the corner of the desk. He wished that she wouldn't do that. It drove him crazy.

Angelina pressed her palms into the desk's edge and leaned forward, her eyes fixed on his. 'You need to know something. Things have changed around here.'

'What do you mean, changed.'

'Dad's been lying, Lee.' Her dark eyes flashed. 'Lying to us all. Even Mum.'

Lee Farrell's face registered disbelief. In all the years he had known Dominic Lorenzo, his wife's interests had always been placed above everything else. It was clear that he was crazy about her.

'What do you mean?'

'You don't know about Kilkenny then.'

Lee was puzzled. 'No. Should I?'

'Dad's out to sell it.'

There was a stunned silence. Kilkenny meant everything to Jennifer.

'Surely not. Angie. What has your mother got to say about this?'

'Let's just say Dad's about to have the biggest fight on his hands.'

Lee's mind began to race. If Dominic had plans to do that, what else was up his sleeve, he asked himself.

Until now he'd never considered the security of his job.

He'd held a managerial role within the company for the past fifteen years, one that he performed with precision and efficiency. Content with his role there'd been no need to aspire to greater things. He had figured that with more responsibility came more stress. It also came with more money, but Eleanor's considerable wealth and his generous wage provided him with more than enough.

He'd learned to be discreet when it came to Dominic's business affairs, offering an opinion only when it was asked for. That was the way that Dominic liked it and it ensured a healthy relationship.

However, of late Lee had sensed something different about Dominic. Angelina was right.

Ill at ease, he recalled Dominic vaguely alluding to the sale of his yacht. Who could blame him? After all, he rarely went near it these days and the cost of berthing, general maintenance and insurance would have been hefty. The *Jennifer's* estimated valuation was around seven hundred thousand dollars, if his quick scan of similar versions on the net was anything to go by.

If Dominic was ready to part with Kilkenny, the *Jennifer* could be next. Lee's stomach tightened. He'd taken his role aboard Dominic's yacht for granted. The thought of losing it altogether was too painful to contemplate.

Angelina interrupted his thoughts. 'And there's more, Lee.' She gave a defiant toss of her head. 'I've just paid a visit to our Mr. Anderson.'

As she related what the business manager had told her,

Farrell sat motionless with his elbows on the desk, his chin resting on clasped hands.

'So you're telling me that what they're up to has nothing to do with Dominic's wineries.'

Angelina nodded.

Lee took a moment to reflect. He'd taken an instant dislike to the new business manager, yet at the time was too caught up in other things to give it much thought. Perhaps he half-expected that that Paul would soon become just another victim of Dominic's ire and be sent packing. He seemed cocky enough. Many an ambitious new employee found they were quickly tossed aside like junk mail. Little did Lee know of the pair's prior three-year connection.

'Paul's not stupid, of course.' Angelina continued. 'He stopped way short of telling me what I wanted to know. But I'll find out, don't you worry. At this stage, I can tell you that not much of it is legit.'

Lee took a deep breath. 'So, where to from here?'

'I've come up with a plan, Lee, that involves both of us.'

'Oh?'

'I really don't want to talk about it here. How about we meet up on the *Jennifer*. I could do with a sail. It's been a while now.'

Lee's mind went into overdrive and his pulse raced.

He'd been captivated by Angelina ever since he first set eyes upon her, when she'd glided up the catwalk as a twelve-year-old. And as time went on and her beauty enfolded like a rose coming into bloom he'd stood by as a trusted family friend, dreaming of what could never be.

And now? Lee was not foolhardy enough to believe there'd be any hope of a relationship but a chance to meet alone like this might never come along again and he wasn't about to pass it up.

He managed to keep his voice steady. 'Which day would suit, Angie? I'd need to get down to the moorings and check things over first.'

'Why not make a weekend of it. I'm free this one coming, if you are.'

Lee sat dumbfounded, not just at the words but the look in her eyes as she spoke.

'I'd have to check the weather conditions,' was all he could think of to say. 'It may not be suitable for sailing.'

'We'll just stay at the marina then.'

He could only nod as Angelina walked out of the room.

35

Lee sat aboard the *Jennifer* in a galley off the main one and waited, heart pumping. As he left for the marina that morning, he had a wild impulse to purchase a bouquet of roses to await her in the dining nook, some French champagne perhaps, and a seafood hamper from the shop on the jetty. But he thought better of it. Best to act low key. Truth was, he felt like a lovestruck teenager about to embark on a first date. But he was not about to let Angelina see that.

Conflicting thoughts raged through his mind. *What in the hell are you getting yourself into?* If Dominic became the least bit suspicious … or Jennifer for that matter. Shit! he thought, what then? But it was Angelina who'd called the shots by suggesting the weekend's sail. There'd been no mistaking the look in her eyes. He couldn't back down now, even if he wanted to.

Lee leaned back into the cushions that were covered tastefully in muted aquas, lilac and grey. Everything about the yacht's interior was tasteful. Hands behind his head and legs outstretched, he surveyed the surroundings to which he had become so accustomed — had taken for granted perhaps. He stirred uneasily. The thought of having this all stripped away from him didn't bear thinking about.

He recalled that day all those years ago when he first boarded the *Jennifer*. He remembered stepping onto the stern and following Dominic as he unlocked the wheelhouse, slid back the hatch and descended the four steps to the main galley. The first thing that struck Lee was the warm ambience of the polished Kauri wood that adorned the walls. The smaller galley in which he now sat, was two steps down and equally as pleasing. In front of this dining nook where Lee now sat, was a compact but all-inclusive galley and beyond that a pantry, a large sleeping berth and a closet.

The smaller galley had always been Lee's favourite. It was where he spent most of his time during his stays. But it was the main stateroom above that he now found himself fantasising about. The large, king-sized bed that lay aft had never so much as raised a glance until this weekend. Earlier in the day when he pulled out the crisp white sheets from the mirrored closet beside the bed, he had felt a pang of guilt. This was Dominic and Jennifer's bed. Yet the feeling dissipated just as quickly, transformed by a heady anticipation of what might transpire. There would be no pressure on his part. His bed was already made up in the galley below and the door separating the two was lockable. The weekend's outcome would be of Angelina's choosing.

There had been a last-minute change of plans. Angelina had some unfinished work to do at the office and wouldn't be leaving now until late afternoon. Not that it mattered. It gave him a few more hours to get things ready.

Lee glanced at his watch. It was already seven. *She should be here by now*, he thought with a frown. Reaching for his mobile, he messaged: Is everything OK?

The response came soon afterwards: All good. Sorry — got held up. Just leaving now. Angie x

He rose and made himself a coffee. That meant, another half hour at least until she arrived. Opening his iPad, he clicked on a work document to fill in the time.

❡

It was after eight when he heard the distant footsteps on the well-lit, wooden pier. His heart leapt as he jumped up and rushed to the main deck, then onto the landing. A slight smile crossed his face. She was still attired in her business suit and was clearly flustered as she negotiated the uneven surface in her high heels, juggling a cabin bag in one hand and tote bag on the opposite shoulder.

'Here, let me grab something for you,' he rushed forward to help.

'Great, thanks.' She dumped her bag at her feet and

wiped a hand across her forehead. 'What a bloody awful day I've had, Lee. I can't begin to tell you!'

'Sounds frustrating,' he said, as he reached for her bags. 'Come on, let's get you aboard.'

She gave a nod. 'Sorry, I didn't even say hi.'

Lee felt his heart skip a beat as her lips briefly brushed his cheek. With one hand on his shoulder, she bent over to pull off her shoes.

'Ah that's better,' She gave a sigh of relief and rubbed her reddened toes.

Lee gave a quick grin, to which she responded with a playful punch of his arm. 'I know, I know. Why didn't I take them off when I got out of the car?'

'No comment.'

'Hmm. Sensible answer.'

The feel of her hand in his was electric as he helped her aboard. For a moment he gazed up at the blanket of stars and took an involuntary breath. This was all too surreal …

As he left Angelina to settle in, Lee leaned back against the galley's kitchen bench to sort out his thoughts. *Where to from here?* He asked himself. Best to back right off, he decided. She was clearly rattled by a hectic day at work, with gridlocked traffic to follow. Now was not the time to make a move. He had learned long ago not to rush things when it came to women. And it had paid off. *I snared Eleanor, didn't I?*

Lee already had a plan in mind by the time she appeared in the doorway.

'Take a seat, Angie. Can I fix you something to eat or drink?'

'Just a coffee, thanks,' she said, sliding behind the galley's table. 'I've already grabbed something to eat at a service station on the way.'

'No worries. Just sit and relax. It sounds as though you had a cow of a day.'

She rolled her eyes. 'That's an understatement. And just as I was leaving, Dad of all people called from Bangkok.'

'Oh? Why?'

'Just checking up on things at work. You know what he's like.'

Lee's heart beat quickened. 'You don't think he suspected anything? About this weekend, I mean.'

'No. I didn't mention a thing.'

Lee gave a nod. Both were well aware of the risks involved but he had Eleanor to consider. He'd used the 'last minute work' excuse in the past and it had been accepted without further question. But Angelina had Dominic and Jennifer to think of. Then, there were the colleagues at work. If one of them got the slightest whiff of a scandal …

Lee occasionally took Jennifer, her family and friends out for a sail. There had been times when the weather had cut up rough and they'd been forced to head to the nearest marina until it was safe to continue. Sometimes it meant an overnight stay. At a pinch he could feign the same excuse should he and Angelina be sighted by someone they knew upon their return. In the meantime, he planned to make their sail appear like a day's outing. Hopefully, there'd be few people up and about when they headed off.

'I plan to set sail early, if that's okay,' he said.

'Fine by me. How lucky are we with this weather?'

Lee gave a nod. 'It's unusual to have a spell of warm days like this in winter. The cold change isn't due until Tuesday.' He paused. 'I hope you brought some warm clothes with you. It'll be cold at night.'

Angelina nodded. 'I've been caught out before.'

'We all have,' he gave a smile as he handed her a mug.

'Thanks,' she said. 'I needed something to wake me up. It's like being bloody jet lagged.'

Lee grinned. He had never seen Angelina any way but impeccably groomed. Wisps of hair had fallen from her bun on to her face and her mascara was smeared. She appeared vulnerable and he rather liked the effect.

'So, tell me about your day,' he said.

'You know what Fridays can be like. Two called in sick and it went from bad to worse from there: an abusive phone call, a computer crash in the afternoon and –'

'No need to go on. Forget about work for now.' Lee said. 'How about I outline our plans for tomorrow and then we both have an early night.'

Angelina sighed with relief. 'Thanks. I could do with one.'

So far, so good. Lee thought. 'Okay, I plan to set sail around 7 am. That'll give us ample time to make it past Port Phillip Heads to the Apollo Bay Harbour to moor for the night. Have you been there before?'

'No.' She added a teaspoon of sugar to her coffee. 'What's it like?'

'Picturesque is the word I'd use. Rolling hills in the background, that sort of thing. Quite different from other marinas.'

'I can't wait to see it.'

'I think you'll like it,' he said. 'I reckon we should get there around three, so there'll be plenty of time to look around or just laze on deck, if you wish. The fridge is well stocked.'

¶

Late that evening, Lee lay wide awake, hands clasped behind his head, listening to the gentle creak of the boat as it rocked against the waves. Morning could not come soon enough.

He awoke to the sound of gulls. Sunlight spilled around the edges of the galley blind as he rolled over to look at the clock. It was already six; later than planned, but everything was ready to go. As he swung his legs over the side of the bed, stood up and stretched, he heard the shower in the main galley's bathroom.

Minutes later Angelina appeared dressed in denim shorts and pink singlet top covered by a loose, white windcheater. She was towel drying her hair with one hand as she spoke. 'Morning.'

'Morning. How did you sleep?'

'Like a log. I can't remember a thing once my head hit the pillow.'

'Good. A decent sleep is what you needed.'

His eyes lingered on her for a few seconds. It had been some time since he had seen her out of her office attire. He quickly looked down.

'So,' she said, grabbling a piece of buttered toast, 'what are our plans for the day?'

'A quick breakfast first then we'll get going.'

'Sounds good. What's on the menu?'

'How does poached eggs on toast with avocado with spinach sound?'

'You can come again,' she quipped.

He stopped himself short of stating the obvious and she shot him a wry smile.

The day was ideal for sailing with a fifteen-knot breeze and minimal swell. A deal had been struck not to discuss business matters for the day. A good ploy on his part. It was a long time since he had felt so carefree, or seen her so relaxed. At one stage he watched riveted, his hand on the tiller as she sat on the deck, tanned legs dangling over the edge with her head tilted up towards the sun and eyes closed. He wished the trip was for a week, not just a day.

She was so close, yet so far. Just having her there was a dream come true, yet it was as if she was teasing him. At times her gestures seemed intimate enough — a touch of the hand on his cheek, a head on his shoulder as he steered. Yet his arm around her shoulders was met with little response.

It was unusually hot for winter but June sometimes produced short spells in the twenties.

Angelina had obviously checked the forecast and packed accordingly. She must have known that the sight of her scant, white one-piece would send him wild and yet she teased some more by sunbaking on a sheltered part of the deck, within arm's reach. And just when he thought he could take no more, she passed him the sunscreen to rub on her back.

As the day wore on Lee felt frustrated and edgy, unable to decipher her mixed signals.

Yet once they motored into the harbor at four, things turned for the better. It was clear by her appreciative glance at the hilly backdrop against the sleepy marina that he had made the right choice.

'Come on, Lee,' she said excitedly with a tug of his hand. 'Let's go and explore.'

As they walked hand in hand along the pier, he noticed the admiring glances of men towards her as they passed and the frosty stares of their female companions. He was used to that. That's just how it was when Angelina was around. If he was twenty years younger, his ego would have blown sky high. But now he felt a sense of vulnerability. Even if their relationship became intimate, how long would it last?

'Feel like a run along the beach?' Angelina's words

interrupted his thoughts, 'I can't wait to feel the sand beneath my feet again.'

He nodded. 'There's nothing like it, is there. 'Come on, let's go.'

Angelina tugged off her sandals and he followed her down to the water's edge. The tide was out and their feet sunk only slightly in the firm sand as they jogged, side by side.

'Do you run much when you go back to Kilkenny?' he asked.

'Not really,' she replied. 'The beach near us is only small. To get to a stretch of sand like this, you have to walk around the cliff face first. And it can be quite rocky.'

Lee nodded. 'And what about the path along the clifftop?'

'Past our place it gets pretty rugged and uneven in parts and the bushes can be overgrown. Most people out for a walk turn back at our place. So to answer your question I tend to slouch around a bit at home.'

Lee grinned. 'Probably does you good. Your workouts at the gym before work are more than enough.' *Just as well I've kept my fitness up,* he thought. Running had always come easily to him and right now he could easily have gone another ten kilometres. He had always been proud of his lean body — it had served him well over the years, particularly when it came to charming women at the yacht club. He could never quite understand why so many of their husbands had let themselves go.

Angelina stopped to fling a handful of water and he was quick to respond. It soon became a full-on water fight, as he picked her up, ran to where the water was deeper and unceremoniously dumped her.

'Oh no you don't,' she pulled herself up, gasping and spluttering. With one hard shove on his chest she watched as he fell backwards into the water. But he was quick to recover and grabbed at her arm, pulling her in beside him. There they frolicked and splashed in the water like children, until it became too cold to do so. And as they made their way back up the jetty, dripping wet and laughing, Lee was buoyed by the change in her. It was as if he had wasted the afternoon worrying about nothing. The looks he gave were now reciprocated. And as the evening set in, things only became better.

The full moon bathed the marina in luminous serenity, creating a perfect back drop for romance. After an early feed of fish and chips on the beach, they headed back to the yacht and sat in a sheltered part of the deck, lost in time with Angelina's head on his shoulder, his resting against hers. The ocean breeze soothed his soul as he gazed at the proliferation of yachts, row upon row of them; silvery mirror images of the moon.

All was quiet except for the occasional bursts of chatter from a nearby yacht and the distant footsteps of those out for a late-night walk.

It was after ten when Angelina nodded towards the wheelhouse. 'Fancy a drink? Dad only keeps the best of our reds in there.'

'Mm. Your room or mine?' The words tumbled out before he could stop them.

'Mine.'

Lee felt his legs go weak as she squeezed his hand and led him towards the main hatch.

He could only follow in disbelief as they entered the main galley and she led him towards the bed.

'You choose the wine and I'll wait here.'

Lee's heart was pumping wildly as he headed towards Dominic's wine cupboard. He was not sure of what to do or say when he returned and a glass of red could not come quickly enough. However as they sat side by side on the bed, backs against the pillows and wines in hand as they talked, being with her felt the most natural thing in the world.

All sense of inhibition flew to the wind as the wine's soothing effect kicked in. Rolling over to face her, he brushed her lips with his and gently stroked her face. His heart gave a lurch when her arms reached up and he felt her fingers lace behind his neck. He slowly unbuttoned her blouse, planting soft kisses over her breasts and up her neck until he found her mouth again. And she kissed him back with the kind of desire he would never have dreamed possible. As her hands slipped up under his t-shirt and across his chest, the words she whispered were all he'd wanted to hear.

'I need you, Lee. I always have.'

As she pulled off his t-shirt, his heart gave a lurch and he reached down to unzip her jeans.

The hours of passion that followed overwhelmed him and he knew that the memory would stay with him for the rest of his life.

¶

In the early hours of the morning, Lee was still wide awake, almost pinching himself to see that he was not dreaming. Angelina lay asleep in his arms, her head against his chest, long black hair spilling over the pillow and her skin soft against his. Never had he seen her look so beautiful.

For the first time that weekend, his fears were put to rest. But it wouldn't be for long.

36

Lee rose early, carefully removing his arm and slipping out from under the sheets so as not to disturb her.

Up on deck a strong, northerly wind had sprung up as expected after a full moon and sailing conditions would be far from ideal. They would be faced with big tides and have to tack their way back to Port Phillip Heads with possibly three further hours to the Brighton Marina.

Conscious of their 7 am start the following morning at the office, he packed things the best he could so that as little time as possible would be spent at the marina once they berthed.

As they headed towards the Southern Ocean, they were hit with a thirty to thirty-five knot wind. Not good, he thought grimly as he stood at the wheel, legs spread, eyes fixed on the choppy seas ahead. A hangover didn't help.

There was a sense of unease for things to come. Angelina was yet to outline her "plan." From what she had said at the office, things were spiralling out of control and drastic deeds called for drastic measures. Whatever that meant. Something wasn't right. Why all the secrecy? Why did it take a weekend away for her to say what was on her mind?

He wiped the sweat from his brow with the back of his hand.

As his head slowly cleared and images came to mind of the night just past, Lee frowned. He recalled the conversation after they'd just made love and lay in each other's arms, watching the moonlight streamed through the porthole.

'You meant what you said, before didn't you? About me being the only one you've ever wanted.'

'You know I meant it.'

'So, Lee are you prepared to leave your wife?'

The comment was so unexpected, it had left him speechless. The rollercoaster weekend had barely been enough to process. The last thing he had thought of was, where to from here.

'I'm serious, Lee.' She turned on her side to stroke his face. 'I don't want this to be just a fling on the side. I want more than that.'

'And so do I.'

'Well?'

'And you, Angie? If I made such a commitment, would you be willing to do the same?' It was the first thing that had come to his mind.

'Would I have asked you in the first place?' Her voice was soft and he felt his mouth go dry. It was all he could ask for at this stage.

Lee's eyes darkened as he focused on the wild waves ahead. He was glad he had encouraged Angelina to rest below. Conditions were too blustery to stay on deck for long. Plus, it had given him the chance to think.

Hours had passed since she sat down beside him and went through her plan. By the time they moored at the marina, Lee's mind was in turmoil.

9

The late afternoon sun blazed through the windscreen as Lee drove home, and his body was soon bathed in sweat. As he reached for the air conditioner, he paused to reflect on the weekend past. Things had been so perfect the day before, a stark contrast to the turmoil that was rapidly unfolding and the fear of what was to come.

By the time they had had packed up, showered at the marina and washed away the tell-tale signs of salt and sand, their departure was two hours later than expected. Angelina's trip along the bay and across the city to her apartment would be relatively quick but his journey home would be much longer. The weekend traffic had all but come to a standstill on the main arterial, and he was weary: in no way ready for his wife's probing questions.

At the next service station he pulled in for a strong coffee. As he sat on a red plastic chair and reached for some sugar to stir in the takeaway cup, he flicked on his mobile to check his voice mail. There were two messages, one from Eleanor: Where are you, for God's sake. Ring me. *As if I'm going to do that,* he thought. The other was from Angelina: Thanks for an amazing weekend gorgeous guy … exciting times ahead.

You've got to be kidding, he mumbled, as he reached for his car keys.

37

The leader of the small Peruvian gang couldn't believe his good fortune when he received the anonymous phone call from Australia. His was but one of the many foreign criminal gangs operating in Thailand. Those referred to as transnational criminals took advantage of the country's easy entry by arranging safe havens for foreign criminals fleeing from the authorities. Others dealt predominately in drugs and money laundering. Latin American gangs like his focused mainly on robberies and thefts, particularly from wealthy residences, exclusive hotels, resorts or jewellery fairs.

Rodriguez had no idea where the caller got his number but the money was too good to refuse. A third was to be paid up front into his bank account, with the remainder deposited on the job's completion. The only stipulation was "no questions asked" and no further contact to be made with the caller. The request was nothing unusual and Rodriguez was happy to comply. The job was no more dangerous than the others but Rodriguez could see a way of making a significant amount of money on the side. *The Langdon* was renowned for its wealthy clientele, ripe for the picking.

He had quite a bit of research to do on the workings of the place but knew just the right person to call on.

As far as he knew the place hadn't been targeted before. That was a good thing. By the time his gang had finished there'd be adjustments to security, and whoever made a move there next time would have a job on their hands.

Two nights later, Rodriguez rolled a cigarette as he crossed his legs on the table and looked out the filthy window to the dingy street below. It was nearing 11 pm and the street walkers would be soon be out. He gave a satisfied smile as he thought of the seventy grand that would be sitting in his bank account within the next twenty-four hours.

ᚴ

Dominic switched off his iPad and looked out over the city lights from his executive suite on the fifty-second floor of *The Langdon.* The upmarket five-star hotel was set in a tree lined avenue in the middle of Bangkok's CBD.

Paul Anderson had told him of the place not long after they met and numerous business deals had been clinched there since. The facilities were world class: an executive club lounge, fitness centre, heated pool, spa and a Business Centre equipped with conference and banquet rooms.

The elegant hotel suites blended oriental and contemporary décor.

It was 1 am but Dominic was unable to sleep, nervous with anticipation over the deal he was to about to sign within a matter of hours. Slipping on his shoes, he rose and headed out the door to the lift. The foyer was deserted, except for the receptionist who gave a wave as he crossed the floor to the revolving glass door. A gush of humid, steamy air hit him as he stepped onto the pavement.

There was a steady stream of traffic — cars, scooters, tuk tuks, and hot pink taxis and horns honked constantly as he weaved his way through the passers-by along to the next block. A mixture of familiar smells hung in the air: exhaust fumes, cigarette smoke, stagnant water and sewerage plus the tantalising smells of coconut curry and sticky mango rice from the street vendors.

Loud music blared above the muffled voices and laughter in the bars he passed and neon lights flashed like beacons in shop windows.

In a nearby doorway stood a petite street walker in her skimpy top and ridiculously high platformed shoes. She was pretty enough; many of them were. But they lacked class.

It was an hour before he made his way back to the hotel, glad to get back to the peace and quiet of his room. Stripping off his sweat drenched clothes, he had a shower and put on the hotel's white robe. Pouring himself a brandy, he sank down in to the leather lounge, reflecting on the deals he was about to sign.

The thought of taking out such an exorbitant loan had jangled his nerves for weeks, despite Paul Anderson's reassurances. There was enough for a decent deposit from the sales of his Bangkok office block, some shares, and a small winery that was no longer profitable. But it was a drop in the ocean. Millions were needed to pay out the loan.

Dominic had lied to Jennifer when he said the proceeds from Kilkenny's sale would go directly into the purchase of the penthouse at Benton Towers. There would be a separate loan for that. The proceeds of Kilkenny would go directly into paying off this deal.

Kilkenny would be snapped up quickly. He had no doubts about that. He thought about the expressions of interest from private buyers over the years. For him, the matter would be straightforward. It never crossed his mind that Jennifer would react to his proposal with such resistance and hostility.

Dominic scowled as he swished the ice around in his glass. He'd been so preoccupied with the deals at hand, he'd scarcely thought about Jennifer and what he was up against once he returned. This was about more than Kilkenny. His marriage was at stake. Never had he seen such an expression of loathing on his wife's face as when they'd last spoken on the beach. There was no going back now. Their relationship was all but over. The last thing he wanted was a divorce. The thought of being dragged through the courts by lawyers fighting over who received what of his hard-earned money made his blood boil.

But if divorce is what the bitch wanted, he'd end up the winner. He'd drag their separation out for as long as it took. This would give Paul ample time to make sure that the books were squeaky clean and transfer money from their illegitimate operations into offshore accounts. Jennifer would only get a smidgeon of what he really had.

Dominic leaned back and crossed his arms behind his head. Divorce may not be that bad after all. He'd be free to come and go as he wished, with no one to answer to.

9

At 3 am, all was quiet at *The Langdon.* Not many checked in at this time of the morning and the two desk staff were bracing themselves for a few more tedious hours until their replacements arrived at six.

The thirty-five-year-old security guard had been on duty for barely half an hour when he began to feel dizzy. Normally he came straight from his apartment downtown to start his shift, but he'd been out on the town with a young woman he'd met at a bar. Initially, he was dubious when she struck up a conversation. The city was rife with con artists and criminal gangs and he was wary of approaches from anyone. However, he was entranced by the nineteen-year-old South American beauty with the liquid brown eyes who told him she was backpacking around Asia during her university gap year. He could hardly believe his luck when she arranged to meet again the following evening.

On the thirtieth floor, he felt the passageway swim before his eyes and he grabbed at a nearby door. Waves of iridescent colours swirled around in his head as he collapsed on the floor.

At that moment three men dressed in black with balaclavas covering their faces burst through the entrance door and into the foyer, brandishing sawn off shotguns. One fired three consecutive shots at the three security cameras, while the others rushed up to the two staff on duty.

'You two, hands in the air,' the taller of the three shouted at the terrified night manager and receptionist. 'And back away from the desk.'

They did so, white faced and shaking, as he pushed past to shut down the alarm system at the main control board.

All the while the manager's eyes were darting to the foyer and passageways beyond.

'If you're looking for your security guard, don't bother,' the tall man smirked, 'you know, I'd have a word to your boss about him. No good having someone who likes to sleep on the job.'

He seemed to enjoy the look of panic on the night manager's face. 'Don't worry,' he waved his gun carelessly in the air, 'he's still alive, if that's what you're worried about.'

There was a laugh from the other two.

'Okay,' he continued, 'do as you're told and you won't get hurt. Got that?'

The employees nodded quickly.

'First up, we want to know where the twenty safe deposit

boxes are … the ones belonging to the Thai Tourist Bureau.'

Neither moved.

The man barking the orders pointed to the young female receptionist. One of his accomplices scrambled over the counter, jerked her arm back viciously by the arm and smashed her in the face. She collapsed on the floor stunned, blood streaming from her nose.

'Shit!' The night manager paled and rushed to offer assistance but was hurled into a nearby door.

'Look — we mean business.' The leader's voice was ominous. 'Do we get some co-operation here, or what?'

The young man nodded, his hands trembling violently as he led the two down a flight of stairs and keyed in a number. The other stood guard in the foyer, one foot placed in the small of the back of the receptionist, who lay terrified, unable to control the sobs that wracked her body.

Within a matter of minutes, the three returned carrying calico bags laden with tightly rolled wads of Thai baht, jewellery and documents. Rough hands shoved the traumatised staff towards a back office, where they were bound securely to a pylon and gagged with duct tape; but not before the gang had the code numbers to every door on the top two levels of the building.

9

Dominic swilled the last of his brandy and with a contented

sigh, placed the empty brandy balloon on the coffee table before him. At last he felt ready to sleep. Walking barefoot across the white marble floor to his bed, he turned down the sheets and glanced at the orange numbers on the bedside clock. It was later than he would have wished but the meeting at nine had been rescheduled to later in the day. The pressure was off. In his relaxed, sleepy state he was oblivious to the slow turn of the door handle, but was shocked into terrified awareness by the black clad figures who swarmed silently into the room like FBI agents, guns poised.

Dominic was momentarily frozen. One man kept a gun trained on him while the others rushed around the room, ransacking drawers, rifling through his wardrobe and throwing his belongings about like a couple amid a full-on spat.

A few seconds passed before the reality of what could follow sank in and then Dominic's mind swung into action. 'Look, stop. There's no need for this,' he said quickly. 'I'll give you whatever you want. Money, credit cards, passwords you name it.'

'Good,' his guard said with an unnerving quietness as he held a hand in the air to stop the others.

Dominic took a silent breath of relief as he reached in his pocket for his wallet. The bank cards he used for travel were set up for such emergencies, with ten thousand dollars, give or take on each one. Before he travelled, he always deleted his banking apps off his phone and iPad, just in case. Street robberies were common in Bangkok. Best to take no chances.

The gang's leader grabbed the wallet and ripped out the two bankcards. 'Passwords?' He grabbed the hotel notebook and pen from the bedside table shoved it under Dominic's face.

Dominic could feel the sweat pouring down his back as he scribbled the numbers on the pad.

'Good.' The man ripped off the top page and shoved it in his pocket. 'All we need now is the code to your room safe and then we'll leave you alone.'

This was unexpected and sent Dominic into a panic. Under normal circumstances it would not be so much of an issue. But the safe contained highly confidential papers and a laptop with details of his unscrupulous dealings which, if leaked out, could bring him to his knees.

His heart raced but he managed a nonchalant shrug. 'There's been no need to use it. It's a rushed trip this time.'

The response was chilling. 'Oh, really? Then it should be open, the way it was found. Correct?' He nodded towards the ensuite cupboard where one of the gang headed.

Dominic felt himself tremble as he watched the man pull the pillow off the safe.

'Liar!' A savage punch in the stomach sent Dominic reeling, then he was jerked back by the collar of his robe and smashed into the wall. Suddenly he was overwhelmed with fury. No one treated him like that. No one! Like an enraged bull, he lurched forward and grabbed the arm holding the gun. But the assailant in the doorway fired three quick shots into his back. His body gave a jerk before he collapsed, face down on the carpet.

'Not quite as planned,' said Rodriguez. 'But mission accomplished. Let's get going.'

38

When Angelina's mobile rang in the city apartment, she jumped off the sofa and snatched it off the kitchen bench.

'I see.' There was a slight quaver to her voice. 'Thank you for letting me know. I'll ring you in an hour to discuss the final details, okay?' She pressed the end button and leapt in the air with excitement. 'Yes, yes, *yes*! We pulled it off, Lee. We bloody well pulled it off!'

There was an uneasy silence.

'Well come on,' she gushed, 'Aren't you going to say something?'

There was a nod. 'It'll take time to sink in, that's all,' came the shaky response.

'You don't have any regrets, do you? I didn't want it to come to this. Of course I didn't. But it was the only way.'

'Yes, yes it was.' Lee fought to steady his voice.

In truth, his mind was in turmoil. It was one thing to get even. After all, his job was seriously in question and

Dominic appeared on course to ruin anyone or anything that stood in his way. And that included Jennifer. But murder? His mind whirled.

If only Angelina hadn't walked into his office that day. But he had been too enraptured, too swept up in the moment not to succumb. And then there'd been the weekend on the yacht: the magic of having her so near, the scent of her perfume, the toss of her dark hair, the night's wild love making and hope of things to come. No, in hindsight he would have done it all again. Well, he was up to his neck in it and there was no turning back. His thoughts began to race. Where in the hell were they headed from here? Angelina didn't seem to share his concerns. He had no doubts that she had her own carefully worked out agenda.

As if reading his mind, she stepped lightly across the room, settled on his knee and put her arms around his neck. 'Now listen here, Lee,' her dark eyes demanding his attention, 'I've already given this a great deal of thought. But I need you to work with me. Okay?'

He nodded. But fear tightened his stomach. If she was capable of having her father murdered …

Angelina reached up and whispered in his ear. 'By the way gorgeous guy, you ever mention anything of this to anyone, ever, I'll be back to get you. Now I've got one last minute thing to attend to.' She climbed off his lap and padded down the hall to Dominic's office.

❡

Paul Anderson was at home alone drinking a scotch on the sofa when he decided to check his emails. Reaching for his laptop, he opened his mail box and scrolled through his messages. One stood out. It was from Dominic. Paul was instantly alert. He hoped everything was all right. He wasn't expecting to hear from Dominic for another few hours, once the deal was signed.

The message sent his heart hammering.

Paul, I need you to consign the attached transaction immediately. There's been a change of plans. It appears that a Chinese company is vying for our second deal. If we don't get in first, there's a strong chance we'll miss out. I've brought forward Thursday's meeting to tonight at 8. I'll fax the documents and receipt to you later this evening.'

'Christ, Dominic!' he thought aloud. 'Twelve million dollars? And you expect me to sign it here and now?'

Calm down Paul, he reasoned. *You were going to do it anyway in two days.* With shaking fingers, he typed in his signature.

9

It was three hours later when Jennifer's front door bell rang. Looking up in surprise, she placed her book on the table beside the sofa, uncurled her legs and headed for the door. When she turned the handle, and faced a police constable and a young female assistant, she knew something was wrong, very wrong.

'Mrs. Lorenzo?'

'Yes.'

'I'm Senior Sergeant Galbraith and this is Senior Constable Allen. May we come in please?'

'Of course.' Jennifer stepped aside to usher in the pair. 'What is it?' she could feel her heart pounding in her chest. 'What's wrong?'

'I'm afraid there's been some bad news. Your husband was killed in his hotel room early this morning. It was a random attack apparently, part of a large-scale armed robbery at the hotel. He was one of three victims.'

Jennifer's hand flew to her mouth. 'There … there must be some mistake.'

'No, sadly not.' The constable's voice was gentle. No matter how many times he faced this task it never got any easier.

He nodded to the female constable who placed an arm around Jennifer's shoulders and led her to the sofa.

He waited until they were seated before continuing. 'Investigations are currently underway. The Australian Embassy passed on to us what they knew.'

Jennifer sat in a blur, too stunned to think, barely absorbing the sketchy details that the constable was able to provide.

'We will keep you updated of course, Mrs. Lorenzo,' he said in conclusion, 'now who can we call to be with you?'

❡

It wasn't until later that night when Jennifer sat with Angelina and Cara at the kitchen table and turned on the news that the details became clear, as footage showed *The Langdon's* roped off foyer, damaged security cameras and trashed hotel rooms.

'I just don't understand,' she said pointing to the screen, 'I know that Bangkok can be dangerous but I thought the hotel Dom chose was one of the safest.'

'It probably was,' Cara said, 'but I've heard about the gangs operating in Bangkok. They're highly organised, ruthless criminals capable of finding their way into any place.'

'She's right, Mum,' Angelina added as she gently placed a hand on Jennifer's, 'Dad couldn't speak highly enough of *The Langdon*. He just happened to be there at the wrong time, that's all.'

❡

In Bangkok, the Chief Criminal investigator in charge of the case slumped wearily as he sent the last of the carefully worded details to the Australian embassy to forward to Jennifer. It had been two full days of crossing the t's and dotting the I's. Almost a pointless exercise. It would soon recur in another part of town, carried out by another gang. They seemed to sprout up overnight.

The families of the three hotel victims were told that police would stop at no lengths to trap down the culprits.

The small, bald investigator gave a snort. Those responsible would either have fled the country or gone underground for as long as it took. After all they made off with enough cash. Not that the police would reveal the exact amount to the media. That was the usual precautionary measure to discourage copycat crimes.

Now there were just the last-minute details to sign off, the release of the bodies to their next of kin and the return of their personal belongings. He chewed on his tasteless gum, thoughtfully, as he shut down his computer.

39

Dominic Lorenzo's funeral was held at the same city cathedral where his son's had been. Against Jennifer's wishes the whole thing was larger than life, an almost ostentatious affair: the who's who of the business world and well-known socialites, a concoction of young couples in designer clothes and balding men with their glamorous wives. During the service Jennifer sat in the front row flanked by Cara, Angelina and her sister and brother-in-law who had flown out from London. The coffin sat before them, draped in lilies and roses. Her eyes were fixed straight ahead as she listened to a succession of speeches extolling the virtues of the man who had become all but a stranger to her. She stiffened as a company executive spoke of Dominic's generosity and great love for his family. *If only they knew half of it,* she thought with bitterness.

The service was followed by a ridiculously large gathering at *The Sheraton,* many of whom she had never seen in her life. There she was greeted by a seemingly endless stream of people offering their shallow, obligatory words of comfort. For the first time in her life Jennifer felt a hypocrite as she played the role of a devoted, heartbroken wife. It was easier this way. It was what was expected and then she could be left alone.

Once it was all over, there was a private burial service at Kilkenny's family graveyard. Kate was quick to note Cara standing away from the others as Dominic's casket was lowered into the plot beside Joseph's and she instinctively moved to her side. Her heart bled for the young woman who through no fault of her own was scarred by the lives of the two whose graves stood before her.

On the walk back to the house, Jennifer turned to her sister and brother-in-law. 'Thanks for flying out. It means so much to me that you're here.'

'As if we wouldn't come.' Kate placed an arm around Jennifer's shoulders. 'In any case, it's been far too long since we've been together.'

'Yes. But it's not as if I didn't try ...' Jennifer's v voice trailed off.

Kate stopped and turned to face her. 'You mean Dominic?'

There was no response.

'Jen,' the words were gentle, 'if's there's anything you'd like to talk about, let me know, okay?'

Jennifer ran a hand through her hair and gave her sister a hug.

Kate sent her husband a concerned look over the top of her sister's head. There'd been the odd hint dropped over the years. There was far more than met the eye, things that she may never be privy to. But she could see that her sister was at breaking point and needed someone. As far as she knew Jennifer had no close friends to confide in. Dominic had seen to that.

As if reading her mind, Peter added, 'that goes for me as well of course.'

There was a momentary pause. 'Actually, there's something to do with the business that I'd like to discuss, Peter.'

'Not a problem, Jen,' he replied. You've got a big task ahead, taking on Dominic's company.'

There was a smile. 'You're not wrong. I'm looking forward to the challenge though. Angelina's input will be invaluable. She knows the workings of the place inside out. To this point I've left instructions for things to continue as normal, until I've some time to think. And then I'll consult with the family lawyers and take it from there.'

Peter nodded. 'Sounds like a good plan to me.'

There was a pause and when Jennifer spoke her eyes were troubled. 'If only things were that straightforward, but there's more to it I'm afraid. It's taken Dom's death to find out.'

'I see.' Peter chose his words carefully. 'So, when would you like to talk about it?'

'How about in another day or two? The past week's been so draining, I can barely think straight.'

'Of course. Let me know when you're ready.'

That night, a makeshift dinner and early night was agreed upon. As the housekeeper popped her head around the door to say goodbye, she said, 'everything should be in order now. Let me know if there's anything you want done tomorrow.'

'No, we'll be fine, 'Jennifer said. 'Thanks for all that you've done, Meg.'

'No worries. Oh and I forgot to mention, Cara, a young man came looking for you today while you were at the funeral. Tall, dark haired. Asked you to contact him.'

All eyes turned to Cara but her face registered little. She simply nodded and mumbled, 'Okay. Thanks.'

What young man? Jennifer wondered in surprise, but she said nothing.

As Jennifer put away the last of the dishes and turned off the light, she gave Kate a hug in the doorway. 'God It's good to see you again. I'm so glad you're staying for another two weeks.'

'Me too. Peter has plenty of leave up his sleeve and things have been flat out at work. We could both do with a break. And thanks again for the offer of your apartment. We're looking forward to catching up with some old friends while we're in town and then there's Peter's parents.'

'Of course. I forgot all about them. How are they?'

'As good as can be expected. Old age is catching up; not that they'll admit it of course. I'm not sure how longer they can remain in that big house,' she paused, 'not that I'd dare mention it. They're as stubborn as hell.'

Jennifer smiled. 'Yes, I remember.'

'Anyway, Peter will attend to what needs to be done, before we head back. It'll have to do for now.'

Jennifer gave a nod. 'I'll make a point of dropping in from time to time.'

'Thanks. We'd appreciate that.'

As they headed up the stairs towards their rooms, Jennifer gave a sigh. 'It's been such a long day,' she said, 'I'm so glad it's over.'

'I bet you are. You did an amazing job with the funeral, Jen. Everything went beautifully.'

'Thanks. It was a blur to be honest.'

'I can imagine. Now you get some rest. We'll talk again in the morning.'

Jennifer paused as she turned on her bedroom light, reflecting on the night just past. With a pang of regret, she realised how little she knew of her daughter. The identity of the young man who'd visited was immaterial but it hurt to know that Cara had confided in her little over the years regarding her boyfriends, dreams, aspirations. She should have tried to get closer, should have made the effort years ago. It wasn't too late, she thought wearily. Was it?

Peter was already asleep when Kate climbed into bed. She lay reflecting on Jennifer's words that afternoon. What was going on at the company that was causing such concern? Then she began to think about her nieces, who'd barely spoken to each other at the funeral and she noted a simmering tension between the two as they prepared dinner. How on earth would they go working side by side in the company? Jennifer faced a daunting task indeed.

Cara took her iPhone from her pocket and flopped down on her stomach on the bed, legs dangling in the air. With trembling fingers, she scrolled through her old text messages. For years she'd considered deleting his text. The thought of it sitting there became too raw at times. And now she was glad she hadn't.

Her heart began to beat wildly as she found it. For a moment, she sat forehead furrowed, then began to type: Sorry I missed you today. Can we meet?

What she really wanted to say was, *I can't believe you came and I wasn't here. It's been so long and I've missed you.*

She held her breath and hit the send button.

Within seconds there was a beep and the words she dreaded appeared on the screen: Message not delivered.

She thumped the pillow hard, tears stinging her eyes. *Goddamn you, Will,* she muttered, *You said to contact you, but how the fuck do I do that when you've changed your number?*

All those years ago, he'd said he'd be back. Would he give them one more chance?

❡

Jennifer rose early to get breakfast and found her brother-in-law already up.

'Morning, Jen. How did you sleep?' he asked.

'Like a log, surprisingly enough. How about you?'

'Had a good one as well, but as usual I woke at six. It's a hard habit to break. Kate's still asleep so I let her be.'

'Good. I told her to have a sleep in. Are the girls up yet?'

'I haven't spotted Angelina yet but Cara's up and gone already.'

Jennifer nodded as she turned on the coffee machine. 'She's been asked to fill in at the stables for the next week or so. And that means early morning starts and long days. I've got to hand it to her Peter, she's a hard worker.'

'Good for her. You don't see that in kids much these days. Kate told me of her decision to defer her uni course.'

Jennifer nodded. 'Dom wasn't too happy about it; I can tell you.'

'I can imagine. Did she give a reason?'

'I think she was over the study thing and in need of a break, that's all. I did the same at her age. A year's travel around Europe was the best thing I ever did. I came back so refreshed.'

Peter nodded. 'I wish I'd done that. Twelve years at school then four years study on top of that can be a bit much. The irony is,' he said as he pulled out a stool, 'the moment I got my degree, I landed a job in a university.' He paused. 'It's as if I've never seen anything but the inside of a classroom.'

'It's what you love doing though,' Jennifer said. 'You're a natural teacher.'

'No, it's time for a change,' he said. 'Once my contract has run out that will be it.'

'Oh,' Jennifer sounded surprised. 'How long have you got to go.'

'Another three years.'

'You're coming back to Australia, I hope.'

Peter nodded. 'The kids will probably stay in the UK, though. They're happy in their jobs and it's where their friends are.'

'Well, they've spent most of their lives there.'

'Exactly. Now tell me what Angelina's been up to. From what I gather, she went to work with Dominic once she left school.'

'That's right. It's all she's ever wanted to do. It didn't take her long to pick things up, I can tell you. She was all but running the show within a matter of months.'

Peter laughed.

'She hasn't looked back since, really. Simply loves the place.'

'That's good,' he said. 'I imagine you'll be looking to her once you step in.'

'That's an understatement,' Jennifer remarked. But there's Cara too, don't forget. She may not be familiar with the workings of the place but she'll bring a wealth of knowledge. Dom made sure she was enrolled in the best business course around.'

'I bet he did.'

'Did you know that she gained distinctions in every subject?'

'Kate did tell me that. Pretty impressive! So, it's her

Masters she's yet to complete.'

Jennifer nodded.

'Do you think she'll go back to it?' he queried.

'I doubt it, not now that Dominic's no longer here. Why should she? Unless of course she wishes to.'

'Probably not. It may be less useful than a few years of work experience.'

Jennifer gave a grin as she reached for two mugs from the shelf. 'How do you like your coffee?'

'White with one thanks.'

'And what can I get you to eat? There's eggs and bacon in the fridge.'

'No, thanks. A couple of slices of toast will do fine and then I'll be off. I thought a bit of golf wouldn't go astray. It'll give you girls a chance to catch up.'

'Any excuse eh?' she said with a laugh.

Two hours later Jennifer and Kate were still in their pyjamas at the kitchen table, giggling like schoolgirls.

'Remember that night when I snuck out with my boyfriend?' Kate said, as she layered a thick spread of jam on her toast, 'and you were left to cover for me.'

'Do I what!' Jennifer rolled her eyes. 'What an ordeal that was!'

'And how about the night before your wedding when we had a few too many chardonnays.'

There was a groan. 'I wasn't in the best headspace the next morning, I can tell you.'

Kate grinned. 'And how about when we were teenagers.

We were pretty bad weren't we. Poor Mum.'

'And she didn't know half of it. What were your two like at that age?'

'Ashley wasn't so bad, just a string of outrageous hairdos and threats of tatts but Olivia, well that's another story.'

'Go on,' laughed Jennifer, pulling her legs up under her on the sofa.

'Olivia had the "know it all" attitude, the "I'll do as I like" thing. Girls can be such cows!'

'You can say that again. But I'd have to say, my two were a bit different. They had attitude, don't get me wrong, but they weren't caught up in the bitchy girl things that go on at schools. Angelina preferred the company of boys.'

'Nothing's changed on that front,' Kate joked. 'And Cara?'

'Kept to herself, mainly, apart from a one-off stint with a Goth group. God you should have seen the makeup, the outfit!'

'Cara? Who would have thought –'

Jennifer nodded. 'But there's been no mention of a friend since.'

'No boyfriend?'

'Not that I know of'

'You might be surprised. Cara's an attractive young girl. Who knows what she got up to when she was at Uni?'

'I'd like to think she had someone she could talk to, share things with.' Jennifer said. 'God knows, she's been a closed book to *me* these past few years.' There was a pause. 'I've tried so hard to get close to her but nothing's worked.'

'I know,' Kate said gently, thinking back to the conversations she'd had with her sister over the years. 'But she'll come around. Give it time. I'm sure you two will have plenty to talk about once she joins the company. In the meantime, how about you and I take her out to a few places before I head back.'

'That sounds good. Thanks.'

'No worries. Now let's get these dishes cleared so we can get dressed and go for that walk you told me about.'

¶

That night, Peter returned to the golf club with Kate and Jennifer for dinner. 'They're having a seafood buffet,' he explained, when he arrived home at five. 'If the meal's anything like the steak I had at lunch, we can't go wrong.'

'I'd forgotten how lovely this place is,' Jennifer said, as they took their seats at a table by the window. It must be five or six years since I've been here.'

She glanced across the vast lawn that adjoined the exclusive course. Few locals were paid up members, due to the club's extravagant fees. However, it was a popular place to meet for dinner.

The evening was spent catching up over old times, with the food every bit as good as Peter said. Instead of staying for coffee, they decided to return home.

Around midnight, Angelina's silver Lexus pulled up in the driveway.

Peter raised an eyebrow. 'Home from another date?'

'Most likely, 'Jennifer said. 'They don't last long, though.'

'I can imagine.'

There was the sound of a key in the front door and Angelina walked into the room with the grace of a dancer. *Nothing's changed,* Kate thought. Even in jeans, sandals and pink t-shirt the girl was a stunner. Kate was quick to note the look of admiration on her husband's face, yet she felt no envy. Angelina was not making advances when she gave him one of her smiles. It was just who she was.

'What, still up you three?'

'Just sitting, waiting for you.' Peter said. 'I've got the shotgun handy, just in case.'

Angelina gave a merry laugh.

'So, when are you bringing him to meet us?' Peter continued.

Her eyes danced mischievously. 'Who said it's serious?'

'Hmm.'

Angelina crossed the floor to give each of them a quick peck on the cheek.

'About time you two rocked up for a visit,' she said.

Kate nodded. 'I know. Time's just slipped away.'

'So, when are you coming back for good?'

'Once Peter has seen out the last of his contract. Not long to go now.'

'Awesome. We've missed you, haven't we, Mum.'

'Yes,' Jennifer said with a smile.

'Here,' Kate patted the sofa, 'sit down for a chat before you head off for bed, will you? Let's find out what you have been up to.'

Angelina flopped down beside her and settled into the cushions.

The conversation soon turned to the couple's children and Angelina leaned forward with interest, bubbling with exuberance at the stories they told. It was only later when the subject changed to Cara that Kate noticed a slight shift in Angelina's demeanour: nothing she could put a finger on, but unsettling, nonetheless.

Later, she turned to Peter as he turned down the doona. 'Did you notice anything different about Angelina tonight?'

'No. When?'

'Just before she said good night.'

'Not that I can think of. Why?'

'Oh nothing. Probably imagining things.'

9

After breakfast, Peter accompanied Kate and Jennifer for a walk down to the beach. As they headed up the steep track back towards Kilkenny, Kate turned to look below at the small, sandy stretch of private beach from where they'd come.'

'You're so lucky to live in this part of the world, Jen.'

There was a nod. 'I know. Having lived here for so long

now, I wouldn't want to be anywhere else. The same goes for the girls. It almost tore my heart out to learn that Dominic was planning to sell Kilkenny.'

'Yes, I couldn't believe it when you told me,' responded Kate. 'Surely he knew you wouldn't agree to it.'

'No, but he gave it a damn good try, resorting to the usual smooth talk and charm. When that didn't work he stormed off, packed his things and headed for town. A good thing when I think about it. Gave me time to think.'

'And what did you come up with?' Peter asked.

'Nothing really. My mind just went around in circles. However I can tell you one thing, I wasn't about to go down without a fight. Not about that, not about anything.'

There was a pause. 'I didn't tell you about the other women, did I.'

The couple looked at each other in surprise.

'What women?' Peter was the first to ask.

'Dom had a series of affairs, none of which I knew anything about,' came the bitter response. 'Not cheap trash mind you, but sophisticated, intelligent women. No surprise about that of course. Nothing but the best for Dom.'

'How long had this gone on?'

There was a shrug. 'God only knows.' She paused for a moment. 'Years, probably. More fool me for not suspecting. I just blindly let him go away for days, often weeks at a time. Heaven knows what trysts went on and where.'

'For heaven's sake, Jen. Don't berate yourself like this. Kate said. 'Men who cheat become pretty damned good at covering their tracks. Until they get caught out of course. It only takes one slip up, one look. '

'I know.' Jennifer thought of the warning signs she'd seen but had chosen to ignore.

'So how did you find out?' Kate asked.

'Angelina told me.'

'Angelina!' Kate was incredulous. 'How did she find out?'

'Just before Dom left for Bangkok, Angelina headed back to the office late one night to get something and she heard voices coming from Dominic's office. Thinking he was with a client, she went to knock on the door and introduce herself. But when she got there,' Jennifer closed her eyes for a moment, 'Dominic was making out with someone.'

'Oh my God,' exclaimed Peter.

Jennifer nodded. 'The thought of it sickens me. The office of all places!'

Kate took her hand. 'So, when did Angelina tell you about it?'

'She was too devastated to say anything to me at the time. It was only when we were making Dom's funeral arrangements that she mentioned it. She'd done some investigations of her own and sure enough, there'd been others.'

'Oh, Jen,' Kate sympathised. In truth she was thinking, *You rotten bastard. What goes around ...*

There was an uncomfortable pause before Jennifer spoke. 'There's more, I'm afraid.' She pointed towards the veranda. 'I think I'm ready for that chat about the business, Peter.'

Peter nodded. 'Okay, let's go.'

As the three settled into the white wicker chairs, Jennifer took a deep breath and looked out across the ocean before she turned to face them.

'The Bangkok police informed me that Dominic had gone to Thailand to sign off on two major contracts.'

'Oh, you mean with the winery?'

'Try entering into a partnership with a Korean company, buying up vast areas of land in Borneo.'

'Borneo?' Peter looked puzzled. 'To do what?'

'Set up palm plantations.' Jennifer gave an involuntary shudder. 'You know, bulldozing miles of forest dead smack in the middle of Orangutan country, or what's left of it. The other was a similar deal: ripping up large stretches of pristine jungle in the Amazon for logging.'

Jennifer's words rendered them speechless. Peter was the first to speak. 'He didn't get to sign them, did he?'

'No, they were found in the safe and returned to me untouched, amongst his other belongings.'

'Thank God for that.'

'Have you told the girls any of this?'

'Not at this stage.'

He nodded. 'Probably best it stays that way for the time being. You've enough to think about already.'

He wiped his brow with the palm of his hand and sat to reflect for a moment. 'Had Dominic mentioned going into property development prior to this?'

'Only in a passing comment, when he'd had drink or two

too many. But I didn't give it too much thought, to be honest,' she remarked. 'He'd been considering the purchase of a few smaller, well known wineries to strengthen his supply business overseas. From what he said, Australia has overtaken France to become the biggest exporter of wines into China over the past year. I thought that's what he'd been working towards.'

Peter stopped to reflect. He knew that his brother-in-law was a highly ambitious business man and being ruthless came with the territory. But he didn't think that he would stoop this low. He had known Dominic for some time. Projects as unconscionable as this were simply not his style. Someone had influenced him: someone with connections. And if that sort of person was part of his company, they needed to be weeded out fast. They were the last people Jennifer needed on board. He turned to face her. 'Something doesn't add up. Are you familiar with how Dominic's company is run?'

'From what I can gather, everyone's roles are clearly defined and followed to the letter from the executives downwards.'

There was a nod. 'And the finances?'

'The books are all in order, as far as I can gather. When the Australian Tax Office did a compliance check on the company last year, everything was above board.'

'Was there any reason that Dominic's company was targeted?'

'Not really. From what I've been told, the ATO are

having a blitz on large scale businesses at the moment. It seems that many have been avoiding tax by hiding their profits in offshore accounts, complex trust funds and the like.'

'I see. I presume that Dominic was in charge of the decision making within the company.'

She gave a nod. 'Dom had to be in control of everything he did. However, I know that he worked closely with his Business Manager.'

Peter nodded. 'I recall meeting him once when I visited the office. James. That's his name isn't it?'

'No, I'm afraid James Stanton is no longer with our firm.'

'Oh?'

'Dom had him replaced.'

'Why?'

'He said that it was time for some younger, fresher ideas.'

'How did you feel about that?' Kate asked.

'To tell you the truth, I was furious. James Stanton had been with us for the last twenty years and was highly respected by everyone he worked with. The company wouldn't be where it is today without his vision and hard work.'

She paused for a moment. 'It wasn't as if he didn't come out if it well. From what I have heard, he received a more than generous redundancy package. And he'd have little trouble in finding a new job. It's just the way it happened I suppose. He would have been devastated.'

'When did this all take place?'

'A few months before Dom left for Bangkok.'

Peter looked up sharply. 'As recently as that.'

There was a nod.

'Well that puts a different slant on things. Tell me what you know of his replacement.'

'Only the little that Dom told me after the appointment was made. His name's Paul Anderson. Apparently, he has extensive experience in the corporate world, comes with an impressive resume and spent the last five years living in Singapore. That's about it. Oh and,' she said with a laugh, 'he didn't make much of an impression on Angelina, that's for sure.'

'Did she say why?'

'Not really. She just said that she didn't trust him.'

'And you. Have you met him yet?' he asked.

'Only once, when I visited Dom at the office, a month or so ago.'

'And?'

'He appeared nice enough. Why?'

'Have you got Dominic's office number handy?'

Jennifer nodded. Reaching in her pocket for her mobile, she tapped in her password and scrolled through the contacts.

'Thanks.' He took the phone. 'If it's all right with you, I'll make an appointment to see him.'

She nodded.

He hit the call button and waited.

'Good afternoon, my name's Peter McFarlane,

Dominic's brother-in-law. I'd like to be put through to Paul Anderson.'

There was a pause.

'What? When? No, no that's fine.' He hung up.

'Shit, you're not going to believe this. Paul's no longer working there.'

'What!' Jennifer gasped in disbelief.

'He cleared out his office soon after news came through of Dominic's death. The girl I spoke to said he forwarded you his immediate resignation.'

Jennifer frowned. 'No, I received nothing. In fact, I was surprised not to see him at Dom's funeral.' She paused. 'Far out. He got the hell out of there pretty quickly, didn't he. What in the hell were he and Dom up to, Peter?'

'God only knows, if the Bangkok deals were anything to go by. It'll be most interesting to see what our Mr. Anderson has to say. Do you have the investigator's number handy?'

'Yes, it's inside.'

As she rose to get it, Peter's brow furrowed. It was a week and a half since Dominic's death. Paul Anderson could be anywhere by now. It was possible that he'd skipped the country, given his Asian connections.

He watched a seagull soar above the horizon. One thing was for certain, from now on everyone in Dominic's company would have to be made accountable. There'd been too many loopholes, too many avenues for corruption. No other business he knew of was run by the one person. He knew little of the company's board structure or if one was even in existence. He knew that there'd been meetings from time to time between Dominic, Madeleine, Jennifer and the business manager but from what Jennifer told him, they only discussed dividends and profits. But there had been no such meetings since Madeleine's death.

After dinner he discussed his concerns with Jennifer.

'You're right,' she said gravely. 'I'll book an appointment in the morning to speak to my lawyer.'

40

A few days later Angelina made breakfast for Jennifer, Kate and Peter who were heading off for the day, seeing the local sights.

'So what time will you be home, Mum?' she asked.

'Late, I imagine. It depends on where we end up. Don't worry about dinner. We'll get something on the way back.'

Angelina nodded, turning to Kate. There's lots of great little cafes and restaurants to choose from now.'

'I imagine so,' she said. 'Are you sure you don't want to come with us?'

'No. I've got things to do around here.' Angelina replied. 'Maybe next time.'

At around ten, Peter headed upstairs to collect the car keys.

'Make sure you two have your raincoats with you,' he said upon his return. I just checked the weather forecast and it looks as though we could be in for some wild weather. Take a look out there. The wind's already whipping over the ocean.'

Angelina watched from the window of her upstairs room as Peter's hire car headed down the drive way. A smile crossed her face.

Late that afternoon, Cara was mucking out the last of the stables when her mobile rang. *I wonder who that is,* she thought as she wiped her hands on the back of her jeans and reached for the phone in her coat pocket. Her expression darkened as Angelina's number came up on the screen. It was rare that her sister rang her unless she was after something.

'What's up?'

'You need to get home.' The voice was urgent. 'There's been an accident. It's Mum.'

Cara felt her heart race. 'What do you mean? What happened?'

There was a crackling on the line and a muffled voice.

'I can't hear you. Speak up, will you?'

'She went for a walk along the cliffs and she fell.'

'Is she all right?'

'I don't know. She's on a ledge, halfway down the cliff. I can't possibly reach her. I saw her arm move slightly but it looks as if she's unconscious. She's not responding to my voice.'

'Fuck! Have you phoned for an ambulance?'

'Yeah, they're on their way.'

'I'm leaving now.' Cara hit the off button, ran around to

her quarters to grab her bag and out to her car.

'Shit, shit,' she muttered as the rain started pelting down. She threw the car into reverse and there was a squeal of tyres on the gravel as she flew around the circular front driveway towards the road. A bay thoroughbred jumped sideways in its stable as she passed.

Cara had made the trip from the stables to home many times over the past few months but this one seemed like the trip from hell. The rain became heavier and the windscreen wipers struggled to cope. High winds off the ocean buffeted her black Honda, which felt like a small boat struggling to hold its moorings.

'Come on, you friggin' rain. Just ease off so I can see!' she muttered in desperation but the rain became torrential and the road ahead a blur.

Cara was on the most treacherous stretch of road that required careful driving, even in idyllic conditions. It wormed downwards, like a huge black, curved snake to a precarious, hairpin bend and then up again. She recalled learning to drive the family Range Rover on this narrow stretch of road. It had been the most harrowing experience of her life. Now, she was forced to slow right down, rely on her memory as to where the danger spots were and ride things out.

Flicking on the aircon to clear the condensation from the windscreen, she made out a sign to her left that pointed to Kennedy Bluff. 'Thank God,' she muttered. She was almost home.

She screeched to a halt in the driveway, yanked on the handbrake and tore down the cliff pathway to where Angelina stood in the distance, frantically waving her arms.

'Where is she?' Cara yelled as she approached, the rain stinging her face like pellets.

'Down there,' Angelina gestured, with a nod of the head. 'Actually, she doesn't appear to be moving any more. See what you think.'

The words were so calm, so indifferent that for a moment Cara thought she'd misheard. But the look in Angelina's eyes told her otherwise.

Sickened and numb, she rushed to the cliff's edge and forced herself to look.

'There's no one down there!' she swung around in bewilderment.

Angelina took a step towards her. 'Not yet there isn't.'

On instinct, Cara threw herself away from the cliff's edge, to the safety of the path.

'Remember this place, Cara?' Angelina took another step closer. 'It's the exact spot that Joe fell,' she paused her eyes glittering, 'let's say with a little help from me.'

'What! *You* pushed him!' Cara exclaimed in disbelief. 'Why?'

'Let's just say he stood in my way.'

'He was just a boy!' Cara's face was full of anguish. 'A four-year-old boy!'

Angelina shrugged. 'It would've been quick.'

The detached way she spoke sends chills coursing through Cara's body.

'Why are you telling me this now?'

'Why not? Angelina took a step forward. 'You won't be telling anyone.'

Cara desperately looked around for a plan of escape.

Angelina watched with an expression of mild amusement.

'Poor, misguided Cara,' she soothed, 'So tragic that you chose to end your life this way. I told Mum only last week that you'd been depressed for some time; made her promise not to tell. And when this is all over, I'll tell her about the suicide note I found in your room. The one I screwed up because I didn't want her to see. She'll be devastated that she wasn't there when you needed her the most.'

'You're insane!'

'Don't you *ever* say those words to me!' Angelina shrieked.

Cara's mind was working fast. Her only option was to knock her sister over then make a run for it. But then she caught sight of something metallic in Angelina's hand. This was serious.

'I just don't get it.' She stalled for more time, heart hammering. 'Mum and Dad gave you everything. They adored you. You had the world at your feet.'

'Perhaps, but I'm still just the daughter of a servant who screwed around with God knows who.'

'Don't say things like that.'

'Why not!' Angelina's eyes blazed. 'I've heard the stories. Don't pretend that you haven't.'

Cara felt her anger rise. 'Get a grip. The past is the past. If anything, *I* should be the one to feel hard done by. Imagine living in the shadow of someone as beautiful as you. It's hurt. But have you ever heard me complain?'

There was no reaction. Cara shuddered at the glazed eyes before her. The wind whipped up and Angelina's voice rose above.

'I may have come from nothing but I will *never* be a nobody. All my life I've dreamed of taking over this place, of taking over Dad's business.' Her eyes flashed. 'And I will. With Joe gone, and you, there'll be nothing standing in my way.'

Cara knew she was looking into the face of madness. Her mind whirled.

As Angelina lunged, knife in hand, Cara made an instinctive grab for her wrist, struggling to keep her balance.

'Drop the knife, Angie.' A familiar voice cut the air, causing Angelina to spin around wildly and allowing Cara to break loose and run to where Lee Farrell stood, his dark eyes fixed on Angelina.

Cara watched transfixed as her sister's eyes changed from evil to doe-like.

'Lee!' Angelina cried out. 'Thank God you've come. Cara's just tried to kill me. She waited until Mum left for the day and lured me down here. I managed to grab the knife from her. See?' She waved it erratically through the air.

Lee slowly stepped forward, arm outstretched. 'It's all over, Angie. Now give me the knife.'

'You don't believe a word I just said!' she screeched. 'Bastard!'

Looking around wildly, Angelina made a run for the path slashing Lee's arm as he stepped in her way.

Cara screamed and ran towards him. 'My God. Are you okay?'

'Yeah,' he clutched his arm, cursing the opportunity missed. Yanking the scarf from her neck, Cara made a crude tourniquet to staunch the blood oozing onto the sand.

High above, Angelina stood against the darkness, hair billowing in the wind like some sort of wild apparition. Her words were lost in the wind. 'This isn't the end of it,' she screamed. 'Not by a long shot.'

Shoving the knife in her pocket, she disappeared from sight.

'We can't let her get away, Lee!' Cara went to give chase. 'She's out of her mind!'

Lee was quick to restrain her.

'No, leave the police to deal with it.'

He dug in his pocket for his phone.

Once he'd finished the call, Cara turned to face him, her words barely audible.

'You know that time when Joe fell over the cliff when we were kids.'

He nodded.

'Well, it was no accident, Lee. Angelina told me, just before you arrived. She pushed him.'

'Why?'

'He stood in her way. That's what she said.'

'My God!' Lee's mind began to reel.

'She's insane!' Cara exclaimed. 'Why didn't we see it all this time, Lee?'

Lee thought of the beautiful, vivacious woman he'd held in his arms on the deck of the *Jennifer* under the moonlight.

'I wish I knew, Cara,' his face was dark. 'I wish I knew.'

There was moment's silence.

'Come on,' he took her arm, 'let's get back to the house. The police will be here soon.'

9

Angelina cursed as the car swung dangerously around the slippery bends. Things that had gone like clockwork for so long had suddenly given way like a sandcastle underfoot. Damn Lee. Damn him to hell. For a few minutes, she spat profanities like bitter fruit. Then, as if nothing had happened she took a deep breath and began to consider her next move.

Just as well I have alternatives she thought, with a quick glance at the passport and papers beside her. No, that would come later.

As the oncoming blue light flashed past, her pursed

lips gave way to a twisted smile. 'Perfect,' she muttered softly.

Lee's ears pricked up as he heard the police siren approaching in the distance. *Come on, faster* he willed them. There was only one road between Kilkenny and town, after which Angelina could make her escape from a number of exit points. In the meantime, Jennifer should be arriving at any moment. It had been difficult making a call without alarming her. It was a relief to know that Peter and Kate were with her. He ran a hand through his hair. What a mess.

¶

After the police left, Jennifer sat with the others in the lounge room, her mind in a daze. She barely heard the conversation, offering only a brief word here or there. It seemed no time at all before Lee rose to his feet and said, 'It's time I got going. If you'll excuse me, I'll just step outside for a breath of fresh air before I head off home.'

'Why don't you stay?' Kate said. 'It's late and there's plenty of room.'

'Thanks for the offer but best I get home.'

'Well, you must promise to get that arm seen to first thing in the morning.'

'It should be fine. You did a great job of fixing it up.'

'Mum was a nurse, don't forget. She trained us well.'

'I'm still waiting to hear your promise, Lee,' Kate

continued, 'that gash could be deeper than you think and a course of antibiotics wouldn't go astray.'

Lee threw his hands up in mock resignation. 'Okay. Okay. You win!'

Jennifer managed a wan smile. It was good to have some light hearted banter after what had taken place.

'Now off you go,' Kate nodded towards the door. 'I'm about to make coffee. I'll let you know when it's ready.'

Lee stood still on the lawn, his mind in a turmoil.

There'd been two Angelina Lorenzos: the captivating, vivacious beauty and the ruthless, cold hearted killer. *How could I have not seen,* he thought. *How could I have been so easily deceived. Believed every word she said, gone along with her plans?* He thought of the phone call from Bangkok. The cool, detached response of the beautiful woman sitting cross-legged on the chair beside him as she listened to word of her father's death. Angelina had connections, probably far more sinister than he could ever imagine. If she could push her brother off a cliff and arrange her father's execution, how much further was she prepared to go?

He thought of Cara, who'd come to within an inch of losing her life. If he hadn't arrived when he did, she'd be dead, with Angelina spinning lies about a suicide and Jennifer left broken hearted. He knew Angelina would have planned things well beforehand. Her knife was probably a ruse to goad Cara towards the cliffs. If it were to look like a suicide, Angelina would want no trace of her DNA on her sister's body.

She'd come *so* close to getting away with it.

It was only by chance that he'd come when he did. Angelina had made plans for a weekend rendezvous aboard the *Jennifer*. And when she hadn't turned up, he knew that things weren't right. Angelina was punctual to the minute; never forgot an appointment. But in retrospect, the weekend's arrangements *had* been made weeks before-hand. And she had more important things on her mind, he thought grimly. He'd tried calling a number of times, only to reach her message bank and his texts went unanswered. Definitely out of character. He'd given it a few hours then jumped in his car and driven to her apartment, hoping to find her there. But the apartment was empty. It was only at the last moment he decided to head to Kilkenny.

Shit! A thought suddenly struck him. If Angelina had pulled off Cara's murder, she would have become sole heir to the Lorenzo fortune and he none the wiser; probably sleeping with her and making plans to leave Eleanor. Lee's mind was in a spin, his body bathed in sweat despite the night chill.

As Kate reached for the cups on the shelf, Jennifer glanced out the window, frowning at the figure standing motionless under the moonlight.

'Help with the coffee, will you?' She turned to Cara, 'I'll just go and get Lee.'

At first, he was unaware of her approach and she gently shook his arm. 'Are you okay?'

He turned to face her. 'I should be saying the same thing to you.'

There was a momentary pause. 'It's Angelina. Isn't it?'

'What do you mean?'

'I know that look,' she said softly. 'Were you in love with her, Lee?'

'To be honest, I believed I was, yes.'

'And this has been going on for a while, I take it.'

There was a nod. 'I tried so hard to fight it. I knew it wasn't right. She was so much younger than me but –'

'But she bewitched you. Like so many others before you.'

'How could I have not seen, Jennifer?' Lee's voice choked with emotion as he spoke.

'How could we all not have seen?'

For a few moments, neither spoke.

'Jennifer, there's something you need to know. It's to do with Dominic. Something that I was involved in.'

'Dom is in the past, Lee. Whatever it is, lay it to rest. You saved my daughter's life and I'm eternally grateful to you for that. Now, best we head back to the house. Coffee's ready.'

But Lee knew that nothing would ever be laid to rest. The memory of the call from Bangkok would haunt him for the rest of his life. He didn't know how long he could keep up the facade and when he'd eventually crack.

As they stepped on to the porch, Jennifer turned to face him. 'Can I ask one thing, Lee?'

'Of course.'

'What made you come when you did?'

'Just luck, I guess,' he lied. 'I had nothing planned for the day so I thought I'd take a drive to Kilkenny to catch up with Peter and Kate before they left.' He paused. 'They're not about to leave yet, I hope. At least not until this is all sorted.'

'No. They're staying for a while longer.'

There was a nod. 'Not that there's need to worry,' he was quick to reassure her, 'she certainly won't be bold enough to head straight back here and from what the police said tonight, I'm sure she'll be found soon.'

Lee was surprised at how easily the words had rolled off his tongue. In fact, he was overcome with trepidation. After what had transpired over the last eight hours, there were no guarantees for anyone's safety, and with Angelina's connections who knows where she might be hiding out.

41

Two days later, Jennifer received a phone call.

She sat bolt upright on the chair. 'Are you sure?'

Peter raised an eyebrow as he passed.

'I'll tell you later,' she mouthed the words as she quickly headed out of the room to take the call.

Five minutes later, she returned and slumped onto the sofa, her face registering confusion and disbelief.

'That was Xavier, my lawyer. A fiscal audit's just been completed on Dom's company. It appears that a considerable amount of money has been siphoned from the bank accounts over the past few months. It's been traced to Angelina.'

'You're kidding. How much?'

'Around two million, give or take.'

'But how's that possible?'

'Dom had more things on the go than I was aware of, things that Angelina was privy to. Two years ago he gave her control of three portfolios, none of which were on the books. God knows how she did it, but she managed to bleed all three accounts dry.'

'A few months. That was about the time that Paul arrived wasn't it?'

'That's right.'

'You don't think that he was involved in this?'

'Not a chance. Angelina despised the man.'

'That's right. You did mention that when we first spoke of him.'

'Dominic and Paul were collaborating on new projects: things she was not privy to. She mentioned it a few times and I can tell you, she was ropeable.'

'I see. Did Xavier say whether a check been done on her finances?'

Jennifer nodded. Her bank accounts have been emptied. And you know the family trust fund that Madeleine set up for the girls once they turned twenty-five?'

'Don't tell me.'

'Yes, she wiped out the entire account: one million dollars.' She shook her head. 'You know, I said to Madeleine when she established the Trust, "Do you think that's wise? Why not set a partial amount, or provide ongoing access to the interest or something." But for some reason she'd have none of it. More fool me for not checking up on things. Madeleine had spent considerable time with both girls on wise investment choices and I assumed that it was things had been set in order long ago.'

'You *have* frozen Dominic's assets, I hope.'

'Yes. Xavier did that immediately when he learned of Dom's death.'

'Shit, Jennifer.' Peter rubbed a hand through his hair. 'What a mess!'

'You're telling me.' She paused. 'What in the hell is Angelina up to, Peter? God, I hope they find her soon.'

'They will, don't worry. Give it time.'

But what if they don't, he thought.

42

It was a chilly winter's day and Cara curled up in bed, covers rolled up to her chin. It was uncharacteristic of her to sleep during daylight hours but the events of the past two weeks had left her exhausted and unable to sleep at night. Consequently, she often found herself dozing off during the day. The last of the sun's rays filtered through the window and she welcomed the bliss of drifting into a deep sleep as her eyelids became heavy and the bed's warmth enveloped her like a soothing bath.

Sometime later she was jolted awake by a rattling of the window. She had no idea how long she had been asleep. Was it six o'clock, seven perhaps? She felt cold with fear, her hands clenching like a vice. Angelina would not return. Would she? The police said she wouldn't be that game. It was little comfort to know that they were out searching for her and a that a security guard had been stationed around the clock at the main gate, upon Peter's insistence.

No one would know of Kilkenny's back entrances and secret passageways. But Angelina did …

The rattling grew louder and the wind began to howl. Cara pressed a hand to her chest. She could feel her heart racing like a runaway car. Suddenly it hit her. She and her mother were all alone. Peter and Kate had headed off to the apartment for the weekend.

Flinging off the covers, she fled down the stairs in search of her mother.

'Cara, whatever's wrong?' Jennifer cried out in alarm, as her daughter rushed into the lounge room, eyes wide with terror and hair askew.

'I had a bad dream, that's all.'

It suddenly dawned on Jennifer that Cara, the stalwart one, was as fragile and vulnerable as she.

'It was a dream, that's all darling,' she soothed. 'Now come and sit with me for a while.'

For the first time in as long as she could remember, Jennifer found herself reaching out and pulling her daughter into her arms. And for the first time, Cara did not withdraw.

As they sat, side by side on the sofa, Jennifer cradled her daughter's head, taking in the scent of her newly washed hair. 'Are you up for a walk?' she asked. 'There's someone I'd like you to meet.'

It was getting dark as they headed towards the path that encircled the cliff face. The incessant crash of waves boomed in the distance as they walked on, collars turned up and hands in pockets.

Jennifer stopped at the rusted gate of the Zielinski house, taking Cara by surprise. It was the last place she expected to visit. Childhood memories flooded back of the times she sneaked away from Kilkenny with her sister and cousins to get a peek of the phantom resident. "I dare you to go inside the gate." Ashley had said. And with each visit, the dares became bolder.

The grass swished underfoot as they crossed the lawn towards the house. As they stepped onto the veranda, Cara felt an involuntarily shiver. After all this time she found her eyes darting in all directions, as if she expected someone to jump out from the shadows.

Suddenly the porch light flickered on. The door inched opened and a stooped old lady with faded blue eyes peered around the edge. 'Oh, it's you, Mrs. Lorenzo,' she said. 'Good evening.'

Jennifer's heart sank as and she noticed the gnarled, red hands as she opened the door. How long since she'd seen her?

'Good evening, Alice. This is my daughter Cara. I wondered whether David is busy. I'd like a word, if that's possible.'

There was a nod. 'He's in the basement.'

The old house's interior was musty, cold and dark as they followed Alice along a narrow, dimly lit passageway. There was the smell of mould that comes with houses locked and windows closed. Doors flanked both sides, all shut. At the end of the passage the old woman stopped before a staircase that led to the basement.

'I'll leave you here, if you don't mind. I find the stairs a bit difficult these days.'

Cara's heart pounded as they descended the stairs towards a faint light that spilled under the door. For years she had entertained wild childhood fantasies of the phantom in the Zielinski house, of what went on there.

She watched, transfixed as her mother gave the faded door a soft rap.

'David, it's Jennifer. I've brought Cara to see you.'

There was a slight pause, followed by the scraping of a chair and footsteps across a wooden floor.'

The old door groaned opened and Cara's heart stopped, as she caught sight of a pair of sea-green eyes like her own.

'Mum?' she swung to face her mother.

Tears welled in Jennifer's eyes. 'Cara, it's time you met your father.'

'What!'

Jennifer eased her to a nearby chair, where she sat, stunned and bewildered. Finally, it was the grand piano in the centre of the room that captured her full attention. Atop was the framed photo of a handsome young man, resplendent in tails, performing before a packed concert hall.

'Is that you?' she looked down at the man crouched before her, face etched with concern.

'Many years ago, yes.'

'Where?'

'The Musikverein Auditorium, Vienna.'

'But I don't understand!' Cara's voice choked with emotion. 'Why did you two hide this from me. I've spent my whole life with someone I believed to be my father but who never loved me.'

Jennifer looked at David with consternation.

'We've much to tell you now,' she said. 'There was never a good time for that but it's time you learned the truth.'

David pulled up two chairs and Cara noted the missing three fingertips of his right hand.

'Soon after Dominic and I married,' Jennifer began, 'I was invited to a charity function here at Helena's house. Dom hated those occasions, so he had engineered a five-day business trip. I was introduced to David by his mother, after his piano recital in the drawing room.

'A chance meeting next evening on the clifftop led to an affair that neither David or I sought, yet were powerless to stop.'

Jennifer closed her eyes for a moment, recalling the two nights of love making on the moonlit beach. Never had she experienced such passion, such tenderness.

'And then, Dominic arrived home earlier than expected. He seemed so much in love, so happy to be home. Overcome by a deep sense of shame, I contacted David to end our relationship but he'd already gone. I wanted to tell him face to face but perhaps it was better that way. We both knew that it was wrong.'

'I discovered I was pregnant with you after a whirlwind trip to Paris with Dom. "A second honeymoon," he called it. I never considered the possibility that I could be carrying David's child and not his.'

The thought that Cara *could* be David's daughter *had* flashed through her mind in the early days of her marriage when she witnessed Cara as a child, humming along to a tune on the radio then playing what she'd heard, note perfect, on Madeleine's piano. But there were no further signs and the incident was soon forgotten and Cara's attention turned to horses.

What hadn't occurred to her was that Dominic knew of their affair. How naïve could she have been? Nothing escaped him.

It wasn't until the first signs of tension in their marriage that she suspected he knew; the odd cryptic, snide remark when music was mentioned.

She turned to Cara. 'It was a long time before I was convinced you were David's daughter. Remember that evening two years ago, when we arrived home early to find you playing a Beethoven sonata?'

Cara nodded.

'That's when I knew for sure. I recognised in your playing, a gift. A gift I've heard only in David's music.'

There was such a lack of awareness on her part. Neither she nor Dominic possessed musical talent. Her ineptness was made abundantly clear at a high school musical audition. She recalled how her cheeks burned with shame as she struggled to sing in tune and the sniggers of her classmates as they lined in the passageway to await their turn. On the other hand, Dominic showed no interest in music whatsoever.

Jennifer held out her hand. 'I came so close to telling

you about David. It took the shock of Dominic's death to determine that enough was enough. You needed to know. That's when I contacted Helena regarding David's whereabouts, unaware he was here all the time. And when I came to tell him about you …'

'I already knew.' David said softly.

'But how?'

'I too, heard you play. One evening, months ago when I was walking past Kilkenny. 'You were playing Debussy's *Claire De Lune*. I can recall that night as if it was yesterday, how that haunting melody drew me into the garden where I sat spellbound in the darkness.'

David held Cara's eyes. 'I knew there and then that you were my daughter.' There was a pause. 'After that, I came many times to hear you. Although I doubted that we'd ever meet, it was enough to know you were close.'

Cara sat still, listening. Not once had Dominic spoken to her like that.

'You did love her back then, didn't you?' were the next words that she spoke.

'Yes, yes, I did.' David glanced at Jennifer who quickly averted her eyes.

'In truth I never stopped loving her. She kept me going through his darkest years. Just to be near her when I came back to this house gave me the will to live and whenever I walked along the stretch of beach we once shared, I felt her presence.

'Then why did you leave her without so much as a word?'

Cara persisted.

'Let's say it wasn't of my doing.'

David spoke of the threats made on his life by Dominic when he discovered the affair; his promise to leave the country and not contact Jennifer again.

For a moment everything was silent, except for the faint tick of a clock on the mantlepiece.

David took a ragged breath before recounting the events of that fateful night in Prague. Never in his wildest dreams did he expect Dominic to carry out his threat, three years after he'd left the country. He'd kept to his side of the bargain: he'd not contacted Jennifer again. Had Dominic been envious of his success?

The random decision to head out for a walk that night would haunt him for the rest of his life. He should have known that the alleyways near his hotel were no place to wander. He would never forget the words in broken English, before the knife slashed his face, searing into his flesh. "I've got something to give you, Zielinski," he hissed, "from a friend of yours, let's say. I heard you had pretty hands. Well not anymore."

Cara's hand flew to her mouth as David spoke of the cold- blooded assault that left him scarred, and robbed of his career. One look at her face and he cut short the mention of the ensuing years: the revolving door of institutions, depression and addiction to prescription drugs.

'It's all right,' he comforted her. 'This house became my refuge. It's here that I found peace.'

'It was you!' Cara gasped. 'You who came and went all these years.'

He gave a nod.

'And you never knew he was here, Mum?'

'No,' she said. 'I knew of a visitor who stayed from time to time. But from what I gathered it was some distant relative of Helena's who'd been through troubled times and came here for respite.'

Cara reached across and gently lifted David's hand. 'How could he do this to you. How could he?'

The poignant gesture caused pangs of pain through Jennifer's heart.

'What's done is done,' David said. 'It could be worse. The damage is to my right hand but I'm left-handed. I'm still able to compose and improvise.'

'There's one thing Dominic could never take from David,' Jennifer said softly. 'And that was his music. Look.' She gestured towards a bookcase against the far wall.

Cara stood and slowly walked towards the collection of CDs, and ran her fingers across the top, pulling one out at random.

'Can you play it for me?'

'If you wish.'

As the dramatic notes of a Rachmaninov concerto filled the room, Jennifer watched the two, overcome with emotion.

It was only after David had left the country that she realised how much she missed him. She'd come so close to flying half way around the world to watch him play. But in all likelihood Dominic would find out, especially if she travelled by herself. The other option was to take the girls with her, under the guise of a cultural experience. That wouldn't work either. He'd want to know every place they visited, everything that they did. Besides, she wanted to attend his concerts alone. Many times, she had fantasised about seeing him perform in the concert halls of Europe. She closed her eyes, imagining herself watching him in the darkness as he played, wanting so badly to reach out to him. She envisaged waiting outside the foyer long after the concert had finished and when he headed out, she would call his name softly and watch his face as he turned …

But she was married, with a family. As he most likely was. Jennifer often wondered what his wife would be like. Beautiful, probably. An artist like him perhaps or the daughter of a European aristocrat. There'd be children, no doubt. She wondered in which country David and his family lived. And why he'd never contacted her.

If only I'd known what he did to you, she thought with a deep pang of regret. *Known you were here.* For a moment, she envisaged a life without Kilkenny. A life with David. Yes, she would have left.

When the CD had finished, Cara eagerly reached for the next.

Jennifer smiled. 'How about we leave the rest until next time. It's getting late.'

'When's next time. Tomorrow?'

'Tomorrow it is,' David said.

Cara walked to the Steinway and pressed a few keys. Turning to David, she said, 'Can you teach me to play? Show me the things that you learned?'

David nodded, barely able to speak. 'It would be my pleasure, Cara.'

He slowly rose and fetched a brown paper parcel from a table near the window. 'Perhaps you might like to start with this,' he said as he handed it to her.

Cara opened the string with unsure fingers. Inside was a handwritten manuscript that read, *Rhapsody in F minor. Dedicated with love to my daughter Cara.*

She looked up, eyes shining with tears.

It was after midnight when Jennifer and Cara headed along the cliff path towards home, guided by the narrow beam from David's small torch. Against the stillness of the night, the distant ocean boomed with soothing regularity. Jennifer's heart ached as she stole a sidelong glance at her daughter who clutched the brown paper parcel to her chest as if it was her only possession.

'This is a new beginning for us, Darling,' she said softly. 'Everything will be all right. You'll see.'

But is it all over? Cara thought.

They walked on in silence.

Jennifer Lorenzo knows it is only a matter of time before the killer returns and this time around there won't be any mistakes…...

I'M BACK

The continuation of the chilling
Dark Illusion Trilogy